PRAISE FOR SA

"Sara Goodman Confino's writing shines as bright as her characters' sparkling personalities in this clever and satisfying story of moving on. With Confino's trademark wit and humorous one-liners, readers are sure to delight in this uplifting tale of finding love after grief, even in the most unlikeliest of places."

—Heidi Shertok, author of *Unorthodox Love*

"Sara Goodman Confino is a force of literature. In her latest, *Good Grief*, protagonist Barbara navigates the treacherous sea of mourning after the loss of her spouse, including a not-so-welcome visit from her late husband's mother. This is a touching tale of learning to live and love again, told with Confino's trademark heart and wit. Delightful, poignant, and rife with humor—a not-to-be-missed book of the summer!"

—Aimie K. Runyan, bestselling author of *The Wandering Season*

"Barbara and Ruth share a similar pain. Living under the same roof, the widowed mother and daughter-in-law butt heads as they wade through loneliness and grief. And when they each scheme to find love for the other one, Confino does what she does best: crafting a brimming tale of family and second chances while finding joy through our sorrows. Special nod to the tiny gems from former books Confino has sprinkled within the pages. But mostly, readers will fall in love with this bighearted story full of hope."

—Rochelle B. Weinstein, bestselling author of *This Is Not How It Ends*

"*Good Grief* is not a romance, but it's a love story at its core . . . between a young widow and her pushy but well-meaning mother-in-law, who moves into her house uninvited. I cackled at their secret attempts to set each other up with the town's available men, fist-pumped the air at their strength in challenging situations, and shed more than a tear as their friendship flourished. Sprinkled with romantic side plots for both mother-in-law and daughter-in-law, and cameos from beloved characters of the author's previous books, *Good Grief* is another winner from Sara Goodman Confino and guaranteed to delight her large existing fan base and bring in new readers who have yet to experience her charming and hilarious stories."

—Meredith Schorr, author of *Roommating*

Good Grief

OTHER BOOKS BY THE AUTHOR

Behind Every Good Man

Don't Forget to Write

She's Up to No Good

For the Love of Friends

Good Grief

a Novel

SARA GOODMAN CONFINO

LAKE UNION
PUBLISHING

This is a work of fiction. Names, characters, organizations, places, events, and incidents are either products of the author's imagination or are used fictitiously.

Text copyright © 2025 by Sara Goodman Confino
All rights reserved.

No part of this book may be reproduced, or stored in a retrieval system, or transmitted in any form or by any means, electronic, mechanical, photocopying, recording, or otherwise, without express written permission of the publisher.

Published by Lake Union Publishing, Seattle

www.apub.com

Amazon, the Amazon logo, and Lake Union Publishing are trademarks of Amazon.com, Inc., or its affiliates.

EU product safety contact:
Amazon Media EU S. à r.l.
38, avenue John F. Kennedy, L-1855 Luxembourg
amazonpublishing-gpsr@amazon.com

ISBN-13: 9781662527531 (paperback)
ISBN-13: 9781662527524 (digital)

Cover design and illustration by Philip Pascuzzo
Cover image: © Kupalina / Getty

Printed in the United States of America

For Jennifer Lucina, without whom I could do none of this

1

My mother hugged me again. "I don't *have* to leave yet," she said for the third time. "If you're not ready—"

"I'm ready," I said quickly. Too quickly. A wounded expression crossed her face, and I felt guilty. As much of a struggle as it could be to live with my mother at thirty-two, I did know that I couldn't have survived these last two years without her. "Thank you. For absolutely everything. But it's time that I try to figure out how to do this myself. Whether I'm ready or not."

Her chin trembled slightly, but she nodded.

"Now go on," I said, gesturing to the waiting cab. "You're going to miss your train."

She nodded again and turned, before two small bodies came barreling past me and almost knocked her to the ground in a tight hug. And for a moment, I questioned whether I should be sending my mother home or not. Susie and Bobby needed stability after losing their father two years ago, and my mother, while not always easy, had certainly provided that.

But no. We needed to do this. And my mother had her own life to live in Philadelphia. Although after several visits from my father, I certainly understood why coming to live with me, where she only did half of the housework instead of doing EVERYTHING herself, could feel like a vacation. Even with little kids running around the house.

Granted that was then. Now, Susie was eight, Bobby was six, and they were both in school. And I was finally starting to feel like I was coming out of the cocoon of grief. I wasn't a butterfly yet by any stretch of the imagination, but I was starting to feel like maybe someday I could grow some wings. Just not with my mother living in my house.

I had gone from my parents' house to college to marrying Harry. And then when he died, my mother moved in. "Just until you get back on your feet," she assured me.

The prospect of being alone was terrifying. There had always been someone else in charge. Someone else to share the burden of being the adult. Someone whom I could ask when I was unsure. And I didn't know if I could fill that role on my own, either for the kids or for myself. But it was time to try—and if I failed, well, Philadelphia wasn't *that* far away.

"Okay, give Grandma one more kiss and then say goodbye. She's got to get home to Grandpa after all."

"You'll come visit us, won't you?" Susie asked.

My mother opened her mouth to reply, and I could see she was going to say she would stay. "She's going to come visit," I reminded Susie before I wound up unpacking suitcases. "And we can go visit her in Philadelphia too."

"On the train?" Bobby asked. There were few joys in life that trumped a train ride for a six-year-old boy.

"Of course on the train," I said, ruffling his hair. He beamed up at me. "Now go on. One more hug and kiss, and then Grandma has to go." Both kids complied, and I hugged her as well. "This was a mitzvah," I whispered into her ear.

"You're my daughter, Barbara," she replied, squeezing me. "All you ever need to do is say you need me."

Finally, she released me and made her way down the front walk, waving as she took her seat in the back of the taxi. The three of us watched as the car pulled away from the curb, and I saw Susie surreptitiously wipe at an eye with the back of her hand. In some ways, losing Harry was hardest on her. He had been wrapped around her little finger since she was born. And while we talked about him a lot to Bobby, he didn't *really* remember his father the way that Susie did. He had only been four when Harry died, and two years was a long time for him.

What they needed was a distraction. "You know what would be perfect right now?" I asked, taking their hands. They both looked up at me. "Ice cream."

"But we haven't had dinner," Susie said suspiciously.

I crouched down. "What if ice cream"—I paused for dramatic effect—"IS our dinner tonight?"

"Can we do that?"

I winked at her. "If we all agree not to tell Grandma when she calls to tell us she made it home. We're a team—we can do whatever we want as long as we do it together. What do you say?"

"Ice cream! Ice cream!" Bobby shouted.

"I *guess*," Susie said, drawing it out to three syllables. "Just this once."

"I'll sweeten the pot," I said, still at their level. "What if we eat it—just this once—while we watch television?"

"That's against the rules," Susie said primly.

"And that's why it's a special treat," I said. "One-time offer—yes or no?"

"YES!" Bobby said. "Say yes, Susie!"

Susie agreed, and I parked them in front of the television while I went to get bowls and trays. We were going to be just fine.

Which wasn't what I was saying at ten that night, when my kids were still awake. Bobby had begged for a second bowl of ice cream, then threw up after his bath, and Susie was lying on my bed, holding her stomach and moaning dramatically. She hadn't even finished her first bowl, but there was no way to convince her that her brother eating too much ice cream was not contagious.

By eleven, they were both asleep, albeit in my bed. I, however, lay awake, staring at the ceiling, wondering if I could actually raise two children all by myself.

When you say your marriage vows, *until death* sounds so far away. You assume you'll be a little old lady with white hair and seven teeth left, with scores of grown children and grandchildren who will welcome you into their homes and take care of you by the time you have to face the world alone again.

But the best-laid plans of mice and men and all that jazz. And if I'd had it all to do again, the only thing I would have changed is I would have tried to take in more of the joy that we had. A mental snapshot of every smile, laugh, and gesture to flip through like a scrapbook in the times when it felt overwhelming. And there had been so very many happy moments. But we were young and thought we were immortal, as all young people do. Harry's father had died young, but that wouldn't happen to *us* because we were too happy to let something like death stop us. I let out a heavy sigh at the thought. If he were here, he would smooth my worried forehead with a kiss, spreading the lines with his fingertips to make me laugh if the kiss didn't do the trick. *You don't need to worry,* he'd whisper. *I'm not going anywhere.* And wrapped in his strong arms, I could believe that.

But in the end, our love was no more a match for death than anyone else's.

Bobby mumbled in his sleep—a trait he got from his father—and I leaned over to kiss his forehead, a gesture I repeated with Susie before snuggling into my pillow. "Good night, Harry," I whispered as I did every night. I no longer told him what he had missed each day—a habit that likely hurt more than it helped. But we were firm believers in not going to bed upset with each other, and I had found I couldn't sleep if I didn't say good night. Whether he could hear me or not.

2

I woke up to find a foot in my face. Bobby had flipped completely upside down in the night, and the arch of his foot was pressed up against my forehead. He was taking up most of the bed, while I slept on a sliver at the edge. Susie, however, looked comfortable on Harry's side. She lay on her stomach, her face pressed into his pillow. It didn't still smell like him—I did check from time to time—but Susie swore it did.

She hadn't slept in my bed for months now, but she'd frequently sneak in while I was sleeping and take his pillow. I offered to let her keep it, but she didn't want that either. I had caught her standing at my bedside with a hand on my chest several nights, making sure I was breathing. She was too young to understand that Harry had died of a heart attack—the same thing that killed his father at a similar age—and that I couldn't have inherited that.

The kids sleeping in my bed wasn't about Harry though—I understood that Grandma leaving was another loss, even if it was just the next step for us.

But as I eased myself out of the bed to avoid waking them, the crick in my neck reminded me that they were going back to their own rooms the following night. Thirty-two certainly didn't *sound* ancient, but I was finding that I turned into Methuselah very quickly if I didn't get enough real sleep anymore. I slipped on my bathrobe and slippers and padded downstairs to make the kids a special breakfast.

I flipped on the lights in the kitchen and began gathering the supplies for pancakes. The calendar on the fridge caught my eye, and I set the eggs on the counter. It was Sunday, March 3. Still jarring to see that we were in 1963. It felt like time had stopped two years ago in so many ways. Those early days of grief were so overwhelming—even more so because I had to stay upright for the kids. Not for me the luxury of wallowing in bed. No, I had to propel myself through the appearance of a normal day, taking Susie to school and pretending to be too busy to chat with the other moms so I wouldn't have to hear their expressions of sympathy that would send me spiraling into sobs. Passing Bobby to my mother when it became too much and crying in my closet to avoid detection before washing my face and reapplying makeup to hide the evidence. Death and taxes may have been the two certainties in life, but if I were in charge, husbands and pets would live exactly as long as we did.

But that kind of thinking got us nowhere.

Although it did remind me that I would have another battle on my hands soon—a dog was ostensibly off the table while my mother was here. She wasn't allergic, but the idea of a creature tracking mud into the house practically gave her the vapors, and that was a good excuse to avoid decisions I couldn't handle yet.

And puppies could be as hard to keep alive as toddlers. I didn't need that much extra responsibility.

Which was a problem to be dealt with when it arose, not now, I thought resolutely.

Instead, I grabbed a pen from the junk drawer next to the refrigerator and circled the date, writing the number one in the box. Today was the first day of our new lives. We just had to keep putting one foot in front of the other and someday, hopefully within this calendar year, we would stop having to remind ourselves to do that.

"Mama?" Susie's voice called from upstairs. Then more frantically before I could respond.

"Making breakfast," I called up sunnily. She appeared at the top of the stairs in her nightgown, her hair a halo of disarrayed brown curls, which she had gotten from me.

"I didn't know where you were," she said.

I climbed the stairs and cupped her chin in my hand. "Mommy isn't going anywhere," I said. "You know that."

"But—"

"No buts. My mother is still fine. My *grandmother* is still fine. And Bubbie—"

"Mama!" she said insistently. "You're not listening to me."

I straightened back up. The pediatrician had said it was important to listen to their concerns so that they felt they were getting a full answer. "You're right. What's wrong?"

"Bobby wet the bed."

I slapped the heel of my palm to my forehead. "My bed?" Susie nodded. "Okay, plan B. Pancakes can wait."

"I can get the sheets," Susie said.

I pulled her in close and kissed the top of her head. "Call me if you need help." I turned from her and raised my voice toward the bedroom. "Bobby, go put your pajamas in the washing machine for me, please."

"I'm sorry, Mommy," his mournful voice replied.

"Happens to the best of us," I said, with a cheer I didn't feel. If I remembered my Heloise, I'd need to clean the mattress with baking soda and vinegar, which was only a SLIGHT improvement on what it would smell like if I didn't clean it at all. "Now hurry up. I'm making pancakes."

"Ooh, pancakes!" He scampered out of my room and down the hall.

"Day one," I said quietly to myself as I poured flour into a bowl. I took a deep breath and let it out, feeling like it was the first real breath I could remember taking.

By the time the kids were downstairs, I had the first batch of pancakes on the table. Perfectly golden brown with the crispy edges that they loved. I returned to the stove to make more while they tucked in.

I opened the window over the kitchen sink and felt the breeze that swept in. March in the Washington, DC, suburbs tended to flip-flop wildly, from balmy to snow, and the sunlight was often deceptive. A bright red cardinal landed on the branch closest to the window, and I smiled when it chirped like it was speaking to me. The air was crisp, but not cold, with the promise of a lovely lamblike day before the lion roared again. *Lions.* Now that was an idea. We hadn't been to the zoo since before Harry died. Bobby probably didn't even remember it. What better way to start our new adventure as a family of three? "What would you think of going down to the zoo today?" I asked.

I should have waited until they were done eating, because the pancakes were abandoned immediately. But I made some sandwiches as they scurried off to get dressed and then fielded their complaints about how slow I was as I put on my makeup and dressed as well. Completely unfounded, I might add. I was ready to leave in under an hour, and off we went. And at least they wouldn't want ice cream after last night.

3

The National Zoo was one of the activities that had seemed too daunting without Harry, with the big hill in the center. I couldn't swing Bobby onto my shoulders when he got tired of walking like Harry would have. But at six, he insisted he could walk the whole way. And except for a cotton candy break, he did.

The kids oohed and ahhed at the lions and tigers and bears, but all I could see were the families. Complete and whole with a mom and a dad, some smiling, some annoyed over an unseen grievance, but all present. We would never be that again. And I wondered if I could ever walk into a room again without being reminded of that loss.

We drove home after our adventure, the kids tired and happy, each clutching a new stuffed animal from the gift shop. I couldn't dangle ice cream, dinner in front of the television, and new toys forever, but I made it clear this weekend was a special treat because it was our first weekend on our own. And as I glanced at them in the rearview mirror, I felt a sense of satisfaction. I had taken them to the zoo by myself without tears (theirs or mine) or losing anyone. And if Susie or Bobby noticed all the happy families with fathers, they didn't let on with so much as a sigh or wistful glance. They just enjoyed the new memories we were making.

We were going to be all right.

I lowered my sunglasses to see better as we neared the house. Something was on the front step. Something . . . large.

"Did we get a package?" Bobby asked.

"Not on a Sunday," I said, still trying to make out what it was.

My eyes widened as the image came into focus. Harry's mother, Ruth, was sitting on a suitcase—one of five—on our front step. Her dark hair was streaked with more gray than the last time I had seen her, and she wore a look of impatience as she squinted at the car, determining if it was us. Harry said she had needed glasses since his childhood but refused them because they made her "look old." I had seen pictures, and she was stunningly beautiful in her youth, with large brown eyes that Harry had inherited, a brilliant smile, and porcelain skin. She was still a handsome woman now, though the grief of losing first her husband, then her son had etched lines on her face.

"Wha—?"

Susie cut me off, rolling her window down frantically. "Grandma Ruth!" she called excitedly. "It's Grandma Ruth!"

I didn't mind my mother-in-law—much. Though the phone calls where I needed to comfort *her* for the whole first year were a bit . . . intense for a grieving widow. But the volume of suitcases, as well as the fact that she had neglected to call and tell me she would be stopping by, made me nervous.

The kids hopped out practically before the car was in park, throwing themselves at the grandmother who, despite living only half an hour away in the District of Columbia, they saw far less often than my mother before she had moved in. She returned their hugs, peppering them with kisses that left a seemingly unending trail of lipstick marks across their faces, before pulling hard candies from her purse to slip into their expectant hands.

I took a deep breath to steel myself before stepping out of the car. "Mother Ruth," I said as warmly as I could, using the name she had asked me to call her. Honestly, I tried to avoid saying her name whenever possible. *Mother Ruth* was far too formal, and, despite her intentions, I felt it kept me at arm's length. "We didn't know you were coming," I said. "We would have been home if we had."

"I suppose I'll need a key that actually works," she said without malice in her voice, which bore the slightest hint of an accent. She had come over at six, the youngest of five daughters, from a border town in what was either Ukraine, Russia, or the Soviet Union, depending on what year you were discussing.

I had forgotten she had the old key. My mother insisted, early in her residency, that we needed stronger locks with no man in the house, so she had hired a locksmith. "Of course," I said smoothly, while silently thanking my mother. I didn't need Ruth letting herself into my house day or night at will. Though this was the first time she had attempted to use the key since Harry's death.

Moving around her, I unlocked the door, and the children poured inside, Susie taking her grandmother's hand and asking her to help find a place for her new stuffed elephant.

"Bring my bags in, won't you?" Ruth called over her shoulder. "I can unpack down here if they're too heavy for you to bring upstairs to my room."

"Your room?" I asked, looking from the suitcases to her.

She extracted her hand from Susie's and turned back to look at me. "Yes," she said. "Your mother told me she was moving home, so I'll take the room she used."

I could feel my eyes widen, and I tried to lower the lids to a normal height. "For a few days?" I asked thinly, knowing this was too many bags for that.

"For as long as I'm needed." She smiled innocently at me.

"That—that's just it," I sputtered. "I told my mother she could go home because we're—we're fine. We have everything under control."

Ruth leaned down to Susie and told her to go on upstairs, and she'd be up in just a minute, then walked back to me, placing a hand on my cheek. "No," she said. "You don't. But don't worry. I'm here now. And mother knows best."

She reached around me in the doorway and grabbed a carpetbag that had been on top of one of the suitcases, heaving it over her shoulder and taking it up the stairs with her, calling Susie's name as she went.

At a loss, I brought her bags into the front hall, then glanced up the stairs before going to the kitchen, where I immediately placed a long-distance call to my mother, who answered on the third ring.

"Mom," I said by way of a whispered greeting. "Did you tell Ruth to move in?"

"Did I what?" she asked over a slightly staticky line.

"Ruth," I whispered slightly louder. "She just showed up. With suitcases. Five of them. And announced she's moving in indefinitely."

"I told her I was going home and to check in on you from time to time," my mother said. "I'm sure that's all she's doing."

"Five suitcases," I hissed. "What did you do?"

"Do you want me to come back down there? I'm sure she wouldn't stay if I was back."

I was less sure of that than she was. And the absolute last thing I wanted was to live in a house with the both of them. "No," I said. "I'll . . . handle it. Somehow." I told her I'd call her the following day and hung up.

Then I marched myself upstairs to face the issue head on.

The issue was in the room that was practically still warm from my mother living in it, sitting on the edge of the bed, then rising and sitting again. "How *did* your mother sleep on this mattress for two years?" she asked me. "Her back is only a few years younger than mine."

I had a tart reply on the tip of my tongue, but I swallowed it. She had lost her son. If "helping" us helped her through her own grief, who was I to take that from her? No. The best thing I could do was act grateful and then let her know, gently, as I had with my mother, that it was time for us to be on our own.

I wasn't going to take two years to do it this time though. A couple of weeks of Ruth Feldman in my house wouldn't be the end of the world. Though more than that might be. So that was the trick, then—make sure she saw we could do this ourselves and promise to visit with her more frequently. I would be able to do that in two weeks.

"The *guest* room doesn't get used that much," I said with a shrug. Did I put that little emphasis on *guest* as a pointed dig? Yes. I'm no saint. Even if they did canonize Jews, I doubted I'd be in the running—though not ceremoniously throwing her out might get me a nomination. "I'll bring up what I can carry," I told her. "And then I'll start dinner. Are you hungry, Mother Ruth?"

"I could eat." She cocked her head at me. "I suppose just 'Ruth' will do. 'Mother Ruth' is a mouthful when we're living together. Unless you'd rather call me 'Mother'?"

I studied her for a moment. Was that in response to calling it the guest room? She turned her back on me and began opening dresser drawers and examining the space, humming softly as she did so.

After lugging her bags upstairs, I returned to the kitchen. The calendar caught my eye with its circled number one. *Two weeks,* I thought through gritted teeth. *Then we start the "on our own" count again.*

I leaned my forehead on the smooth, cool surface of the refrigerator next to the calendar, wishing for the millionth time for some kind of sign from Harry. Could he see us? Did he even know that I was humoring her for his sake? But that was the worst part about death— if we knew the person wasn't really completely gone, it wouldn't be so hard. And after so long without a peep from Harry, my faith was shaky at best.

But I took a deep breath, steeling myself, and blinked away the tears that threatened my eyes. If I could make it through the first two years of widowhood, and I had, I could do anything. These next two weeks would be a breeze. An unpleasantly hot one, but a breeze all the same.

4

I hadn't planned on a full dinner after the zoo trip, so the leftover lasagna that my mother had made Friday night sounded absolutely heavenly.

But I couldn't very well serve Ruth leftovers when she was moving in because she didn't think I could handle motherhood on my own. Instead I took stock of what we had that I could throw together quickly and decided on chicken breasts and canned vegetables.

While she unpacked, I dipped the chicken in breadcrumbs and got the whole mess into the oven, keeping an ear out for her footsteps.

It wasn't that I disliked Ruth specifically. Her version of how things were done and mine just never quite lined up. And she didn't seem to understand that raising children in 1963 was different from how it had been in the throes of the Great Depression. Yes, my kids had to hide under their desks for bomb drills, but we had ample food and money for the necessities.

My relationship with Ruth started as I imagine most mother/daughter-in-law relationships do. By which I mean, I tiptoed as carefully as I could around her for the first couple of years, trying desperately to make sure she saw me as the perfect wife to her son and perfect mother to her future grandchildren, while she eyed me vigilantly for missteps.

At least that's how it felt.

She was neither the demon that I saw some of my friends describe their husbands' mothers as, nor the warm, second mother that I had imagined.

Warm wasn't a word I would use to describe Ruth Feldman. Even Harry, when asked about her in the early days, stumbled over how to characterize her. Involved? Yes. Nurturing? No. Though she did have a flair for the dramatic.

"You have to understand," he had said, beginning with a phrase that, had I not been a naive twenty-year-old in the midst of her first—and only—love affair, would have warned me of the power struggles that were coming. "She didn't grow up like we did. Coming here so young, losing everything, then losing my father . . ." He had paused there, remembering. "She did everything to make sure I had what I needed every single day."

We had been in his car, the night before he first brought me to her house. A meeting that I understood the importance of. "She sounds incredible," I said. And she did. The greatest hardship I ever saw my own mother witness was when her hairdresser retired to Miami. Oh, the indignity!

I hadn't been expecting the slight woman who greeted me—Harry stood a proud six feet tall, towering over his mother by a foot—by looking me up and down, sighing exaggeratedly, then announcing that there was no meat on my bones, so she would clearly have to teach me how to cook properly or else her Harry would starve.

"Barbara is a great cook, Ma," Harry had said, brushing it off playfully. "And she can eat as much as I do—she's just got a great figure."

I had never cooked for him, nor eaten anywhere near the quantity I had seen him put away, but I beamed up at him, grateful for the defense. Harry was her only child and the light of her life. No one could defuse her the way he could.

Of course, her stated intention to teach me to cook was laughable as her culinary skills were . . . interesting, to put it kindly. I remembered looking over at Harry, wondering how he grew so tall on food like this, before gnawing on a half-frozen Passover cookie that Ruth proudly said I wouldn't have known was for Passover if she hadn't told me.

I definitely would not have guessed Passover, as I wasn't sure it was food, but I smiled and politely agreed, which meant I received her seal of approval.

According to Harry. Because all I got to my face was criticisms. Ostensibly playful criticisms, but when it's your future mother-in-law, you can't exactly play back yet. And we never warmed to the point where I could.

And the censure only intensified after we got married. I confessed, just two months after returning from our honeymoon, that I was worried our new home was haunted. I would come home from an errand or lunch with a friend and find a plant had moved from one room to another. Our bookshelf was rearranged. Even our bed, which I made each morning, was made *differently* from the way I had made it. Harry listened, first concerned, then amused.

"I think I know who your ghost is," he said, crossing to the kitchen phone. He dialed, waited, then said, "Hey, Ma. Have you been to our house recently?" He nodded, then chuckled. "Yeah, let Barbara know before you come over next time, please. She thought she was going crazy."

I would have preferred a ghost, honestly. But it only took two more warnings from Harry about not meddling too much in our lives before she started calling before she came over—or at least knocking before she came in.

"Dinner will be ready in ten minutes," I called upstairs. "Susie, come set the table, please."

No one answered me.

"Susie!" I called again. I heard a muted laugh, and I sighed. Then I checked the timer on the counter, peeked in the oven—serving burnt chicken wouldn't help my case that Ruth's presence was unnecessary— and then climbed the stairs to find my wayward daughter and remind her that no chores meant no allowance.

The doors to both children's rooms were open, with no sound emanating. Granted, it wouldn't be the first time they'd hidden under a bed or in a closet, waiting to jump out and try to scare me. I always played along, even though their giggles as I entered their rooms gave them away every time. But the door to the spare room was closed, with muffled voices trickling out.

I hesitated, debating the etiquette of knocking in my own home when my children were inside, but ultimately opted for politeness over asserting dominance and rapped lightly.

No one answered, so I opened the door. Susie was wearing a matronly dress, complete with a wide-brimmed straw hat adorned with flowers that made her look like a miniature Minnie Pearl. Bobby was draped in a tweed suit older than I was, complete with a bow tie and a fedora.

Confused, I turned to Ruth. "You packed a men's suit with you?"

"It was his grandfather's," Ruth said, waving a hand. "He can wear it for his bar mitzvah."

In seven years, I thought. But it wasn't worth arguing.

"Get changed," I told them. "Dinner will be ready in . . ." I glanced down at my watch. "Seven minutes. And the table isn't set."

"They're having fun," Ruth said, putting a hand on Susie's arm as she started toward the door.

"One of Susie's chores is setting the table."

"And if she misses it one night, will it be the end of the world?"

I wanted to reply sharply that children needed structure. That the entire purpose of chores was to teach responsibility. Not to mention that I had just cooked a meal—albeit a simple one—that I didn't want to entirely because *she* had shown up unannounced on my doorstep and that Susie not setting the table meant I had to do yet another task.

But Susie looked up at me with Harry's big brown eyes, and I found myself acquiescing. Her straight nose, high cheekbones, and plump, rosy lips were mine, but her eyes were all his. "Just this once," I said to her.

She threw her arms around me in a tight hug, and I felt some of the tension leave my shoulders, relishing that I didn't have to be the bad guy when pitted against Ruth and her bag of dress-up clothes.

Then I went down and set the table.

～

Bobby wrinkled his nose at my chicken. "Can't I eat Grandma's lasagna instead?"

"I didn't make lasagna," Ruth said. "You'll eat what your mother made you." She cut a piece of her own chicken, then held it up in front of her face to inspect it.

"Our *other* Grandma made lasagna," Bobby explained, still making a sour face at the chicken. "Before she left."

"I'm sure that will make a wonderful lunch for tomorrow," Ruth said. "But tonight, we clean our plates." She pointed with her fork.

My toes positively curled in my shoes. "Ruth," I said quietly. "We don't follow the clean plate rule."

"What on earth do you mean?" She turned back to the children. "You'll finish your food. There are starving children."

Both little faces turned to look at me. Harry's doctor had been crystal clear that his best chance of avoiding his father's fate was being active and keeping his weight down. From that day forward, we had to untrain ourselves from our Depression-era upbringings. Not that it had made a difference for him in the end, but meals stopped being a struggle once we allowed the kids to stop eating when they felt full.

Now, however, I was torn between showing respect to my mother-in-law, who had suffered from actual hunger, and standing up for my kids.

Talk about a rock and a hard place.

Bobby pushed his plate toward the center of the table, then crossed his arms defiantly. "You can send it to the starving children," he said. "I want lasagna."

"Then you'll go to bed hungry," Ruth warned.

I made a T with my hands to signal a time-out. "We don't send children to bed hungry in this house either," I said, more firmly this time. "Bobby, you know the rule. If you don't want to eat what I've made, you can make yourself a peanut butter sandwich." He glared at me for a moment, then pushed his chair back and went into the kitchen, where the telltale screech of a chair being dragged across the linoleum floor told me he was getting the bread and peanut butter.

"The chicken *is* rather dry," Ruth said in a loud whisper. Susie looked from her to me with wide eyes, but I shook my head at her.

Then I took a deep breath, counted to five, and exhaled. "The chicken isn't the issue," I said calmly. "I am just raising them with values that don't match the Depression upbringing that Harry and I had because they aren't living in that world. And assuming things don't come to a head with the Soviets, they're going to grow up in a world where they hopefully won't ever have to worry about food."

Bobby returned to the table with the sloppiest sandwich I had ever seen, jelly dripping out of it at crazy angles, and a big, self-satisfied grin. "Better?" I asked him.

"Better," he said through a mouthful of peanut butter, his blue eyes, the same shade as mine, crinkling at the corners.

Ruth started to say something, but I beat her to it. "Don't talk with your mouth full," I said.

"Then don't ask me questions while I'm eating," he said, still chewing.

I couldn't help but smile, though I tried to hide it from Ruth.

Ruth grumbled through much of the rest of the meal, then reached for Bobby's plate when she was finished with her food and ate his chicken as well.

She had a hard childhood, I remembered Harry telling me. *Her family had been wealthy in the old country, but that all changed when they came here. They escaped a pogrom with only what they could carry.*

My shoulders sank, watching her finish Bobby's unwanted chicken. The last thing I wanted was to be unkind to Harry's mother—even if I didn't invite her to be a guest in my house.

Ruth retired to her room to finish unpacking while I bathed the children—a bit of a misnomer as Susie had become self-conscious about bathing with her brother in the last year and now took a shower by herself in my bathroom while I sat on the closed toilet seat next to the tub as Bobby washed himself, having also rejected my help. He didn't actually need me in there at all, but he was a little skittish about being alone.

I brought both kids to Ruth's room to say good night before reading them their bedtime story and tucking them in. Susie went down easily. Bobby still wanted me to sit in the rocking chair in his room until he fell asleep.

When his eyes finally fluttered closed and I heard his breathing settle into a slow, regular pattern, I tiptoed out of the room, shutting the door quietly behind me.

I wanted nothing more than to soak in a hot tub and just exhale, and I debated doing exactly that as I crept past Ruth's room, where a light peeked out from under the door. I went as far as turning on the water in the bathtub before the guilt hit me.

No, I didn't want her there. Especially not when my own mother had just left. But she lost her only son and was here to help. I turned off the water and pulled the stopper, letting it drain. The least I could do was be kind. I looked up at the ceiling. "You owe me for this one," I said quietly.

So instead of relaxing, I went downstairs, made up a glass of Alka-Seltzer, and brought it to her room, knocking softly.

When she opened the door, I held out the glass. "I thought you might need this."

"Thank you," she said, taking the glass and bringing it to her mouth to sip. "I do have heartburn from whatever was on that chicken."

I blinked at her. It was literally egg and breadcrumbs. But I could let that go. "Just so you know, there's no need to finish the kids' food. I won't throw it away. I save what they don't eat for leftovers."

"You couldn't have told me that before I ate two dinners?" she asked, patting her practically nonexistent stomach. But there was a mischievous twinkle in her eyes—Harry and Susie had inherited that same glint when they caused trouble too—which both made me feel better about giving up my bath and told me this wouldn't be an enduring issue.

"Would you like to watch some television with me?"

"No," she said. "Thank you. It's been a long day. I'm just going to go to sleep."

"Of course," I said. "There are more towels under the sink in the bathroom and just let me know if there's anything else you need."

"I'll be fine," she told me. "Good night, Barbara."

"Good night, Ruth."

5

As the hot water of the shower caressed my shoulders Monday morning, I leaned my tired forehead against the cool tile wall. Susie woke up from a nightmare around three, and I had struggled to fall back asleep after getting her settled.

But the cold contrast of the tile triggered a memory—it was an old one, from the early days of our marriage, before kids and responsibilities had sapped so much of our energy. I always woke up before Harry so that I could make him breakfast while he showered. But one morning, he surprised me, pulling open the shower curtain and slipping in behind me. "What—?" I'd said before he silenced me with a kiss, running his hands across my wet body before turning me around, my forehead against the tile as it was now.

I grazed a hand down from my neck, moving lower as I thought about the warm, comforting feel of Harry's body against mine, imagining my hand was his. My breath hitched slightly, and then—

A hand suddenly ripped the shower curtain back.

I screamed, hunching over reflexively and trying to cover myself against the intruder, before looking up into my mother-in-law's face.

"Ruth!" I tried to wrench the shower curtain back into place with one hand, using what I could of the fabric to shield my body, but she kept a firm grip on it.

"Where do you keep the spatulas?" she asked, entirely unfazed by my nudity, the hand that wasn't keeping the shower curtain open resting on her hip.

"Can it wait until I'm out of the shower?" I asked.

"Only if the children will eat burnt eggs. Where are they?"

"The drawer next to the refrigerator," I said, finally yanking the shower curtain from her hand and tugging it closed. "Why didn't you just look in the drawers?"

"Well, I didn't want to overstep."

But opening the curtain while I'm showering isn't overstepping? "Next time, please just look in the drawers," I said through gritted teeth. Then I remembered what time it was. "Wait. The kids aren't up yet."

"They were reading in their rooms and famished. I'm making them eggs."

"They're supposed to stay in their rooms until seven."

Ruth started to pull the curtain back again, but I held it shut with all my strength, peeking my head out from around the side to appease her. "They're too hungry to wait until seven," she said. "I'll go finish making the eggs."

I waited until I heard the bathroom door close before I lowered my shoulders. My eyes drifted toward the shower wall, where my forehead had rested, but the memory was long gone now. And even if it wasn't, the mood was.

What had I gotten myself into?

I tilted my head skyward. "You're in so much trouble that you're not here to deal with this for me," I said, then sighed and turned off the water. "Two weeks," I muttered as I toweled off.

～

I walked into the kitchen to find Ruth at the sink. The air was smoky and both kids looked up at me with matching expressions of concern.

I crossed to the window and opened it to let fresh air in. Ruth glanced at me over her shoulder, but I smiled to disarm her. "It's going to be a lovely day," I said, nodding to the cardinal who was back on his branch. She turned back to the sink, satisfied that I wasn't going to give her grief about the smoke, and I went to the table to kiss the children's foreheads.

"Mommy," Bobby whispered. "I can't eat this."

I looked to Susie, who was cutting her food into teeny-tiny pieces but not eating either.

"I'm sure it's not that bad," I replied in a hushed tone, my eyes on Ruth's back. Then I actually looked at the eggs, which were watery with chunks of red and white in them. "Is that . . . ?"

"He wanted lasagna last night," Ruth said without turning around. "So I put some in the eggs. It's practically an omelet—cheese and tomatoes."

The kids looked at me imploringly, and I hesitated. Respecting elders was such an ironclad law of my youth, but there had to be some kind of line when it came to defending my own children.

I took Bobby's fork and poked at the pile of mush on his plate. "Like an omelet," I repeated optimistically. "Cheese and . . . tomatoes . . ." No. The kids couldn't eat this. But how to tell her that politely?

Of course, if I wanted to get rid of her faster, rude might just do the job. That *was* tempting after the shower. But I looked down at the determined woman next to the sink and found myself wavering. I didn't remember saying that his family would be mine when I said *until death parts us* in our wedding vows. But if the roles were reversed, and I was gone, I knew full well that Harry would ensure my parents were in the kids' lives.

Ruth was abrasive and stuck in her ways, but she had never, to my knowledge, acted maliciously. This wasn't a punishment for Bobby's peanut butter sandwich—it was her attempt at making peace over the night before.

I joined Ruth at the sink. "Ruth," I said quietly. "Did you try the eggs?"

"I had a piece of toast," she said, still working at the burned frying pan with a piece of steel wool.

I turned off the water. "Leave it," I said. "Heloise says boiling water, vinegar, and some baking soda will do most of the work for you. I can do that later."

"I don't know a Heloise," Ruth said, reaching for the hot water knob. Her voice dripped with distrust. "Is she German?"

"I—I don't know her in person. It's a newspaper column on cleaning."

She shook her head. "It's nothing some elbow grease won't fix. I don't need the newspaper to tell me how to clean a pan."

"Listen," I said. "I appreciate that you wanted to feed Bobby what he wanted. It shows how much you care. But lasagna and eggs just don't work together."

"What are you talking about? The children love my eggs." She turned around and took in their full plates. Both kids looked down guiltily. She shook her head and wiped her hands on the dish towel. "You have to try them at least," she told them. "They don't have to finish food they don't like, but they do have to try it." Then she glanced at me. "That one is a Grandma rule."

I bit my bottom lip. "I suppose that's fair—with the condition that if you're experimenting, you try it first."

"We ate boiled cabbage for a full year when I was young," she said. "This is a delicacy compared to that."

I took Susie's fork from her hand and held it out to Ruth. She crossed to the table, took the fork, speared a large bite of lasagna eggs, brought it to her mouth, and chewed, her face remaining neutral as she swallowed.

"Well," she said, reaching for her coffee and taking an inordinately long sip. "Of course we didn't like these. Whoever heard of Jews eating lasagna in their eggs? I'll put a little gefilte fish in next time, and they'll be a delicacy."

"Can I just have cereal?" Bobby asked, his eyes wide. "Please, Mommy?"

"Me too," Susie said, looking slightly green.

"Yes," I said. "Grandma was just kidding about gefilte fish. Weren't you?"

She looked like she was considering it. "Maybe for Passover." I shot her a sharp look as I poured Sugar Frosted Flakes, which the kids had talked me into letting them get, into two bowls.

"Why don't you come grocery shopping with me today and we can pick out some things they'll like?"

"They'll never eat well if you only make things they like already. They need to try new things, even if they aren't their favorite."

I held my tongue, assuring myself as I packed lunches for school that I would be the first Jewish candidate for sainthood by the end of these two weeks.

6

After I took the kids to school, I returned home to pick up Ruth to go to the store.

I saw her looking at me from the corner of my eye as I drove toward the grocery store near my house. "You don't need to pretend you like me," Ruth said. "I know what it's like to live with a mother-in-law. We lived with Abe's parents when we got married."

"I like you just fine, Ruth," I said, desperate to ask why she was here if any of what she had just said was true.

"You'll see I'm right eventually. About needing help. Though I'm an absolute pleasure unlike my mother-in-law. Dreadful woman."

If she was a pleasure, Abe's mother must have been an actual demon. As for help, so far she had only been more work. But I was confident in my ability to do it all myself. And she would soon see that she hadn't been right after all.

"You're welcome to come visit us anytime," I said.

Ruth flipped on the radio, and we were spared the need to speak for the rest of the drive, by the Exciters singing "Tell Him."

∼

"Morning, Barbara," Eddie said pleasantly as Ruth poked and prodded every single melon in the produce department.

Eddie was my best friend Janet's brother, and he owned and ran Greene Grocers, which his parents had opened twenty years earlier, making the transition from a produce cart down in the Northern Market on O Street in DC to an actual storefront in Silver Spring, before eventually moving to the current location in Rockville. The name was a clever play on their last name and the original cart's selection.

Most people I knew preferred the bigger and newer Giant grocery store up at Congressional Plaza, but I was loyal to Janet and her family. And I had known Eddie for fourteen years now. I still remembered him carrying Janet's trunk into our shared dorm room, and the smile that lit up his whole face as I introduced myself to him. He was three years older than us and lived off campus by then, but he popped by frequently to see his little sister—even if the two of them squabbled like cats and dogs. Truth be told, I'd had a bit of a crush on him that first year. Not that I could act on it—nothing would have soured my new friendship with Janet faster than admitting to liking her (in her words) annoying older brother. And then I met Harry, pushing Eddie firmly into the category of things that weren't meant to be.

Eddie knew a lot about things that weren't meant to be. After college, he served in Korea, planning to use the GI Bill to go to medical school. But a mishap in a plane left him with severely impaired vision in one eye, crushing his dream of being a surgeon. When he returned, he went to work for his father, taking over entirely when his mother died.

"Eddie," I said. "How are you?"

"Doing well," he said. Then he looked down and noticed the apron he had on and quickly removed it, shaking his head slightly. He always dropped what he was doing when I came into the store, making me feel like part of the family—maybe even more so, since Janet usually just got a nod if her kids weren't with her. Then again, I didn't criticize changes he made in the store, like she did. I actually preferred Eddie's little touches to their father's way of doing things. "And yourself?"

It was one of the great mysteries why no one had snapped Eddie up, though I did sometimes wonder if he was self-conscious about his eye. You couldn't tell anything was wrong by looking at him, but he did need to close that eye to see more clearly. He wasn't tall like Harry, but he was handsome, with dark, wavy hair and eyes that twinkled when he smiled. Moreover, he was funny and above all, kind-hearted. He provided platters for Harry's shivah free of charge and came over to shovel the snowfalls we'd had in the last two years among other minor household chores that were beyond my skill level. The definition of a mensch.

"I'm . . ." I didn't know how to finish that sentence, honestly. "Well, my mother went back to Philadelphia."

Eddie raised his eyebrows. "Permanently or for a visit?"

"I sent her home," I said. "I'm ready to do this myself." Then I glanced over at Ruth, who stood, a melon in hand, watching us intently. "Well—somewhat. Eddie, I'd like you to meet my mother-in-law, Mrs. Feldman. Ruth, this is Eddie Greene."

"*Greene* as in why there's an *e* at the end of *Greene Grocers*?" she asked.

Eddie grinned a little bashfully. "My father loves a good pun. But yes."

"It's clever," she said. "There used to be a man down at the O Street Market with the same name for his cart."

"That would be my father," Eddie said.

Ruth smiled broadly, then it faded. "Is he . . . ?"

"Still with us," Eddie said, and Ruth exhaled in relief. "He retired, and I took over when my mother passed."

Ruth's face was all sympathy. "I'm sorry. Your father had the best produce in the market during the Depression."

"He did." Eddie nodded. "It's how he was able to expand to a store." He glanced down at Ruth's hands. "Listen, if those melons aren't to your liking, you just let me know, and I'll grab you some from the back."

"Do you do that for all your customers or just the pretty widows?" Ruth asked, nodding in my direction. I felt a flush creeping into my cheeks at the implication.

"Everyone," Eddie assured her, then leaned in closer. "But if I didn't take special care of Barbara, I'd never hear the end of it from my sister."

"Your sister?"

"Janet," I said. "My best friend." Ruth didn't look like it rang a bell. "Matron of honor in my wedding?"

"Ah, yes. Well, the melons are perfect," she said, though she had been complaining otherwise before she knew whose market it was. Then she turned to me. "I'm going to go get some eggs. I noticed you were low this morning."

"I can come with you."

She was already walking away with the cart but winked at me over her shoulder. "You two talk, it's fine."

"She seems nice," Eddie said.

"You think everyone is nice."

He chuckled. "It's the store. Everyone is nice *to me* because no one wants to be rude to the person who could lick all the strawberries before selling them."

"Eddie! You wouldn't. Would you?"

He winked. "Let me know if I have any customers you don't like, and then you can lick them yourself."

I laughed despite myself. "Eddie Greene, I don't believe you for a second."

"No," he said. "You shouldn't." His gaze turned slightly concerned. "You said you were ready to do this yourself though. Does that mean you didn't invite your mother-in-law to stay?"

"That's one way to put it."

"What's another way?"

I sighed. "She showed up unannounced with five giant suitcases."

Eddie's eyes widened. "So I should have licked the melons?"

"Quite possibly," I said. "I'm hoping that when she sees how capable I am, she'll cut it to a two-week visit instead of the indefinite one she's implying it is."

He reached out like he was going to touch my arm, then thought better of it and shifted his apron to the other hand. "She won't be able to help but see that," he reassured me. "She's probably just jealous that your mother got so much time with the kids."

"And it's good for the kids to be around Harry's mom. I know that. But, Eddie, this morning she made eggs and put leftover lasagna in them."

"Leftover lasagna?" I nodded, and he laughed again. "Well, I'm sure your cooking will put her mind at ease, then."

I exhaled audibly. "She's still complaining about the chicken I cooked last night. It's going to be a long two weeks. What's good today that I can impress her with?"

"I'll have Gary wrap up some of the veal," he said.

"Not veal. The kids won't eat it. I need something they'll eat to prove that they're not overly picky."

"Brisket?" I nodded. "I'll make sure it's the best we have."

"You're an angel, Eddie. Truly."

He smiled at me. "It's the least I can do." Then he quickly added, "You know I don't want to make Janet mad."

"Well, I appreciate it, even if it's not strictly from the goodness of your heart."

"Let me know if you need me to take care of anything around the house so she knows you do have help," Eddie said. "I don't mind."

"That means a lot. Thank you. Besides, she was complaining about the guest room mattress—maybe a few rough nights of sleep will chase her out."

Eddie strode across the produce aisle and plucked a single green pea, which he tucked into my palm. "Might want this to put under that mattress."

I laughed as Ruth rounded the corner with eggs and a box of cream of wheat in the shopping cart. She looked from me to Eddie and back to me, her eyes narrowing as she studied us.

"I'll have Gary pack up that brisket," Eddie said quietly, then turned to Ruth. "Did you find everything you needed, Mrs. Feldman?"

"I did," she said. "I do hope I'm not interrupting."

"Not at all," I said. "Eddie was just telling me that they have a great cut of brisket that he's going to have them wrap for us."

"Why are you holding a pea?" Ruth asked me.

Eddie excused himself and walked toward the butcher counter, his shoulders shaking in laughter.

7

Tuesday through Friday, I dropped the children at school and then spent five hours at the hospital, which was a relatively new arrangement. I had started as a volunteer when Bobby went off to kindergarten and I was left alone with my mother and my thoughts, either of which was enough to drive a person mad. I needed to find a way to occupy my time.

My mother suggested charity work, and after a trip to the emergency room to get stitches for Bobby's right ear left me practically hyperventilating, I decided I had to get past my memories of the night Harry died. So I marched up to the door one day, took a deep breath, and walked inside, breathing in the faint scents of bleach, antiseptic, and sadness, and went straight to the nurses' station, where I asked how I could be of any help.

Dressed as a candy striper, I patted the arms of the elderly, fed Jell-O to those with shaking hands, and comforted new mothers. The latter of which was the best balm for my battered soul. It was good to remind myself that hospitals weren't just where life ended, but where it began as well.

But there wasn't much organization to how and when volunteers came and went, and there were days when the head nurse would call, begging me to come in again. So I started a chart, making sure that we would have candy stripers there every day of the week, including weekends, and that they were assigned to the areas of highest need.

Before long, we were running a tight ship.

By the end of my second month there, Dr. Harper, the hospital's administrator, offered me a job. I shook my head at first, thinking he was going to pay me for candy striping. "Mrs. Feldman," he said, leaning toward me over his hands, which were folded on his desk. "You don't understand. While you're useful with patients, you're invaluable in keeping this hospital running. Nurse Frank told me that she was on the verge of quitting when you came in."

Suddenly I was employed. It didn't pay much—the hefty life insurance policy that Harry had taken out (and entrusted to Janet's husband to avoid worrying me) amply provided for us—but I deposited my checks dutifully, watching proudly as the little nest egg of my own earnings grew. And with Mondays off for errands and housekeeping, and the kids in school, it was an arrangement that suited everyone.

I asked Ruth what she was going to do with herself while I was at work. Remembering how she used to let herself in and rearrange things, I didn't love the idea of leaving her home alone, but she told me she was perfectly capable of entertaining herself.

The hospital had rapidly become a comfort zone for me. For five hours a day, four days a week, I could shed my mom skin and be an unencumbered human. There was something so satisfying in knowing that I was helping people beyond my own family and making a contribution to the world beyond the children I had brought into it.

Work at the hospital wasn't easy. There were days when I left only to sit in my car and sob over the news I had seen families experience while I held their hands, feeling their pain on a level that they would never know how well I understood. But there were beautiful moments as well. Miracle births, coma patients waking up coherent, life-saving procedures on people who, moments earlier, had seemed beyond saving. It was a whole world of life, death, and everything in between, and I was proud to be a part of keeping that running.

"Good morning," I said brightly, dropping off a box of Montgomery Donuts for the front desk staff. I had another for the nurses upstairs.

"You're an angel," Delores said, opening the box and letting the heavenly aroma of sugared fried dough overpower the antiseptic hospital smell.

"How busy is it today?" I asked with a wink.

"Not too terrible, but Dr. Howe is in rare form today according to Donna."

I grimaced. Dr. Howe was an absolute menace to every woman on staff. Dr. Harper knew, because I complained about him regularly, but was avoiding the issue as long as he could because there was no denying that Dr. Howe was a fantastic doctor. He was just a terrible human being. And quite often, dealing with him fell to me—not because I cowed him in any way, but because I had nothing to lose by standing up to him. He still pinched my bottom anytime he thought he could get away with it, but I fought back when I could, "accidentally" stomping on his foot or slamming a door in his face. And I had no problem warning him to leave the nursing staff alone or reporting him to Dr. Harper, useless as that was. The rest of the hospital staff relied on the income and therefore couldn't be quite as forceful in their rebukes as I could. Which meant I had frequently taken on the role of protector—which Dr. Howe incorrectly interpreted as flirting.

"I'll keep an eye out," I said as a team of paramedics brought a stretcher in from an ambulance outside. "Hope it's an easy day." I moved past them toward the elevators and went to the third floor, where a supply closet had been turned into a small office for me. Not that I did much in there beyond writing up schedules—I still spent as much time assisting with patients as I could, even if I no longer wore the red-and-white pinafore of a volunteer.

"Barb?" Gloria Ramirez, one of my favorite nurses, poked her head in. "You busy?"

I was, but I never minded helping. "What can I do for you?"

"It's Mrs. Kline again," Gloria said with an eye roll.

I rose from my desk chair. "What is it this time?"

"She's refusing to see Dr. Lefkowitz."

I blinked three times in rapid succession. I knew exactly why she was protesting, but to refuse the best cardiologist in the state was insanity.

Mrs. Kline was always uncooperative with Gloria because she was Mexican—never mind that her parents and grandparents were born here, which wasn't true for most of the white and Jewish doctors and nurses. Not that she responded much better to me with the last name Feldman, but I felt we had made some progress on her last visit to the hospital. "I'll see what I can do."

"You're a godsend," Gloria said with a sigh. "I swear that woman is going to be the death of me."

"And somehow, she'll outlive us all," I said, which got a laugh.

Gloria gave me her room number and I went across the hall, down a flight of stairs, and knocked on the open door. "Mrs. Kline?" I asked.

"Not *you* again," she said as I came into view.

"Me again," I said cheerfully. "We're practically best friends with how often we see each other."

Mrs. Kline sniffed. "I wouldn't associate with you if I weren't dying."

Mrs. Kline had been "dying" for years before I started working here. As far as any of us could tell, her primary ailment was loneliness, perhaps mixed with a bit of hypochondria.

"Mrs. Kline, I hear you won't see Dr. Lefkowitz—"

"I want a Christian doctor."

"Well, Mrs. Kline, you happen to live in an area with one of the biggest concentrations of Jews in this country after New York. And while you're free to select an outside cardiologist of your choice, when you come to the hospital, I'm afraid you need to see whichever doctor is on duty, regardless of religion." *Or of your own bigotry,* I thought.

"Then I'll leave," she said, sitting up in the bed and trying to unhook the wires connected to her.

"You can certainly do that," I said. She stopped and looked at me suspiciously. "But it *is* against medical advice. So if you have a heart attack and drop dead on the street, it's entirely your own decision. And the hospital will not be financially liable if you have a heart attack and live."

She stared at me for a moment to see if I was bluffing—which I was, just not in the way she assumed. I would have bet a week's worth of groceries that Dr. Lefkowitz would find absolutely nothing wrong with her heart. Just as the oncologists had found no cancer, the neurosurgeon had found no tumor, and the pulmonologist had found nothing wrong with her lungs. But I raised an eyebrow and gestured toward the door.

Slowly she leaned back against the bed, pressing a hand to her chest. "Fine," she said eventually. "I'll see that man. But I want a good Christian nurse in here with him, so I have a witness if he kills me."

"I won't do, then?" I was teasing her by now.

"Certainly not," she said. "You'd lie to protect your kind."

"Right. How silly of me. Have a *lovely* day, Mrs. Kline."

"And not that Ramirez woman either!" she called after me.

Gloria was outside the room waiting for me. "She'll see Dr. Lefkowitz as long as a white, gentile nurse is in the room as well."

Gloria closed her eyes and took a deep breath. "I suppose that'll work," she said. "I wish she'd choose a different hospital already."

"We could always refer her to Mount Sinai up in New York, but quite honestly, the Jews have suffered enough in the last twenty-five years. I wouldn't wish Mrs. Kline on anyone else."

Gloria chuckled. "I meant a psychiatric hospital."

I patted her arm. "We can ask Dr. Lefkowitz to suggest that as a next step. Actually you'd better warn him what he's going into anyway."

"She won't let you be in there? She always eventually does what you say."

I shook my head. "Feldman was a dead giveaway. You'd think with a Jewish-*sounding* name, even if it's not spelled that way, that she'd at least question last names, but there's no rationalizing bigotry."

Gloria thanked me and went to go find our esteemed cardiologist, who had survived Normandy, but whose upcoming interaction with Mrs. Kline just might do him in.

Then another nurse came to find me for the next catastrophe, and I stayed busy until it was time to leave and go pick up the kids.

8

"Can I *please* go play at Rudy's house?" Bobby asked. "Please, Mom?"

"After you do your homework," I said as I unlocked the front door of the house. "Just like I said the last two times you asked me."

"I'll do it later, I promise!"

"You know the . . ." I trailed off as we walked inside. Then I leaned back out the door and made sure I was in the right house. Yes, that was our address. And the key in my hand had unlocked the door. But every stick of furniture had been rearranged. The kids looked at me in confusion as well.

Music was coming from the radio in the kitchen, and I steeled myself. "You two go on up to your rooms and do your homework. I'll make a snack and then you can go play." Neither moved, so I pointed to the stairs. "Homework. Now."

I waited until they had scampered up the stairs before I marched into the kitchen, switching off Eydie Gorme, who was singing on the radio to blame it on the bossa nova, as I entered.

"I was listening to that," Ruth said mildly from the stove.

"Ruth," I said as measuredly as I could. "What happened to the furniture?"

"Isn't it lovely?" she asked. "Just the freshening up the house needed."

I blinked at her. "Ruth, you can't just rearrange someone else's house."

"Well, I'm living here now too, and—"

"Visiting," I said, cutting her off. "You're visiting here now. This is still *my* house, and I expect to be able to have the furniture the way that I like it."

"Suit yourself," she said with a shrug as she continued to stir whatever she was cooking. I pinched the bridge of my nose in irritation, then went into the living room to see how much work it would be to move everything back into place.

"I finished my homework," Bobby said, bounding into the room. I always checked it with him, especially when he did it in two minutes flat, but I just didn't have the patience right then.

"Go ask your grandmother for a snack, and then you can go to Rudy's house."

∼

It wasn't until dinner was finished and I was sitting on the closed toilet while Bobby bathed that I realized the kids had eaten Ruth's dinner without complaint. Truth be told, I couldn't remember what it was through the rage of dealing with the furniture, nor if I had actually eaten any of it. My stomach rumbled, and I realized I likely hadn't.

"What was dinner again?" I asked Bobby as he emerged from under the bubbles with a white head and bubble beard.

He looked at me like I was the strange one. "Spaghetti and meatballs," he said.

I nodded. That was difficult to mess up and a guaranteed kid pleaser.

"I like yours better though," Bobby said loyally. "Grandma's spaghetti is kind of crunchy. Like eating bones."

I let out a yelp of a laugh.

"What?" Bobby asked suspiciously.

"Nothing," I said, dumping a cup of water over his head and revealing his brown hair. "I just love you."

"I love you too," he said, dipping his head back into the bubbles. "Do I look like a grandpa?"

"One with very smooth skin," I assured him. Then I realized I had no idea how to shave a face. Legs, sure, but in the next ten years, I was going to need to figure that out. I wondered who had taught Harry to shave. Maybe a friend's husband would step in?

That was what Ruth and my own mother didn't understand: sure, I needed help, but I needed Harry's help, not theirs. More mothers were just too many cooks in the kitchen, quite literally sometimes.

It was an issue Ruth *should* understand, having lived it. But maybe having only one child was different. Maybe thirty years ago was different. Maybe she and I were just different.

Or maybe the reason she didn't have chin hairs was because she taught herself how to shave too.

I dumped another cup of water over Bobby and told him it was about time to get out of the bath. I had a few years before I had to figure it out. There had to be directions somewhere. Maybe a library book on it. Or I could ask Eddie to explain shaving to me sometime before Bobby grew a beard. I would just have to be enough.

Susie was in her room, her grandmother brushing her hair, when I came to tell her it was bedtime. I listened at the door for a moment, jealous and wanting to tell Ruth that that was my job, not hers.

"Really?" Susie was asking. "A pony? Of your own?"

"Of my own. I loved her," Ruth said. Her voice sounded wistful as she remembered the simpler time of her childhood. Not that her childhood *had* been simpler, but when she was just a couple of years younger than Susie, she couldn't have understood how complicated things were about to become.

"What was her name?"

"*Sheyntkeyt.*"

"What does that mean?"

"Beauty," Ruth said. "Like how I call you my *sheyna maidelah*. Pretty girl."

Susie thought for a moment. "What happened to her?"

Ruth grew quiet, remembering. "We had to leave her," she said eventually. "We had to leave everything to come here."

"Why couldn't you bring her with you?"

"We had to leave suddenly," Ruth said. "In the night. The men—"

Knowing the rest of the story, I entered the room quickly. "Ready for bed?" I asked lightly.

"Not yet," Susie said, waving me off. "What men?" she asked Ruth.

"The men said if they wanted to come to America, they had to come right then," I said, not letting Ruth reply. Susie was too young for pogroms. And while the Russians may have taken that pony, it was much more likely that Ruth watched them slaughter it. We had enough issues with nightmares as it was these days. "And it's a good thing they did, or Daddy and I wouldn't have met." I looked purposefully at Ruth over Susie's head. "Isn't that right?"

Ruth studied me for a moment. "I suppose. If you want to look at it that way," she said. "Time for bed, my *sheyna maidelah*."

"Can Grandma tuck me in?" Susie asked.

I felt my body tense, but Ruth shook her head. "That's your mama's job," she said. "Give Grandma a hug, and I'll see you in the morning."

Susie obliged and confirmed that she had brushed her teeth without me needing to ask anymore. Unlike her brother, whose breath I needed to smell if I didn't watch him brush. She climbed into bed, and I tucked the blankets gently around her, brushing a few stray strands of hair off her face. "Did you know Grandma had a pony?" she asked me, then yawned. "Can I have a pony?"

"No, sweetheart, you can't."

"Why not?"

I wished I could say yes. "Where would we even put a pony? We don't live on a farm."

"In the backyard."

"Ponies need more room than that," I said.

"A dog, then?"

I kissed her forehead. "We'll talk about it." She opened her mouth, and I cut her off. "Another day. Right now, go to sleep. You have school tomorrow."

She pouted slightly. "I wish *we* lived somewhere with ponies."

"Dream about that," I told her. "And we'll talk about a dog soon."

∽

Ruth was in the living room watching television when I went to clean the kitchen after the kids were asleep, but the kitchen was already clean.

I debated pouring myself a brandy and then going to take the bath I had wanted to take two nights earlier. But I had to deal with Ruth if we were going to live under the same roof for any period of time. Moreover, I needed to draw my boundary lines. No redecorating and no telling the kids horror stories of escaping pogroms.

But the brandy wasn't a terrible idea for that. I poured a glass, then took a long sip, relishing the burn as it went down. I didn't drink often—it was a bottle left over from Harry's thirty-second birthday party, when we had foolishly celebrated him making it past the age his father had passed at. I didn't want to think about that. But keeping my cool in a conversation with Ruth at this point required fortification.

I refilled the glass and then left the kitchen for the living room, where Ruth was chuckling over *The Red Skelton Show*. "Can we talk?" I asked her.

She didn't even glance up, though I did note a glass of sherry on the table in front of her. "Can it wait until the next commercial?" she asked.

I could give her that much. So I sat in Harry's armchair and waited for the show to go to a break.

When it did, she turned to me. "I was trying to help. With the furniture."

It wasn't an apology, but it was close. "I understand that. But making more work for me isn't helping."

"You could have left it. Then it's not more work."

I sighed and counted to ten in my head before responding. "When's the last time you redecorated your own house?"

"This isn't about my house," she said quickly.

"Then why does it have to be about mine? How would you feel if I went over and rearranged all your furniture?"

She looked like she wanted to say something but kept her mouth shut.

I could feel the brandy loosening me up, and I again wondered if I had actually eaten dinner or if I had just moved furniture in a rage. "Look, Ruth, the kids love you. And I think it's really good for them to learn about Harry's side of the family. But if you're going to . . . visit here, we need to set up some ground rules or we're going to butt heads." I'd started to say if she was going to stay here, but I needed to be clear that this wasn't a permanent situation. Her brow furrowed slightly at my choice of words, and I knew she had caught my point.

"Such as?"

"No redecorating if we don't discuss it first. No telling the kids stories that they're too young to hear."

"I wasn't too young to live it," she said quietly, her eyes fixed on a point over my shoulder, seeing sights I never wanted to imagine.

"And they, God willing, will never have to. They already suffered the loss of a parent. Please don't make them afraid that they'll be forced to run as well."

"They'll need to learn eventually that the world isn't safe for us—"

"Ruth, they're going to learn that on their own. But *this* world is safer. Our world. No, not everyone loves us," I said, thinking explicitly of Mrs. Kline. "But it's not the same world you grew up in. Not here."

We weren't that far removed from the atrocities of Europe. Less than twenty years since it ended. But that was an eternity to small children. Hearing such things from Ruth, someone they knew and trusted, would only instill a fear that they didn't need to have.

"Anything else?" she asked.

"Let me shower in privacy," I said. "And I'll give you the same courtesy."

The commercial break ended. "I assume there are no objections to Red Skelton?"

"None whatsoever," I said. I still would have preferred a bath and a book in bed, but I stayed with her until the end of the episode as a gesture somewhere between a show of solidarity and a show of possession.

Eleven more days, I told myself as I got into bed later that evening. What else could she throw at me in eleven days?

9

Janet laughed over her coffee as I told her about my new roommate. I had stopped by to see her after work on Wednesday both because I needed to vent and because I needed a break before I faced Ruth again.

"Kick her to the curb," she said, shaking her head as she offered me a refill. I declined because I drank two cups at work. Another and I would be up until four in the morning scrubbing the ceilings.

"I can't do that."

"Sure you can. It's what I finally did with George's mother." Janet's mother-in-law moved in to "help" for three months when Janet had her first baby. And apparently by "help," she meant care for George, Janet's husband, *not* Janet and the baby.

"You did not kick her out."

Janet grinned wickedly. "Okay, I made her life miserable until she left. It was all very Shakespearean."

I felt the corners of my mouth twitching into a smile at the idea of Ruth as the shrew. Then I felt guilty. "This is different," I said. "She's a widow who lost her son."

"And you're a widow who has to raise yours," Janet said. "She's never going to leave if you don't make it clear that she has to." She took another slice of the coffee cake I had brought over. I seldom had time to bake anymore now that I was working, but it helped that Eddie had added a bakery to the store and provided some of his and Janet's mother's recipes for the baker to use.

"I think she genuinely wants to help. She's not a bad person. It just..."

"Is grating having someone else living in your house," Janet finished. I nodded. "What if you marry her off?"

I choked slightly on my water. "What if I *what*?"

"It'd get her out of your house," she said with another wicked grin.

I made a wry face. "With my luck, she'd just have the husband move into my house too. Besides, she hasn't so much as gone on a date in . . ." I did the math in my head. "Forty years."

"So? There are plenty of widowers out there who would love someone to cook—"

"I'm going to stop you right there," I said. "Ruth is the most atrocious cook on the planet. And she has the nerve to complain about *my* cooking."

"She's got to be better than what they're making on their own," Janet continued, unfazed. "You should see what my father lives on when he doesn't come to my house for dinner. Anything would be an upgrade. Besides, she's clearly lonely, or she wouldn't be at your house."

I tried to imagine Ruth going on a date. It felt as foreign as the idea of *me* trying to date again.

"Easier said than done," I said lightly.

Janet shrugged. "It's an idea. Or I can just come over and bang two pots together in the middle of the night and tell her it's time to go home. It's not like Paula lets me sleep anyway."

"Mama?" a sleepy voice called from upstairs, right on cue. Janet groaned, and the voice came more insistently. "MAMA!"

"She still won't sleep if you're not in the bed with her?" I asked.

Janet shook her head as the wailing started upstairs. "No. And *this* is what I get when she wakes up and realizes I snuck out." She went to the doorway of the kitchen and called upstairs. "Mama is in the kitchen with Auntie Barbara. Go back to sleep."

"I scared," came a sniffly voice.

"Oh, for the love of—" Janet huffed quietly so that Paula wouldn't hear her. "It's the middle of the day." Then louder, "I'm coming, hang on."

I brushed some crumbs off the table into my hand and deposited them in the trash while I waited for Janet to return, then got a cup of milk for Paula and cut a small piece of cake for her as well. When Janet came back into the kitchen, Paula on her hip, the little girl's eyes lit up, not at me, but at the cake on the table.

"Cake!" she screeched, leaning so far off Janet that I was briefly worried she'd tumble to the floor.

Janet rolled her eyes and set Paula down. The little girl then made a beeline for the cake. "Thank your Auntie Barbara," Janet said. "She's nicer than me."

"Tank ew, 'Tee Bawba," Paula said through a mouthful of cake.

"Bites," Janet said. "We take bites in this house."

Three gigantic bites later, the slice of cake was demolished, and Paula ran off to play with her toys in the living room.

"On the plus side," Janet said, "with how much time I'm spending in her bed, there's no chance of a fourth baby. This one is going to be the death of me."

"Oh shush," I said, gazing fondly toward Paula. A third baby hadn't been ruled out yet when we lost Harry, but that door was firmly shut, locked, and the key thrown away now.

Janet's face softened and she put a hand over mine, not needing to say anything. For a few moments, we sat in companionable silence. It's a rare friendship that can do that comfortably, and I appreciated Janet for it. She could be blunt and brutal to anyone she didn't like—which was a long list—but she would take that same ferocity out on anyone who slighted me, be it a stranger or my own mother-in-law.

Finally, she stood. "Do you need to get home?"

I shook my head.

"Let's take Paula to the park, then go get the kids from there. Give you a break from the old lady."

At almost sixty, she wasn't *that* old, but I'd take the respite. So I cleared the table while Janet got Paula ready to leave.

10

Janet's kids came tumbling out of the school when the bell rang, along with the rest of the neighborhood children.

Mine did not.

A shiver ran down my spine as the wave of students slowed to a trickle and then dried up entirely. I should have gone straight home after work. What if the school had been trying to reach me?

"I—I'm just going to go run into the office and see what's going on," I said to Janet, trying not to alarm her kids.

Janet had no such qualms. "Jeanie, where's Susie?" she asked her eldest.

Jeanie shrugged. "They called for her from the office around lunchtime."

"Who called for her?"

"I don't know," she said. "The secretary said she was leaving."

Ice cubes clinking in my veins, I forced my feet to move toward the front office. I pushed the door open and approached Mrs. Garrison, the secretary.

She looked up from her phone call and held a finger in the air, indicating I was to wait. But this wasn't a time for waiting. "It's an emergency," I said softly but urgently.

Her eyes flitted to my face, and then she told the person on the phone that she would call them back and replaced the receiver. "What can I do for you, Mrs. Feldman?"

"Where are my children?" I blurted out.

She tilted her head, confused. "With their grandmother," she said slowly, clearly annoyed. "She signed them out at noon."

"She—what?"

"I don't know where they went from there. She said they had an appointment."

"They didn't," I said. "And she's not on the list of people who are allowed to sign them out."

"Sure she is," Mrs. Garrison said, pulling out an enormous binder and flipping to the F section. "Says right here: grandmother."

I closed my eyes and pinched the bridge of my nose. "That's *my* mother. Not *this* grandmother."

Mrs. Garrison shrugged. "You should really update their forms, then, to specify. Now if you'll excuse me, that wasn't exactly an emergency, and I do need to return that phone call."

I thanked Mrs. Garrison, though she had been less than helpful, and received a curt nod while she dialed the phone.

My fear turned to righteous anger as I pushed open the door to the front of the school. Janet was waiting for me, the kids running circles around her as she watched for me to re-emerge.

"Ruth," I said, shaking my head as I made my way across the sidewalk.

"Who else would it have been?" she asked, as if that was an obvious person to abduct my children. "Should I get the pots and pans ready?"

"Yes," I said through gritted teeth. Then I forced my tense shoulders back down. "Maybe. If I don't kill her first."

"I'll tell the police you were with me the whole time," Janet said. "All these years of telling George my clothes were on sale were excellent practice at lying."

Normally that would have gotten a grin, but I wasn't in the mood.

My car was still at Janet's, but I walked straight home from the school, my pace brisk in my eagerness to make sure the children still had all ten fingers and toes.

"Susie?" I called as I opened the unlocked door. "Bobby?"

A shrill yipping answered me, and the children came running out of the kitchen, chasing after a small gray streak that jumped up onto my leg. I moved back from the creature reflexively as Susie scooped the . . . squirrel? . . . into her arms, covering its small, bearded face in kisses.

"What on—?"

"Grandma got us a puppy," Bobby said, trying unsuccessfully to take the ball of fur from his sister. "Hey, it's my turn!"

"RUTH!" I bellowed.

She emerged from the kitchen, smiling at the scuffling between the children.

"What did you do?" I asked her.

"Susie and Bobby said you were talking about a dog," she said. "I thought this would be a lovely surprise."

I looked at Susie, who was on the floor, the puppy in her lap.

"Talking about," I said quietly but forcefully, "isn't the same as 'decided to get one.'"

Ruth shrugged. "I thought you'd be happier with this than the pony Susie really wanted." She reached down and ruffled Bobby's hair. "Your father loved dogs," she said fondly. "It's good for children to have a pet," she said to me. "Besides, she's fully housebroken and won't shed."

As if on cue, the puppy jumped out of Susie's lap, came over to me, and looked up with her tongue lolling out happily. She was cute. I did have to admit that. And small. "What's the breed?" I asked eventually, still not sold on this new addition to the family.

"Miniature schnauzer," Ruth said.

"Aren't those German?" I asked pointedly, remembering her objection to Heloise.

She fixed me with a withering look. "The *dogs* weren't Nazis, Barbara."

I sighed heavily, looking down at the joy on the kids' faces. Overstepping was an understatement here. But she had also won, and she knew it because there was no way I was going to be the cause of more loss for them.

"You'll need to feed and walk her," I warned Susie and Bobby. "This is a lot more work than that goldfish from the carnival last year."

"Well, yeah. That fish only lived for a week," Bobby said.

"Exactly. I can't flush a puppy."

"We'll take good care of her," Susie said as the puppy ran back to her lap, sensing an ally.

Pure delight radiated from Susie, and I couldn't help it: the annoyance began to trickle out of me. No one who could make my children smile like that again could be bad, even if this wasn't the dog I might have picked. She was the one they picked. And that was what mattered.

"What's her name?" I asked, crouching down next to Susie and holding out my hand, which the little furball licked, looking up at me with big eyes.

"We waited for you for that," Ruth said. "I wouldn't want to overstep again."

My fingers itched to curl into fists, but I fought to keep them straight. "Any ideas?" I asked Susie and Bobby.

"Pepper," Susie said immediately. "Grandma said her color is called salt and pepper."

I looked to Bobby. "How's Pepper?"

His face fell slightly. "I wanted to call her Spot."

"She doesn't have any spots," Susie said. "That makes no sense."

"Okay, okay," Bobby said. "C'mere, Pepper!"

But instead of going to Bobby, she climbed out of Susie's lap and came over to me. Where she squatted and proceeded to pee on my shoe.

I raised an eyebrow at Ruth. "Fully housebroken, you said?"

Ruth shrugged. "That's what they told me. What does your German hausfrau say about cleaning a dog mess off a shoe?"

I sighed again, slipping the soiled shoe off and picking it up in one hand, the puppy in the other, and depositing her in our fenced yard, the kids fighting to chase after her, while I took the shoe to the kitchen to try to salvage it.

As I scrubbed at the wet spot, I looked up at the ceiling. "You're laughing at me right now," I said. "Don't deny it. I can practically hear you." A flash of red at the window caught my eye, and I could have sworn that cardinal was laughing at me too. I wouldn't have been able to stay annoyed if Harry had been there. He just had one of those infectious laughs. We seldom fought, but when we did, if I could make him laugh, it was always over. I missed that laugh—the way his whole body rolled with it, the crinkles at the corners of his eyes.

I leaned against the sink, closing my eyes as the wave of nostalgia washed over me. Then I sighed and looked back at the bird outside my kitchen window.

What would Harry say if he was here right now?

He would wink, that mischievous twinkle in his eye, and say Ruth had trained the puppy to do that. She would protest earnestly, and he would laugh until we all joined him.

Hmm. Maybe I could train Pepper to pee on Ruth's shoes. That was a thought.

"Oh shush," I said to the silent ceiling. "I wouldn't actually do that."

The cardinal chirped merrily at me, and I abandoned the shoe to join the children in the backyard.

11

Shockingly, Ruth seemed to know a lot about puppies. I watched as she helped Susie and Bobby pack a cardboard box full of towels to make a bed, and then they took an alarm clock and wrapped it in another towel.

"This is to remind Pepper of her mother's heartbeat, so she won't cry all night," Ruth explained.

"Can she sleep in my room?" Bobby asked.

"I named her! She gets to sleep in my room," Susie argued.

"When she's bigger, she can decide where to sleep," Ruth said. "For now, she needs to sleep in an adult's room so we can take her out if she needs to relieve herself."

"Can I sleep in your room with you, then?" Susie asked.

"That's up to your mother," Ruth said, without looking up at me.

"Please, Mama? She needs to know she's my dog."

Bobby opened his mouth to protest, but it dawned on me that if the puppy was sleeping with Ruth, Ruth became the de facto adult. And I needed to make it clear that this was NOT a permanent change of abode. "Actually," I said, "Pepper should sleep in my room. When Grandma goes back to HER house, we don't want Pepper being confused about who her owners are."

Ruth still hadn't looked up. "You heard your mother," she said. "The box goes in her room."

Pleased with myself, despite the shoe that looked like it would retain a stain—maybe I would write to Heloise myself for this one—I went to start dinner. Ruth made no objections to me cooking, but instead took the children and the puppy out to play in the backyard, telling them that a tired puppy is a well-behaved puppy.

～

By 3 a.m., I regretted every life decision I had ever made, from marrying a man related to Ruth to the number of stairs in our house (which I miscalculated on my third trip down them to try to get the crying puppy to urinate anywhere other than on my foot).

"Please," I begged as she stood on the patio with me, staring dejectedly at our lawn as if it didn't meet her standards for defecation. "Just go potty so I can sleep."

The puppy tilted her head at me, then came over, curled up on my slippered foot, and closed her eyes.

This was worse than having a baby. A baby might cry, but a diaper change and a bottle were a relatively easy fix. I wondered if they made diapers for puppies.

No. I couldn't do this. Raising two children on my own was enough. The dog was going back to wherever it had come from the following morning.

A light came on behind me, and I turned around, prepared to shoo whichever child it was back to bed. But Ruth stood at the back door in her bathrobe, with rollers in her hair.

"Did she go?" she asked.

I shook my head miserably. "She just keeps crying and then doesn't do anything when I take her out."

Ruth bent and scooped her up into her arms, cooing comfortingly as the puppy snuggled into the crook of her neck like a baby. "The first night is always the hardest," she said in that same singsong tone she was using to settle Pepper. "They miss their mother and littermates. But they adjust quickly." I had a sharp retort on my tongue about how I would be sleeping if she hadn't decided to bring an addition to our family without talking to me first, but there was no malice in her face, and so I simply nodded. "Come on, *libele*," she said, calling her "little love" in Yiddish. "Let's get you back to bed."

"She's just going to cry again," I said.

"Shh. Let's see what we can do."

Ruth climbed the stairs, and I turned off the living room light. She went into my room and settled the puppy in the towels, tucking her gently next to the one that ticked. Pepper snuggled in and fell right back to sleep. "Keep her by the clock, if you can," she said. "And if that doesn't do the trick, a hot water bottle in a towel should."

She turned to leave, but I called her name, and she looked back at me from the doorway. "Thank you."

"A puppy won't fill the hole left by their father," she said. "But you'll see: puppies make hearts grow so that hole seems a little smaller." And then she was gone.

I thought I would fall right back asleep, exhausted as I was, but instead I lay awake, listening to the muffled ticking and the soft sighing of the puppy as she slept. *How did I get here?* I wondered. This wasn't the life I was supposed to be leading. If I was awake in the night, it should have been because of Harry's snoring. What I wouldn't give for that snoring now. I flipped over, facing Harry's side of the bed, and reached out, though I knew my arm would find nothing but the blanket there. I could have laughed this all off if he were here.

But he wasn't.

I turned onto my back and looked at the ceiling in the dim, ambient light from the street outside my window. A week ago, I'd felt so prepared to handle whatever else life threw at me. But now? So far, Ruth's logic on puppies wasn't working because the hole in my heart just felt larger and larger.

Resigning myself to a sleepless night, I scooted to the edge of the bed and reached my arm down into the cardboard box, resting my fingertips lightly on the soft fur of the puppy's neck. It didn't matter how many sleepless nights I had. What mattered was how my children healed.

"I guess you can stay," I whispered. In her sleep, she stretched her legs and then curled up against my hand. And eventually, I drifted off as well.

～

I awoke to a sharp pain, as tiny, needlelike teeth sank into my index finger. I yanked my arm back onto the bed as the gray light of dawn peeked around the edges of the curtains. I peered down over the edge of the bed, and the puppy yipped at me, then lolled her tongue out and jumped up, trying to get out of the box and onto the bed. And maybe—just maybe—my heart was a little bigger after all. Because instead of being annoyed, I climbed out of bed, put my robe on, and took her downstairs, despite my exhaustion. I wasn't even irritated that Ruth was the one who got the puppy to sleep. "You're not so bad, are you?" I asked as she ran back to me after doing her business in the grass. She gnawed on my slipper in response. But it was a step up from peeing on me. I would take what I could get.

12

There was a knock at the door as I was putting pancakes on the kids' plates. It was silly that my heart still went into my throat two years later at a random knock, but it did. "I'll just be a moment," I told them, wiping my hands on my apron.

But instead of a police officer coming to deliver the worst news of my life, I found Eddie on the doorstep, holding a brown paper shopping bag. I looked at him, surprised, but Eddie was always a welcome surprise.

"Making deliveries now?" I asked with a smile. "Surely you can pay a kid to do that."

"That can be Bobby's job when he's bigger," Eddie said. "I'm sorry I didn't call first."

"Nothing to be sorry for," I said mildly. "Come on in. Would you like some pancakes?"

"Thank you, no, I ate already." I thought of his sister's comment about their father's complete inability to prepare a meal for himself and almost asked if he cooked for himself or if he had stopped at Hot Shoppes or Montgomery Donuts. But I didn't want to pry. Besides, Eddie was quite the eligible bachelor. He probably had a line of women itching to bring over casseroles any chance they got.

Eddie followed me into the kitchen, where he greeted the children. "What's in the bag?" Bobby asked, practically vibrating.

"Bobby," I said warningly. "That's rude. Mr. Greene doesn't have to bring you something every time you see him."

Eddie looked at me guiltily, then whispered, "Is it okay that I *did* bring them something?"

I laughed. He was incorrigible. "Who am I to stand in the way? Just their mother."

He glanced at me quickly to make sure I was being facetious, then slipped Susie a pack of Tammy doll outfits and handed Bobby two Matchbox cars. Both kids squealed with delight, Susie jumping up to get her doll and Bobby plopping himself onto the floor to play with his cars. "Breakfast first," I told them. They sat back in their seats and began eating pancakes as fast as their little mouths could chew.

I shook my head but was smiling at their excitement. "When you have kids of your own, you won't spoil them half so much," I told him.

Eddie shrugged. "*If* I have kids of my own. But I like making them happy."

"What brings you by?" I asked. "Or did you just want to make two kids smile before they go to school?" Heaven knew they could use all the joy they could get.

"Mrs. Feld—uh . . . your mother-in-law stopped by the store yesterday," he said, just as Pepper ran into the room, Ruth behind her. Eddie's face broke into a wide smile as he sat on the floor to greet the puppy. Pepper went right to him and jumped onto his lap, putting her paws on his chest. Eddie pretended to be knocked over, and the kids laughed as Pepper licked his entire face while he lay on my kitchen floor.

"Pepper," Ruth said sternly, and the puppy took a break from kissing her new friend to look up. Apparently she had already picked up her name and what that tone meant. She gave Eddie one more lick, then hopped down and trotted obediently to Ruth, who scooped her up.

"I see she's made herself right at home, then," Eddie said. He picked up the bag, which he had set on the counter. "I just thought I'd stop by with some supplies for her." He pulled out a pink collar with a little bow on it, a matching leash, a set of food and water bowls, and a box of Milk-Bones.

"Eddie," I said, "you didn't have to do all this."

"I know I didn't," he said, slipping the collar onto Pepper's neck while she was still in Ruth's arms. "But I wanted to. It's not every day my favorite family gets a dog." He glanced at me. "Don't tell Janet I said that, please. But you know she loves cats and, well . . . I'm a dog person, myself."

"I can see that," I said, as Pepper licked Eddie's hand. "So far she prefers chewing on me."

"You have to yelp like a hurt dog and then tell her no," Ruth said. "That's how they learn."

"My mother-in-law, the dog trainer," I said wryly.

"I enjoy dogs," Ruth said. "They don't argue."

I counted to five in my head, then ten, to avoid taking the bait. "Maybe," I said measuredly, "you should get another dog when you move home."

She looked at me sharply for a long moment. "Maybe," she said, then hesitated. "But for now, Pepper will have to do."

That emphasis on *maybe* gave me pause, but there was no time to parse exactly what she meant with Eddie there.

"Eddie, this was very kind of you," Ruth said, moving to pat his arm.

"Thank you, Mrs. Feldman. I just wanted to help."

"Ruth," she said. "Anyone who loves dogs is a friend of mine." She looked at me pointedly. I fought the urge to put my hands on my hips. I didn't want to be Ruth's friend. And besides, the pup had grown on me already.

"I should be heading to the store," Eddie said. "I just wanted to bring these things by. If there's anything else you need for Pepper—or in general—just call. I'd be happy to swing it by on my way home."

"Thank you," I told him.

Eddie smiled at me, stopping to scratch Pepper behind the ears before he left.

"That's a good one," Ruth said once the door was closed behind him. "Dogs can always tell."

13

Work had been a respite since I started. Well, okay, not RIGHT when I started, as I was still having heart palpitations every time I walked into the hospital for the first month. But as that faded, it was a space where I was no longer a tragic widow. And there were sometimes whole hours when I was too busy to think about Harry or my circumstances.

And so, four days a week, for five hours at a time, Ruth was the least of my concerns. And when you factored in sleeping, well, that was almost half of the week when I didn't have to think about her. And by that second Tuesday after she had arrived, I needed that break.

"You're getting me all wet!" the patient in room 208 protested. I cursed quietly. I had been daydreaming about getting rid of Ruth again and spilled water from the pitcher I had been pouring from all over her.

Okay, maybe work wasn't a complete respite anymore.

"I'm so sorry, Mrs. . . ." I glanced at the chart on the wall. "O'Connor." I normally remembered patients' names better too. Ruth was seeping into every corner of my life. This wasn't me. It was a byproduct of living with an unwanted guest who had no intention of leaving.

"Are you new or something?" she asked me grumpily as I tried to mop up the spill. She would need a new gown.

"I'm not, actually. But I don't typically fill water cups anymore."

"You'd think you'd have enough practice at that," she said, looking pointedly at my wedding ring.

"Well," I said with a cheerfulness I certainly didn't feel, "my children are old enough now to fill their own water glasses. And my husband passed. So I'm terribly sorry that I'm out of practice."

The annoyance dropped from the bedridden woman's face. "I didn't—I'm sorry—I—"

"It's okay," I said, cutting her off. I shouldn't have brought up Harry. What was wrong with me? "Really. Let me just get you a new gown, and you'll be right as rain. My head was in the clouds, that's all."

I left the room and flagged down a candy striper and asked her to grab the gown and help Mrs. O'Connor change. Knowing me right now, I would mess that up too.

"Barb?" Donna called from the nursing station. "There's a call for you."

I was there in a flash. The only calls I ever got while working were when the kids got sick or injured at school.

"Mrs. Feldman speaking," I said, taking the receiver from the nurse's hand. "What happened? I can be there in fifteen minutes."

"Be where?" Ruth asked.

I held the receiver away from my ear for a few seconds, looking at it as if a snake were inside. Then I heard my name, far away, and brought it back to my ear.

"Ruth," I said through clenched teeth. Then I realized—the school would likely call the house first. "What's wrong?"

"Nothing's wrong," she said, drawing the word out in a way that told me something was, in fact, very wrong.

"Ruth?"

"Well, there was a fire—a small one. But the firemen were quite nice and put it out easily."

"A fire?"

"A small one."

"Are you okay?"

"If I weren't, I think I'd be arriving at the hospital, not calling you there."

If I could have reached through the phone and strangled her with the cord, I would have. "What caught on fire?"

"Well, I'm not used to this electric stove."

I know it's strange to say I loved that stove, but goodness did I love that stove. I knew every one of its quirks, from running fifteen degrees hot to the different sized burners for different sized pots. The double oven with the countertop space next to the burners. It was the first appliance that I ever selected for myself. Harry had surprised me by bringing me to Sears to pick out a new one.

Granted, that was before the kids were born, when cooking elaborate meals was a hobby.

Standing in the department store though, I told Harry I had just been complaining and we didn't *really* need anything new. He pulled me into his arms and told me he'd give me the moon if I wanted it.

Now, all these years later, I was standing in a hospital with tears in my eyes over a General Electric appliance.

I blinked rapidly, and the moisture in my eyes dissipated. "How bad is it?"

"The fire department said it could have been worse."

"That didn't answer my question."

"We will need a new stove," she said. "And probably need to repaint the wall by it. And maybe some new curtains."

My jaw tightened at her use of the word *we*, and I exhaled loudly, thinking of all the things I would say to her if I could.

"At least the children weren't home," I said finally. "The stove isn't salvageable?"

"The firemen didn't think so."

"But the house is okay?"

"Perfectly."

I took a deep breath. It was a small loss. Barely a blip compared to what we had been through. And nothing lasted forever. But it wouldn't have been a loss at all if Ruth had stayed home.

"I'll leave work early and go pick out a new one," I said, more thinking out loud. It was only twelve thirty. There was a decent chance that we could have it replaced by the following day. I would probably have to be there for the installation—I didn't trust Ruth to not have them redo our whole kitchen. And there *was* a set of new curtains that I had been eyeing but hadn't yet bought as the old ones had nothing wrong with them. I didn't remember whom we had used to paint the children's bedrooms—it was someone Harry had hired—but I was pretty sure Janet had used him as well and would know. We could have this fixed by the end of the week.

"I can do it," Ruth said. "You stay."

"No," I said firmly. "This is for my house. I want to choose it."

"But I'm doing a lot of the cooking—"

"Ruth," I said warningly this time. "This is my house."

There was a pregnant pause. "Best get something for supper while you're downtown as well," she said finally.

I said I would worry about that later and hung up. I hated leaving early for a nonemergency, but I also needed to be able to feed my kids and wanted to still be able to pick them up from school. I lifted the receiver and dialed Dr. Harper's office number.

14

By the time I finished at Sears, I needed to pick up the kids, so I still hadn't seen the damage. But I resolved to sit down with Ruth that night, once the children were in bed, and finally have the talk that had been looming since we crept past the two weeks that I had mentally given her. It was time for Ruth to go home.

I warned the children about the fire, knowing full well it could be much better or worse than Ruth had said.

I did breathe a sigh of relief when we pulled into the driveway and the house appeared completely normal. At least it was standing.

The kids scrambled out of the car but ignored my reminder to grab their books and went running into the house, calling for Ruth. I reached into the back seat for their things and went inside, where the smell of smoke hit me immediately.

I coughed, then began opening windows, finally making my way to the kitchen, where I stopped short.

When she had said she wasn't used to my stove, I expected a pan fire. But I realized that had been naive of me. It looked like a bomb had gone off in the oven itself. A singed fragment of my curtains remained, and the wall between the stove and kitchen sink was reduced to blackened exposed beams.

The Formica countertops, however, remained unharmed.

"Ruth?" I yelled, then coughed some more, crossing quickly to the kitchen window to fling that open as well.

"In the living room," she called back. Her voice sounded a little hoarse.

I left the kitchen, wondering how we would ever get the smell out, and made my way to where the children were hugging her on the sofa, the puppy on her lap between them. "Did the firemen examine the wall?" I asked without greeting.

"Yes, yes," she said, waving a hand. "It's fine."

"It's not 'fine,'" I said, anger rising. "Half of the wall is gone. I need to know if the studs are secure or if the house is going to collapse while we sleep."

"They said it was structurally sound."

"You told me it just needed a coat of paint. We need to replace the wall."

"And then it'll need a coat of paint."

I counted to ten in my head to slow myself down. Then I sat on the edge of the armchair. "What exactly happened?"

"I told you: I'm not used to the electric stove. I've always cooked with gas."

I studied her for a moment, but she didn't meet my eyes. "And the oven?"

"Well, there wasn't room in the cupboards when I went shopping."

I blinked rapidly at her as I processed this statement. "So you . . . ?"

"Just put a few things in there. And then I . . . well . . . I may have turned the wrong knob when I went to start some soup."

My mouth fell open. I knew we should have this conversation away from the children, but I couldn't quite stop myself. "What was in the oven?"

"Not much. A bag of flour. Some Jiffy Pop. Crackers."

I pinched the bridge of my nose with my thumb and forefinger. "Popcorn. In the oven?"

"I wasn't going to cook it in there, obviously. I just wanted it to be a surprise, and I knew the children wouldn't look in the oven."

The kids weren't the only ones. It would never have occurred to me to look inside the oven to see if there was anything in there before preheating it.

"Ruth, you *cannot* store flammable things in the oven."

"Well, I certainly can't store anything in the oven *now*," she said. She turned to the kids. "When the new stove arrives, we'll try again on the Jiffy Pop."

She was extremely lucky that the children were sitting there, because the fire looked tame in comparison to what I would have done.

I might have done it anyway, even with the children present, but a knock at the door saved her.

Assuming it was Janet, come to see the carnage for herself, I opened the door and started to say to come in. But instead of Janet, a handsome man stood on my doorstep.

"Yes?" I asked him, not in the mood for whatever he was selling.

"Um, hello," he said, holding out a hand. "I'm Barry Waterman." I looked at his hand long enough that he dropped it, shoving the offending appendage into his pocket. "I . . . uh . . . Is Mrs. Feldman home?"

"I am Mrs. Feldman."

"Oh, I meant the other one. She asked me to come by when I got off work."

"Who exactly are you?"

"Barry Waterman."

"Yes, you said that part already."

Ruth appeared behind me. "Barbara, let Mr. Waterman in," she said, her tone chastising me for my rudeness as if I was supposed to know who he was.

But my house had nearly burned down that day, so I was past being polite. "I don't exactly want guests right now."

"I'm so sorry," Ruth said to the young man. Then she turned back to me. "Did you pick up dinner, like I said? Mr. Waterman was one of the firefighters today, and I thought he might like to join us." She lowered her voice to a loud whisper that Mr. Waterman could clearly still hear. "He's single."

I stared at her as she ushered him into the house. Yes, she was getting evicted this evening. After I figured out how to get rid of the appropriately named fireman.

15

"I suppose sandwiches will have to do," Ruth said with a sigh, looking at me pointedly as it became apparent that I had not picked up dinner. When I said nothing, she turned back to the fireman. "She's quite a . . . decent cook, when she has an oven, you know."

More than I can say for you, I thought, bristling. Then it dawned on me that if Ruth was almost complimenting my cooking . . . "Ruth," I said quietly, gesturing for her to join me in the singed kitchen. She excused herself and followed me.

"You're being so rude to our guest," she chided. "And you should really go change into a nicer dress. You're still in what you wore to work."

"What is he doing here?"

"Well, he seemed so nice that I invited him for dinner. A Jewish firefighter. Who would have thought?"

"Yes, but *why* did you invite him?"

"I just told you. He seemed so nice. And handsome. Just look at him."

She was impossible. "I shouldn't have to say this to Harry's mother, but I'm not interested in this man."

"Well, not to marry, of course. A firefighter would never do. Too dangerous a profession. You don't want to lose *two* husbands. But he's nice to look at, and you could do with a little fun. Loosen you up."

I'd be so much looser without you in my house. "Ruth, your idea of fun and mine are pretty different. Now if you'll excuse me, I'm sending him home." I started to leave the room.

Ruth grabbed my arm. "But I asked him to dinner."

I turned to look at her, and whatever she saw on my face made her drop my arm.

"You're absolutely right," she said. "Much better that he come on a night when we can serve him a hot meal. Don't worry—I'll cook when he comes back. We'll tell him it was you."

If I didn't leave the room, I was going to say—or do—something I would wind up regretting. Eventually. Right then I would have zero regrets. But instead, I demonstrated remarkable control by returning to the living room.

"Mr. Waterman—"

"Barry."

I looked at him again. He *was* handsome. I did have to give Ruth credit for her taste. But he also looked twenty-five at most. "Mr. Waterman," I repeated firmly. "There seems to have been a misunderstanding. I'm terribly sorry, but my mother-in-law isn't feeling well after all the excitement today, and I think it's best if it's just family tending to her."

"No," Ruth said, coming in from the kitchen. "I feel just fine—" I shot her a look sharp enough to cut stone. "Yes," she said uncertainly. "I must have breathed in a little more smoke than I thought."

"You should go to the hospital," Mr. Waterman said. "Smoke inhalation can be—"

"She'll be fine," I said. "But I think it's best if you leave now."

He looked from her to me. "Okay. If she gets any shortness of breath or is coughing up mucus, she should really see a doctor. And not wait until morning."

"Yes, Mr. Waterman, I work at the hospital. I'm familiar with smoke inhalation."

He didn't look convinced. No, I wasn't a nurse, but *he* didn't know that. "Call an ambulance if that happens. Don't drive her yourself."

"I have no intention of driving her anywhere," I assured him as I ushered him toward the door. "Good night, Mr. Waterman." I shut it firmly behind him and leaned on it for a moment with my eyes closed, trying to steel myself for an evening with Ruth before the children went to bed and I could tell her it was time to leave.

"Was he *really* a fireman?" Bobby asked.

I opened my eyes. "I believe he was." Bobby started to laugh. "What's so funny?"

"Fireman Waterman."

It was probably the stress, but I started to giggle as well, and soon I was full-out laughing so hard that I bent over, my hands on my knees. When I finally got myself under control, I ruffled Bobby's hair and told him to go wash up for supper. Then I looked up at the ceiling and shook my head. "I know, I know. You think this is all hilarious."

⁓

Once the children were in bed, I came downstairs and poured myself a drink. If Ruth stayed much longer, I'd have to go buy more liquor. I downed the whole thing and set the glass in the sink. Nope. She was leaving. I couldn't handle another day of this.

I went into the living room and snapped the television off. "I was watching that," Ruth said mildly.

"We need to talk."

She put her hands up in a gesture of surrender. "I learned my lesson. No more using the oven for storage."

"Ruth. You could have burned the house down. You could have killed yourself or me or the kids."

"But I didn't."

"But you could have. And while it's been . . . lovely . . . having you here, I think it's time that you head back to your house."

Her nostrils flared slightly, which was the only indication that she'd heard what I said.

"We can figure out more visits," I said. "I know you want the kids to know you better, and they seem to want that too, so I'm entirely open to—"

"No," Ruth said.

"No what?"

"No, I'm not going anywhere. You still need me and so do the kids. You just don't know it yet."

I sighed. "Ruth, that's just it. I do know what I need. It's why I sent my mother home. I need to be able to run my own home and take care of my kids. My own way."

There was a long pause, where I almost thought I'd won.

"Barbara," she said quietly, but with a steel in her voice that I hadn't heard before. "I had no help when Abe died. None. And I raised Harry the best that I could. Some days, it was enough. Most days, it wasn't. They don't give you a medal for doing everything yourself. And whether you like it or not, I'm not letting you or my grandchildren go through that just because you want to be a martyr. So here I am, and here I'll stay until it's time for me to go." She crossed her arms. "And not a moment before."

She had said her mother-in-law was horrible. "What would you have done if your mother-in-law moved in when Abe died?"

"Probably been pretty frightened as she'd been dead for six years," Ruth admitted.

I stomped my foot, knowing I looked like a petulant child, but unable to stop myself. She was impossible. "You have to go home!"

She cocked her head at me. "The house is gone, Barbara," she said quietly. "Where exactly do you want me to go?"

My mouth opened and closed wordlessly. "Gone?" I finally sputtered. "What do you mean, 'gone'?"

Ruth waved a hand in the air. "Taxes, something." Then she looked knowingly at me. "I gave Harry my savings for a down payment on this house. Didn't you know that?"

I didn't. But my heart sank as I realized I had just lost. I couldn't throw her out, penniless, into the cold.

She stood, scooping the puppy up and patting me on the shoulder as she left the room. "You'll thank me eventually," she said.

I sank down into the armchair, suddenly too exhausted even to go to bed, my head spinning with this new influx of information. Ruth's house—the house Harry had grown up in—was gone. Just like that. Poof.

Could I get it back? My little nest egg from the hospital was modest, but she couldn't have owed that much in taxes, and she had owned the house flat out—if she hadn't mortgaged it for ours. I had learned more than I ever wanted to know about money in the last two years, but I had no idea how any of that worked.

I doubted I could get it back without putting a major dent in the insurance money. And in my mind, that was for the kids, who loved their grandmother and would happily keep her living with us. They deserved to be able to use that money to start their own families, their own lives.

I put my head in my hands, defeated. This was my life now. Enduring Ruth for the rest of hers. With no way out.

But Ruth had one remaining sister, in Boston. *You'll thank me eventually,* she'd said. Well, what if I didn't? What if, instead, I showed her we really did have this all handled and how superfluous she was? I thought of Janet saying how making her mother-in-law miserable was Shakespearean. I grinned at the high school memory of the play. Petruchio gets Katherine to marry him by killing her with kindness before flipping the switch. Well, what if I could get Ruth to indefinitely visit her sister the same way?

And if she wouldn't go stay with her sister, well, the money from the hospital could pay for a small apartment. I didn't love the idea of working just to support Ruth, but in reality, I would be buying my own peace of mind.

She'll never take it, Harry whispered in my head.

I looked skyward and gritted my teeth. "Then I'll tell her you put it aside to support her in her old age."

There was no reply.

Eventually, I heard Ruth's bedroom door close and stood to make my way up to my own room. I needed sleep after all—this was war.

16

I woke up at five, tiptoeing around my room as if the sound of the water running in the shower wouldn't be audible to anyone who was awake. But after I showered, I poked my head into the hall, still wearing my towel, and the house was silent. So I applied my makeup and dressed, then crept down the stairs to—

My shoulders sagged in defeat. I forgot I didn't have a functioning kitchen when I devised the plan to show Ruth I could do everything myself. But I fixed my posture. This wouldn't defeat me.

Instead, I slipped my keys from the hook by the kitchen door and went out to the carport, closing the door softly behind me.

By the time I returned with breakfast in tinfoil containers from Hot Shoppes, Ruth was placing bowls of cold cereal in front of the children, who were staring at the hole in the wall behind the stove, Susie with a wary expression and Bobby with one of awe.

"No need for a cold breakfast," I said brightly, holding up the bags.

Bobby whooped and handed his bowl off to Ruth, who looked nonplussed at the wasting of food.

"Did you get me pancakes?" Bobby asked, crowding me to peer into the bags.

I ruffled his hair, then pointed at his chair, which he obediently sat in. "Of course. I know your order, sweetheart."

"Can we go eat there tomorrow?"

I smiled at the same memory that I knew drove the question. On Sunday mornings, Harry would grin at the kids and say, "Should we—?" He never had to finish the sentence before they both jumped on him and screamed, "Go to Hot Shoppes!" It was a treat beyond measure for them and a break from cooking for me. And a tradition that I should have maintained these last two years, but I hadn't. With my mother there, I had a built-in cooking break, and those first few months, it just felt too raw. But now that I could smile at the memory instead of cry, it was a good way to honor their recollections of Harry.

"The new stove is arriving today, so let's try that out tomorrow morning. Besides, tomorrow is a school day. But what if we started going on Sundays again?"

"Won't it be too sad?" Susie asked.

I slid a plate in front of her with a waffle on it, then handed her the syrup. "Not if we don't look at it that way," I said lightly. "Daddy would have wanted us to still go to his favorite breakfast spot."

Susie nodded, then cut a piece and took a bite. "I think that's true."

Ruth was sitting at her seat at the kitchen table and had a spoonful of Bobby's cereal halfway to her mouth when I placed a plate of eggs and toast in front of her. "Nothing like a hot breakfast," I said, smiling brightly. She eyed me suspiciously. We hadn't exactly parted on good terms the night before. But I merely whisked the bowl of cereal away and dumped it in the trash, bringing the bowl to the sink to rinse. I waited to see if she would argue about the wasted food, but she didn't. It wasn't like you could save cereal once it had milk in it. Though I was sure Ruth would be willing to try.

Once the children had finished eating, I told them to go get ready for school, while I packed their lunches.

"I can do that," Ruth said.

"It's no bother at all," I trilled. "You just go put your feet up."

She crossed her arms, looking like she was ready for a fight, but she stayed in the kitchen watching me until the puppy barked to come in at the back door, at which point she went to retrieve her.

I grinned broadly as I slathered peanut butter and jelly onto slices of bread. She and I were nothing alike. My best on my own *was* enough for my kids. Yes, we all missed Harry. But she was no Harry. She would see quickly how capable I was. And then—I glanced at the calendar on the refrigerator—we'd find her a place to live and start again. On our own this time.

But for now, that gaping hole in the wall needed fixing. I reached for the telephone and dialed Janet's number, cradling the receiver between my ear and shoulder as I continued making lunches.

"Hello?" George answered.

"It's Barbara," I said by way of greeting. His voice became muffled as he called for Janet. Honestly, there was no point to him even answering the phone. We were the only ones who called each other before eight in the morning.

"How bad is your kitchen?" Janet asked immediately—I had told her about the fire when we picked up the kids from school. "Do you want to come for breakfast? Should I get my shovel ready? Ooh, if we make the hole big enough, we can put in a pool!"

Tension immediately drained from my shoulders. Just hearing Janet's voice had that effect. "I picked up breakfast," I said, answering out of order. "There's no history of Jews haunting people if you build things on top of their graves, but I'd still feel bad swimming in a pool made that way. And the new stove comes today, but the wall behind it is much worse than Ruth let on—do you remember who painted the kids' bedrooms? And do you think he can patch a pretty big chunk of wall?"

"I'll call him for you. Will Ruth be there today if he can come take a look?"

"I will. I'm staying home to make sure the stove gets installed properly." I walked to where the kitchen met the hall, stretching the cord with me, to make sure she wasn't around the corner listening in. "So any time works—but the new stove is coming between twelve and two."

"He can always pull the stove out," Janet said. "What a mess though. Does this mean you can send her home?"

I stayed in the doorway, an eye on the stairs, and relayed the saga of Ruth losing her house.

Janet gasped. "What are you going to do?"

"Enact plan B."

"Marrying her off?"

I chuckled. "No. I'm turning to Shakespeare like you did to get rid of your mother-in-law. I'm going to tame the shrew—or in my case, make her feel entirely useless until she leaves."

Janet didn't laugh though. "I don't know," she said slowly. "Won't you feel bad doing that when she doesn't have a place to go?"

"She can go to her sister in Boston," I said. "Or I will rent her an apartment with my money from the hospital." But I couldn't keep the defensive tone out of my voice. On the one hand, I didn't care if she moved in with the devil himself as long as it got her out of my house. On the other . . . I glanced at the ceiling and shook my head. I had never once been on the receiving end of Harry's disappointed gaze, and I didn't like feeling that I was now.

Janet definitely heard the edge in my voice. "Maybe," she said lightly. "But don't Katherine and Petruchio fall in love in the end? Be careful or you'll wind up keeping her until she dies." There was a muffled voice in the background. "What? They know people die." Janet huffed at me. "George doesn't want me talking about death in front of the kids."

"Janet!" I said. "Don't talk about this in front of them—you know they'll talk to Bobby and Susie."

"It's just Paula. It's fine. You can barely understand anything she says anyway."

George said Janet's name loudly, and I laughed.

"I'll send the painter over," Janet promised. "Gotta run. George is shooting daggers at me."

I hung up and glanced at the ceiling again. "Don't look at me like that," I said. "I'm not going to be mean. I'm just going to make sure she knows I can handle this and suggest a nice long visit with her sister or some space of her own. Besides, it's not like you ever wanted her to live with us!"

"Who are you talking to?" Susie asked.

I jumped. "No one," I said. "Did you brush your teeth?"

"Yes, Mama," she said.

We'll finish this conversation later, I thought at the ceiling. That was the one plus of speaking to someone who wasn't actually there—he could hear me without my having to speak out loud.

I just wished he could talk back and help me feel better about all this.

⁓

Once the children were ready for school, I slipped Pepper's leash onto her collar and called to Ruth that I was going to walk Pepper while I dropped the kids off.

"I can walk the dog," she said, coming down the stairs and reaching for the leash, but I held it firmly.

"Nonsense," I said. "This is a good walk for her, and like you said, a tired puppy is a well-behaved puppy. You just take a break. You've worked so hard after all."

She looked at me to see if that last part was said with sarcasm, but I'd kept my tone bright and smiled winningly at her. She clearly didn't trust it, but I was fine playing a long game—provided I would win in the end, that is.

When I returned home after drop-off, I rounded the corner and shrieked at the sight of a man in my kitchen. I grabbed for the nearest weapon I could find, which was an admittedly unintimidating rubber spatula.

But when he turned to face whatever doom I could inflict with a spatula, a familiar and not-unwelcome face greeted me. The burnt stove was pulled away from the wall, and he was fitting metal netting into the hole.

"Eddie," I said, surreptitiously setting the spatula down so he didn't know I was about to try to disembowel him with it. "What are you doing here?"

Before he could answer, Pepper pounced on him, jumping up to lick his entire face. "Morning. Janet didn't want you to pay the painter to fix something I could do."

"But don't you have to be at work?"

He smiled, a childish dimple forming in his left cheek. "That's the benefit of being the boss. Besides, Janet made it sound dire."

"The painter really could have—"

"I'd do the same for Janet," he said smoothly, and I accepted that answer. I appreciated being treated like family.

"Let me pay you at least," I said.

Eddie opened his mouth, then closed it and scratched behind Pepper's ears, and she melted into him, giving his arm long, slow licks. "If you give me money," he said eventually, "I'm just bringing you groceries with it."

I shook my head. "Honestly, I don't know what I'd do without you." Then I glanced over my shoulder. "Just don't tell Ruth that. I'm trying to convince her that I can do everything myself."

He mimed locking his lips. "Your secret is safe with me. Janet said the painter is coming around three. It won't be dry by then, but you won't have a hole anymore, and it'll be dry whenever he comes to actually do the work. Are you going to paint the whole room or just where the fire was?"

"Might as well freshen it all up," I said, looking around. "Now that I'm not paying to fix the wall."

Eddie winked with a smile that immediately made me realize why all the single women in town shopped at his store. Even I wasn't immune to the flutters when he looked at me like that. "That's the spirit."

17

I told Ruth she could go for a walk while the new stove was delivered.

"What about your job?"

"I took the day off. The hospital can function without me once in a while."

She patted my hand. "You shouldn't take so much time off—they could let you go. I can take care of getting the stove installed."

I looked at her hand on mine and then moved my own on top of hers, patting gently. "Honestly, I only started working because I was so bored with the children in school. I'll probably stop when summer rolls around anyway." Which wasn't even a little bit true. I would cut my hours for the summer months, certainly, but I enjoyed the satisfaction of the job so much more than Ruth could ever understand. Yes, of course, I made a difference as a mother. The most important difference. But I couldn't see that every day. At the hospital, I could. And that sense of purpose had been a lifeline when grief felt overwhelming.

She removed her hand from under mine and resumed her patting in a power struggle that was becoming amusing. "You won't need to, with me around. I can watch the children while you work this summer."

"Oh no," I said, reversing the pat again. "I wouldn't *dream* of missing a summer with them. I only get eighteen of them after all—as you well remember, I'm sure."

She pulled her hand back, and I felt a stab of guilt. That had been a low blow. "I'm sorry," I said.

Ruth nodded crisply and said she would take Pepper to the park.

Pepper was sleeping on a towel in the corner, still worn out from her walk to school on little puppy legs.

"She seems so comfortable," I said. "Maybe you want to relax? Or give your sister a call? I don't mind the long-distance charge."

"No," she said. "The children's drawers are too full. I'll go clear out the clothes that are too small for them."

Too much too soon, I chided myself as I watched her scoop up the sleeping puppy and carry her up the stairs. Then I went into the kitchen, where Eddie was squatting by the wall, his bad left eye closed, as he studied his handiwork.

"It looks great," I said. "Once it's painted, you'll never know there was a hole."

His eye sprang open as he turned to look at me. "Not bad," he said, standing up and dusting off his pants. "It'll take overnight to dry, but the painter can come back tomorrow. Or I can paint it this weekend if his price isn't right."

"You've done more than enough, Eddie. Thank you." I leaned up and gave him a sisterly kiss on the cheek.

He rubbed the back of his neck, looking embarrassed. "It's no trouble," he said.

"Whatever will I do when you get married, and your wife wants you doing work around your own house?"

Eddie shrugged, looking down at his feet. "I think you're safe on that front for a while."

"I wish I still had any single girlfriends. I'd set you up." I did know a couple of divorcées, but that wouldn't do. While they'd be happy to snap him up in a second, he deserved someone unjaded.

"It's a bachelor's life for me, I'm afraid. I don't mind though. I've got Janet's kids and Bobby and Susie. And being a fun uncle is a lot less work."

I smiled at him affectionately. "That's certainly true. Can I make you a cup of coffee?" I glanced at my watch. "Or some lunch? It'll have to be sandwiches until that new stove arrives." There was a knock at the door. "Speak of the devil."

"Why don't I stay while it gets installed?" Eddie asked.

As delightful as that sounded, especially with a load of ironing calling my name, I didn't want Ruth to think I couldn't handle an appliance being delivered. "No, I've kept you long enough. Unless you want that sandwich."

The rap at the door came again, and I passed him to open it.

"Mrs. Feldman?" the deliveryman asked. I replied in the affirmative, and he called to another man back at the truck, who began wheeling the new stove on a dolly.

"I don't love leaving you here alone with two strange men," Eddie said.

"I'm not alone. I've got Ruth upstairs. A few minutes with her and they'll be running for the door. In fact, I may have to call you for help later if they don't finish the installation in their rush to get away from her."

Eddie looked at me curiously. "She's not so bad, you know."

"I know," I said, after directing the deliverymen to the kitchen. "She's not. But I don't want her living here. I sent my own mother home—I don't want someone else's, even Harry's, encroaching on my space. I want to be able to put on a face mask and watch whatever I want on television after the kids go to sleep. And I want to cook whatever *I* want to cook without someone telling me I did it wrong. And make my own decisions and redecorate when and how I want."

"All reasonable," Eddie agreed. "But does that mean you'll never get married again?"

I tilted my head. The thought hadn't crossed my mind. Somehow, I still thought of myself as married. And the idea of developing feelings strong enough to even want to go on a date again seemed too foreign to comprehend. "I have no idea. But I certainly won't with Ruth living . . . here . . ." I trailed off as a lightning bolt of a realization struck me. That was the real reason she was here, wasn't it? To keep me from getting married again? But what about that fireman last night?

"My two options if I want her to leave willingly," I said, thinking out loud, "are to either get married or else convince her that I'm not planning to marry anyone else."

I looked at Eddie, and he held his hands up in mock surrender. "Don't look at me," he said. "I'm not part of this."

"I'm not marrying *you*," I said, nudging him playfully with my shoulder. "You're practically my brother. Although . . . a fake engagement might do the trick. She did say you were 'a good one.' Granted that was because the dog liked you, but still."

"You know what?" Eddie looked away and shook his head. "On second thought, you seem to have things under control here. I better go check on the store."

Eddie turned to go, and I wondered if I had offended him. I put a hand on his arm, and he looked down at it. "I'm just teasing," I said. His left eye twitched. I had clearly said something wrong. "Seriously, Eddie, thank you."

"Any time," he said with a nod. Then he poked his head back into the kitchen. "Any problems?" he asked the deliverymen.

"We just finished up," the first man said.

Eddie reached into his back pocket and pulled out his wallet, but I put a hand on his arm. "Don't be silly," I said, going to the hall for my purse, where I pulled out two dollar bills. I handed one to each man and thanked them. Then I looked back at Eddie. "Unless you're actually going to pretend to marry me. Then you can take care of tipping them."

Eddie chuckled and shook his head. "Remind me never to get on your bad side."

"You couldn't if you tried." I smiled at him, and he left with the deliverymen, while I went and peeked in the new oven. I decided to test it out by making a challah for when the kids came home from school. It wasn't a Friday, but Harry used to rub his hands together in excitement when he came home and saw a fresh-baked challah.

Cooking felt like work—it hadn't when Harry and I first got married. Back then, I delighted in making meals for my husband. I practically floated through the kitchen, adding spices and seasonings that could have been as simple as salt and pepper and still impressed him after growing up with Ruth's cooking. But once we had kids, cooking became a chore—a never-ending one like laundry. Every bite of food that met a turned-up nose or got flung to the floor made the whole process less and less gratifying.

But baking—when the kids weren't home to "help," at least—was enjoyable. The act of measuring the ingredients, then kneading the dough to activate the yeast, was soothing in a way that cooking no longer was. I loved the rhythmic motion of flouring the tabletop, kneading the dough, flipping it, and kneading again.

I set it aside to rise, cleaning up as it did. I didn't even pretend it was Ruth's face when it was time to punch the dough down before the second rise. Instead I switched on the radio and sat at the kitchen table with the newspaper, enjoying the luxury of reading more than just headlines.

When the timer went off, I expertly braided the dough, brushed it with egg yolk, and placed it in the new oven. The smell of fresh bread filled the house but also filled something in my soul that I hadn't realized I needed.

By the time I pulled the challah out to cool, perfectly golden without needing to adjust the temperature multiple times, I was glad I had the new oven. I could have lived without the hole in the wall or a fireman coming for dinner, but maybe it was a blessing in disguise. If I was overly sentimental about everything Harry had ever touched, I was on the path toward becoming Miss Havisham. And while my wedding dress was lovely, I wasn't sure I still fit into it after two kids.

Eddie's question replayed in my head, and I realized that it was true. I didn't have any desire to remarry. Or date. Harry had my whole heart. But I didn't know if that was a permanent condition or if what

Ruth said about puppies making hearts grow so loss seemed less would apply to me as well.

I was only thirty-two. I still had a lot of life left to live.

Had there been a catch in his voice when he asked that though? I thought back to the way he'd said it, and yes, there was something—

The doorbell rang, breaking my reverie, and I went to greet the painter.

18

I woke up early again the next morning, tiptoeing down the stairs to make a breakfast feast using the new stove. By the time Susie and Bobby tumbled sleepily down the stairs, I had pancakes, eggs, blueberry muffins, and fresh-squeezed orange juice on the table, with a cup of black coffee at Ruth's seat.

"What a breakfast," she said warmly. She gestured toward the syrup. "I'm surprised this came from a bottle."

"Well, we do have a maple out back, but it's the wrong season to go tapping trees," I said with a levity that I didn't have to fake as the children dug into their food with gusto. Maybe I'd go the extra mile for them more often. Now that they were a little older and no longer flung food they didn't want onto the floor or walls, it *was* more rewarding. "I didn't grow the oranges either."

The phone rang, and I crossed the kitchen to answer it, picking Pepper up on my way so she wouldn't beg for food. "Good morning," I said, assuming it was Janet.

"Barbara," Dr. Harper's voice came across the line. "I hate to do this, but is there any way you can come in for a couple of hours?"

"Um," I said, looking at the white wall that needed to be painted.

"I wouldn't ask normally, but Mrs. Kline is back, and she's already had half the nursing staff in tears, and somehow you're the one she responds to best."

I sighed. I would rather stick pins in my eyes than reschedule the painting over that woman. But my job was being a "patient liaison," and I didn't like the idea of her terrorizing the nurses in my absence.

"I can be in right after I drop the kids at school."

"You're an angel, Barbara. Truly."

I hung up and sighed, pulling the slip of paper with the painter's phone number off the refrigerator. "I hope he's not already on his way," I said to myself.

"Who?" Ruth asked.

"The painter." I cradled the receiver to my ear with my shoulder to dial. "Work needs me, so I need to reschedule."

"No need to reschedule over that. I'll be here all day."

"Rescheduling isn't that big a deal," I said, panicking that my plan to showcase my independence was going up in smoke because of Mrs. Kline. "Or I can just call the hospital back and tell them I can't make it."

"Nonsense," Ruth said, taking Pepper from my arms. "Go to work. This is why I'm here."

I hesitated. To be fair, *she* had caused the current need for help. It wasn't a deficit on my part.

What's the harm in letting her feel a little needed? Harry's voice asked. I shook my head but resisted glancing skyward while Ruth was looking at me. As often as I still talked to him, it so seldom felt like he was talking back that when he did, I tried to listen.

And so I found myself agreeing with her.

"I'll just be a couple of hours," I said.

"Take your time," Ruth said. "Go shopping after. Or to the beauty parlor. I'll try very hard not to start any more fires."

A sharp reply bubbled up, but there was humor in her face. And with Harry's voice still echoing in my brain, I grinned. "Now, Ruth," I said. "Don't make promises you can't keep."

She let out a bark of laughter that startled the puppy. "*That's* the girl my Harry fell for. Now shoo. I can handle a painter."

And leaving the house, I felt lighter. No, she hadn't packed her bags, but the shrew seemed a little more tamed already.

～

The lightness was gone by the time I had finished dealing with Mrs. Kline, who turned even more sour as soon as I walked into the room. And it dissipated further when Dr. Howe slipped into my tiny office behind me and tried to press me up against a wall. I ducked under his arm with a sharp rebuke and left, shutting him in there. I *may* have retaliated by locking him in—the one benefit to my office having been a closet. I kept a key on a wall hook by the door just in case—but I did hope it would take him a few minutes of panic before he found it.

To decompress before I went home, I took Ruth's advice and went shopping—I didn't remember the last time I had bought myself anything. I wasn't wearing black anymore, but even in just two years, my wardrobe was looking dated.

I felt guilty spending on myself despite the life insurance policy and earning my own salary—I wanted to be able to give as much as I could to Bobby and Susie when it came time to start their own lives. That insurance money was for them, no matter what George told me Harry had said when he presented me with the policy. So I limited my purchases to a few updated staples that could be paired with other items that I already had. But a pale pink pillbox hat, just like our first lady favored, caught my eye as I was about to leave Woodies. One little splurge wouldn't hurt.

I found myself smiling on the drive to pick up the kids from school. *Maybe,* I thought, *just maybe, we can find Ruth an apartment nearby. And then I can have her help out. One or two days a week so she feels needed. It is nice to get a break sometimes.*

I still wanted her out of the house. But for Harry, I would try harder to make sure she saw the kids regularly.

That was the solution. Boston wasn't likely to happen. Even if she would prefer to live with her sister, I knew she wasn't going to leave her grandchildren. So all I had to do was convince her I could do this, provide her some independence, figure out a way to involve her more in our lives, and send her on her merry way. As I parked the car, I glanced skyward. "Happy now?" I asked.

No one replied, of course. But I could tell that answer was better.

~

The painter's car was gone by the time the kids and I pulled into the driveway. "Who's excited to see the new kitchen color?" I asked.

"What did you pick?" Susie asked.

I shrugged at her. "Go see for yourself. Just don't touch the walls!" I called after them as I walked around the car, picking up their books and shutting their doors, and followed them into the house.

I went down the hall, the sound of their excited voices drifting toward me, and—

Stopped short in the kitchen doorway.

Instead of the pale yellow that I had selected, bright, patterned wallpaper covered every inch of wall. The base was either yellow or orange. I couldn't actually tell which color was supposed to be the background as the print was too crowded with vibrant fruits, vegetables, and flowers.

"What do you think?" Ruth asked proudly, spreading her arms.

"It's so fun!" Susie said. "It's like living in a Barbie ad."

"Too much pink," Bobby said, wrinkling his nose. "Oh wait, that's a funny banana!" He pointed to a banana with legs and a face. "I like that guy a lot."

Ruth pointed to another dancing banana. "He's got a brother over here."

Bobby grinned, walking around the room and pointing out a strawberry in a hat.

I wasn't smiling.

Susie looked at me and her face fell. "You don't like it, do you, Mama?"

I squeezed Susie's shoulder. "It's—it's a little loud," I said, struggling to see how I could prepare a meal in this room without developing a headache. "But I suppose—if you two like it—then I can learn to like it too."

Susie wrapped her arms around me in a hug, and Ruth looked on approvingly.

∽

I was quiet through dinner—a Ruth concoction of meat loaf that resembled neither meat nor a loaf and that had the unmistakable flavor and texture of coconut flakes in it. Though I did suppress a smile when Bobby went to make a peanut butter sandwich.

I couldn't kick her out with no place to go. But she had proven—repeatedly now—that she couldn't stay unsupervised in my house all day either.

"What would you do?" I asked the ceiling as I got into bed that night. "You always knew what to do."

19

By the time I woke up, I had a plan. "You're right," I told the ceiling. "That's the answer. No need to say I told you so. I'm the one who said you always knew what to do, you big galoot."

When Susie and Bobby went upstairs to get dressed after breakfast, I told Ruth to get dressed too.

"Do you want me to drop the children at school for you?"

"No," I said. "I want you to come to work with me."

Ruth cocked her head. "Whatever would I do there?"

"You can be a volunteer," I said. "It's how I started." *And it'll keep you from ruining my house again,* I thought. She looked uncertain.

"What about Pepper?"

"Pepper will be fine in her box for a few hours. She naps most of the day while the kids are in school anyway."

"I don't know—"

"Ruth," I said, taking her hand with an earnestness that I was far from feeling. "It's good for you. Trust me. Harry wouldn't want you to sit home alone all day."

She looked down at our hands. "I'll get dressed."

~

And that is how I got Ruth into a red-and-white striped pinafore over a starched housedress that was at least a decade old, a nurse instructing her along with a group of much younger women about their duties for the day. I retired to my office to tweak the day's schedule, which I handed to Nurse Jones a few minutes later.

She looked it over, then glanced up at me. "Are you sure sending your mother-in-law to Mrs. Kline is a good idea?"

"Shirley, she rearranged all my furniture, bought a dog without my permission, wallpapered my kitchen with cartoon fruits, and nearly burned my house down."

She tried to swallow a laugh but couldn't quite contain it. "Mrs. Kline is a fitting punishment, then."

"Honestly, it serves both of them right," I said.

"I assume you want her cleaning bedpans next?"

I grinned at her. "I like the way you think."

But by lunchtime, when I had neither seen nor heard from Ruth, I got a little nervous. She wasn't exactly known for following rules. And Mrs. Kline was unlikely to tolerate any nonsense. So with a sigh, I went down the hall toward the room where I had argued her into submission the day before.

The door was open and I heard raised voices from the hall. I took a deep breath and started to walk in, but Ruth's calm reply to Mrs. Kline's strident demand made me hesitate.

"White toast, rye, or a bagel," Ruth said, her voice perfectly measured.

"I *told* you," Mrs. Kline said shrilly. "I am *not* Jewish. I don't eat bagels or rye bread."

There was a long pause. And then Ruth said, quite calmly, "Do I look Chinese to you?"

Another pause. "Of course not," Mrs. Kline said, disgust dripping from her voice.

"That's because I'm not," Ruth said. "But I still enjoy an egg roll and some good lo mein."

"I don't see what that has to do with me."

Ruth's tone didn't change. "It has everything to do with you and you know it."

There was a creaking sound, and Mrs. Kline's voice rose to a panic. "Don't you sit on my bed!"

"It's the hospital's bed," Ruth said. "Why are you here anyway? You seem healthy enough."

"I'll have you know, I am *extremely* ill."

"With what?"

Mrs. Kline began to sputter. "The very nerve! You and that horrible other Feldman—your daughter I assume—to imply that I don't need to be here just because these doctors can't do their job correctly and diagnose me, all because I'm not Jewish and you only care about your own kind—"

"My dear Mrs. Kline," Ruth said, mirth unmistakable in her voice. "If you hate Jews so much, you really shouldn't spend all your time in a hospital. Half of these doctors are Jewish. And for the record, Barbara is my daughter-in-law. Her husband, my son, died two years ago."

Mrs. Kline was quiet for a few seconds, and I wondered if Ruth had placed a pillow over her face. I wouldn't blame her. But I really *should* get her to remove it if so.

"I'm sorry," Mrs. Kline eventually said quietly. I found myself leaning into the room to hear her better. "I lost my daughter six years ago."

"Do you have other children?" She didn't answer. "A husband?"

"Gone twenty years now," Mrs. Kline said mournfully.

"Grandchildren?"

"No. Gretchen wasn't married." There was another pause. "She was my whole world."

"Harry was mine," Ruth said. "But Gretchen wouldn't want you to waste away here. She'd want you to find ways to be happy."

"I don't know how to do that anymore."

I almost jumped out of my skin when Shirley touched my shoulder. "Donna needs help with Dr. Howe again," she said quietly.

I shook my head. "That man is a menace," I said quietly, to not be heard in the room. "I'll handle it."

Good Grief

An hour later, after telling off a handsy doctor and comforting a weeping nurse, I went storming into Dr. Harper's office. "You *have* to do something about that man," I said. "Between Mrs. Kline's abuse and Dr. Howe harassing every woman on staff, you're not going to have any nurses left. Donna is at her wit's end and her fiancé wants to shoot him."

Dr. Harper looked amused. "It would seem one of those problems has resolved itself."

"Tell me Dr. Howe fell off the roof and is in a coma."

He chuckled. "No. Although I think the nurses would have a champagne toast. Mrs. Kline is willingly checking out."

I held a hand to my mouth. "Oh no. What did my mother-in-law do? I should have gone in when she sat on the bed, but she seemed to be making progress."

"I don't know *what* she did," he said. "But Mrs. Kline said she feels better. And that Mrs. Feldman told her that grief and loneliness can have physical symptoms."

"She—what?"

Dr. Harper shook his head. "I don't understand it any better than you do. But bring your mother-in-law back next week. Maybe she can tame Dr. Howe too."

20

As soon as the car doors were shut, I turned on Ruth. "Explain what happened, please."

"What happened with what?" She reached for the window handle and began rolling it down.

"Mrs. Kline. Dr. Harper said she checked herself out of the hospital without even being seen by the doctor. How did you do that?"

"Louise? Oh, she's just a little lonely. That's all. We're having lunch on Monday. I told her I'd try to round up two more for a bridge game soon too."

I blinked rapidly. "Lunch. You're having lunch with the woman who wouldn't even let a Jewish doctor examine her unless a Christian nurse was present?"

"Her parents were from Germany," Ruth said. "She can't help the way she was raised. But she agreed to go to Hofberg's for lunch." Ruth smiled deviously at me. "I promised they won't poison her pastrami if she's with me."

I shut my mouth, which had dropped open. "You're taking a German woman to a Jewish deli for lunch? The woman who wouldn't even eat a bagel because she could be confused for a Jew?"

"Her *parents* were German. She was born here. And people can learn, Barbara. You really shouldn't be so judgmental."

Yes. I was the judgmental one, not Mrs. Kline. "And people called Anne Sullivan the miracle worker. You could give Anne Bancroft a run for her money." I shook my head and started the car, looking behind me as I backed out of the parking space. "Dr. Harper said he wants you to come back next week. Apparently if you can tame Mrs. Kline, the nurses are ready to throw you a parade."

I glanced at Ruth as I put the car in drive and saw her smiling in self-satisfaction.

"You really should think about the reasons people act like they do," Ruth said. "I'm no doctor, but it was obvious that Louise just needed a little attention. Granted, I suppose I understand her a little better than most. It wasn't like I had ever seen someone who wasn't Jewish or European when I came to this country. And losing her daughter, well, I . . ."

But I wasn't listening anymore as the wheels in my head began to turn. *Why was* Ruth *here? Why was* she *acting the way she did?* A lightbulb turned on. *She understands Mrs. Kline because they both lost children and are lonely. That's why she's here. Not because* I *need help, but because* she *needs to feel needed.* I had asked Harry once why his mother never remarried. "I told her she should once," he had said. "But she insisted that she wasn't lonely—that I was enough."

Harry was gone now. *Of course* she was lonely. I thought back to Janet telling me that I should marry her off. I hadn't taken that idea seriously, but maybe . . . maybe that was actually just what the doctor ordered.

At a light, I snuck another look at her. At a couple months shy of sixty, she was far from too old to find love again. After all, she *was* still an attractive woman. Even my own mother was envious of her figure. No, her cooking wouldn't lure anyone in, but . . .

Another lightbulb went on. I actually knew not just one, but *two* widowed men of her generation. Janet's father and Mr. Moskowitz, who lived three doors down from me.

Not that I wanted to foist Ruth on Janet, no matter how much she liked Eddie. And Mr. Moskowitz terrified Susie and Bobby with his yelling that they weren't to play on his lawn—something that, for the record, they had never done. But if Ruth could turn Mrs. Kline into a friend, Mr. Moskowitz would be no match for her . . . charm . . . or whatever one would call it. Besides, wasn't setting people up a mitzvah? I could help two lonely people *and* get my independence back at the same time without having to feel guilty about putting Harry's mother out. I smiled as a plan began to form.

We got home, and I asked Ruth if she wanted to walk with me to pick up the children from school. "We'll bring Pepper with us," I said, scooping the puppy out of her box as she wriggled and struggled to lick as much of me as she could after her first time home alone.

"How lovely," Ruth said. "Let me just change and get a hat."

"Great!" I said brightly. I just had to hope Mr. Moskowitz was outside. But as someone who fussed over his lawn, refusing to let any of the local boys cut his grass for him, the odds were good.

"Isn't the school that way?" Ruth asked, pointing down the street.

"Ye-es," I said, thinking quickly. "But it's such a nice day and poor Pepper was in her box so long, I figured we'd loop the block first so she can get her energy out. Weren't you the one who said a tired puppy is a well-behaved puppy?"

Ruth smiled and held her head a little higher at being quoted. "Quite right."

By the time we were two houses down, I had spotted Mr. Moskowitz pushing his manual mower in crisp lines across his already immaculate front lawn, stopping periodically to mop his brow with the red paisley handkerchief he kept in his pocket. Observing him from a house away, I could see he was definitely older than Ruth by a good ten years. Or maybe he just looked it from making mean faces at children. Either way, I would have picked Mrs. Kline over him in a fight, so Ruth would make short work of this.

"Hello, Mr. Moskowitz," I called as we neared him. "How are you today?"

He turned, pulling the handkerchief out to wipe his forehead. Then he pointed toward the sidewalk. "Don't you let that mutt do his business on my lawn," he said gruffly. "I've found droppings recently."

"Wasn't us," I said mildly. And as far as I knew, it wasn't. Besides, that had become a game in the neighborhood according to some of the other mothers—leaving a present on Old Man Moskowitz's lawn whenever he wasn't looking. I had no doubt that Bobby would bring Pepper to join in as soon as he got over his fear of the man.

He continued to give Pepper the stink eye. "Mr. Moskowitz, this is my mother-in-law, Ruth Feldman."

His eyes traveled up from Pepper, spending a little too long at Ruth's legs and bosom before meeting her face.

"Pleased," Ruth said, sounding anything but, "to make your acquaintance. But we should be going to pick up the children."

"You're heading the wrong way for that," Mr. Moskowitz said, then scowled. "I knew it. It was your dog on my lawn."

"I'll have you know," Ruth said, the hand that wasn't holding Pepper's leash on her hip, "that not only is this dog completely trained, but she has also never even walked down this side of the street. So you and that attitude can *gey kaken ofn yahm*." She switched to Yiddish to tell him to go and do what he had accused the dog of doing on his lawn in the ocean.

The two stared at each other, not off to the start I had hoped. And then Pepper put her front two paws on his lawn and lowered her hindquarters, leaving a puddle all over the sidewalk in front of Mr. Moskowitz's house.

A sound I had never heard before gurgled out of Mr. Moskowitz's chest, and it took me several seconds to realize that wheezing sound was him laughing. Soon Ruth joined him, and then I did too.

"Mrs. Feldman, was it?" Mr. Moskowitz asked.

"Ruth," she said, switching the leash to her left hand and holding her right out.

He took it in his. "Morty," he said. My eyes widened. It hadn't even occurred to me that he had a first name. I knew he was a widower with grown children who seldom visited, but I had never truly thought of him as a person who had a whole life outside of his lawn before, let alone a jaunty-sounding first name.

"Morty," Ruth repeated. "And this here is Pepper."

"More like *pisher*," Mr. Moskowitz said, and Ruth laughed.

Meanwhile, I was looking from one to the other like they were a tennis match. OLD MAN MOSKOWITZ HAD MADE RUTH LAUGH! *Let's see,* I thought. It was late March. If I was lucky, and this worked out, three months was a reasonable timeline for a second marriage among people who didn't have nearly as much time to waste, right? They'd do a small ceremony, either at the courthouse or in the rabbi's study.

And then she would live three houses away from me.

Oh no. What had I just done?

"Well, we should be going," I said, taking Pepper's leash from Ruth's hand. Mr. Moskowitz was still holding her other one. And Ruth was letting him. This was a disaster. What was I thinking?

I wasn't. That's the answer. I wasn't thinking. But three doors down was still better than inside my house.

I thought this was all about doing a mitzvah for two poor, lonely people, Harry's amused voice said in my head. I shot a glare skyward. He and I would have a little talk about that one later.

21

The following Monday morning, I brought Pepper with me to drop the kids off at school, but I took the long way home to walk past Mr. Moskowitz's house again. He was on his front porch, ostensibly reading the newspaper with a cup of coffee, but from the way he peeked over it as I approached, I wondered if that was a pretext to protect his lawn from four-legged defecators.

I waved merrily, and he raised his paper to avoid speaking to me. "Good morning, Mr. Moskowitz," I called. He grunted in return.

Apparently I was less interesting than my mother-in-law. No matter.

"That's okay, Pepper," I said, speaking exaggeratedly loudly for Mr. Moskowitz's benefit. "You can do your business *wherever* you need to."

Suddenly, Mr. Moskowitz's newspaper was on the chair, and he was striding across the lawn with big, angry steps.

"Careful, Mr. Moskowitz. I'd hate to see you step in anything untoward on your lawn."

He reached me and pointed a finger in my face. "Now see here, missy," he sputtered.

"Oh, calm down," I said, scooping Pepper up so she wouldn't *actually* relieve herself on his grass, ruining my plan. "Pepper has never done any business on your property."

"That sidewalk—"

"Belongs to the county," I finished. I stuck a hand in my pocket and pulled out a folded-up section of that morning's *Washington Post* that I had grabbed to protect against his accusations. "And I clean up my messes."

Mildly placated, he crossed his arms. "So you're just here to antagonize me, then?"

"Actually, I'm here to invite you to dinner."

He made a face. "You're too young for me, and I don't approve of forward women."

I resisted the urge to make a face back. "Believe me, you're not my type. But no, I want you to have dinner with my mother-in-law."

This certainly piqued his curiosity. "Really now?" He straightened the collar of his short-sleeved button-down. "I could tell she liked me."

I wouldn't exactly say she liked him. She'd had some choice words about his attitude, and Susie and Bobby now wanted to know what an *alter kaker* was and why it needed to *geh in draint*. I had no intention of explaining that she wanted to tell the crotchety old fart to go to hell, so I told them it meant she wanted our neighbor to be nicer, and they lost interest once the words weren't inappropriate.

But if she could become friends with Mrs. Kline, I didn't see why romance couldn't bloom with Mr. Moskowitz. There was no accounting for taste.

"Yes, well, I made you a reservation at Rive Gauche in Georgetown for six tonight."

"Rive Gauche!" Mr. Moskowitz said. "Absolutely not! I'm not giving her the impression that I'm the kind of man who will spend money willy-nilly like that. No, sir."

"Do you even want to know what kind of strings I had to pull to get you in there?" Technically it was one string—a girl Janet and I went to college with had married the son of the owner, so we were two of the rare common folk who could snag a table on a moment's notice. And our cocktails were on the house. But Mr. Moskowitz didn't need to know that.

"Don't care. No woman is worth a three-dollar piece of French fish."

I put my hands on my hips. "Fine. Why don't you just take her to the McDonald's on Rockville Pike and get her a fifteen-cent hamburger, then? Maybe you can splurge and spend a quarter to get her a Coke too." We glared at each other for several seconds until finally he caved.

"I don't like driving that far at night anymore," he said, somewhat more meekly. "Can it be someplace closer . . . and more reasonable?"

I conceded slightly. "Would O'Donnell's work?"

"The one in Bethesda?"

I nodded.

"As long as she doesn't try to order the lobster," he grumbled.

"She doesn't eat shellfish," I assured him, though I had no idea if that was true. Harry and I kept kosher, but loosely and in the house only. If Ruth wanted to order the lobster, that was going to be her problem to handle. "Pick her up at five forty. She'll be ready."

I turned and walked back toward my house, setting Pepper down as soon as we were no longer in front of his house. She did still have to finish her business before we went inside.

~

Of course, once we were home, I had to figure out how to get Ruth to go on this date. Calling it a date would never work. Harry had been unequivocal that while he wished his mother would find someone, she had no interest in replacing his father. It was one of the few areas where I truly felt I understood Ruth, honestly. When Harry told me that, years ago, I didn't. But now? No one could replace Harry. And the idea of another man in my bed? I shuddered.

But it had been a lot longer since Abe died. And Ruth was lonely. I could definitely see that once the kids were out of the house, companionship would be welcome. Would it be the same passion and love that I had with Harry? No. But a sedate, older relationship formed of a mutual desire for company? There was an air of eventual appeal to that. And while

Mr. Moskowitz was a crotchety old crank, he appeared . . . softer . . . when Ruth's name came up.

Satisfied with that line of thought, I rationalized that a white lie to help these two people find solace in each other was just fine.

Music emanated from the kitchen, and I went in to find Ruth humming along idly as she flipped through the newspaper, a cup of coffee in front of her. Pepper ran right over to her, and Ruth lifted the puppy up onto her lap.

"I ran into Mr. Moskowitz on my way home," I said by way of greeting.

"Oh?" Ruth asked, completely uninterested.

"Yes. He—he actually asked if you'd have dinner with him." She looked up, brow furrowed, but I kept talking before she could say no. "He . . ." I cast around desperately, wishing I had come up with a real plan before I spoke to her. I looked down at the table in front of her and saw she wasn't reading *The Washington Post*, but *The Jewish Week*. A headline mentioned the Jewish Community Center, which was down on Sixteenth Street, just a few miles south of Ruth's house. And an idea formed. "He wants the JCC to open a branch up here. He thinks you'd be perfect to help convince them it's needed."

I crossed my arms and smiled at her, satisfied with my bait.

Ruth contemplated this. "I suppose we *should* have something up here," she said slowly. "Though I think that would only make the situation worse in the District."

"The situation?"

She shot a knowing look at me. "Half the houses on my block are for sale. And they're not moving to Boca for the weather." She shook her head. "They don't realize that they're behaving just like people did when we got here. Did we ruin the neighborhoods when all the 'good Christians' ran away from us? Of course not. All they're doing is driving down property values."

She wasn't wrong. Of course, we had chosen the suburbs because we would have more room for children, and it was more affordable—but we had also bought the house before the schools in DC were integrated nine years ago. That was when the mass exodus really began.

"It would be good for the children to have a JCC nearby," Ruth said, thinking aloud. "And then you could save money by dropping that country club membership. Especially if they build a pool."

I bristled at the mention of the club. The pool was the only reason I still kept our membership, but it wasn't Ruth's place to tell me how to save money—especially not when she had mismanaged her own enough to lose her house. But she also wasn't wrong—I hated the club without Harry. The well-meaning questions that just reminded me over and over again that I was different now. The happy families playing in the water. The men golfing and playing tennis while the women lunched. It was all a reminder of loss. A local JCC *would* fix that at a fraction of the cost.

I shook my head suddenly. There was no plan to move the JCC. It was just my story to get Ruth to go on the date, fall in . . . maybe not *love*, but . . . mutual companionship, and leave my house.

"Exactly," I said. "And—uh—Mr. Moskowitz said he doesn't like driving so far anymore—especially at night . . . So will you meet with him? To help convince the board?"

"If he's not comfortable driving, he shouldn't drive," she said. I had let Ruth drive to the store the previous week in her boat of a 1946 DeSoto Suburban, and I personally felt she was a little too comfortable driving, but I kept my mouth shut. Then she agreed, but with a slightly sour face. "Why dinner though? Can't he just stop by the house? I can make coffee and a babka."

If he tasted her cooking, the whole plan fell apart. I shrugged. "If he's willing to buy you a meal, what's the harm?"

"He's probably lonely," she said with a sigh. "When does he want to meet?"

"Tonight," I said confidently.

"Well, that won't do. I have lunch with Mrs. Kline today. I can't eat out for two meals in a row."

"Sure you can. What would you do if you were on vacation?"

"If this is a vacation, the maid service is severely lacking," Ruth said, though there was a glint of humor in her eye. "I've already started two loads of laundry this morning."

"You don't have to do that, you know."

"And you don't have to refuse all help," she replied tartly. Then she sighed in resignation. "I suppose I can have dinner with the man, though I would guess he wants someone else to do all the work, while he takes all the credit, or he wouldn't be asking for help at all." She leveled a finger at me. "That's the real difference between men and women, you know." She stood and shook her head. "It's going to be a long day. I'd invite you to lunch with Mrs. Kline, but she doesn't seem to like you. Will you be all right on your own?"

I can't wait to be on my own, I thought. "Perfectly so."

～

After Ruth left for lunch at Hofberg's with Mrs. Kline, I genuinely debated calling the restaurant to warn them. I wouldn't wish those two together on my worst enemy . . . Then again, those two together *were* my worst enemy so maybe they deserved each other. Either way, I was free for an entire glorious midday and evening.

It was a beautiful day, so I tied a scarf around my hair and rolled the windows down in the car to drive to Greene's for the weekly shopping. The sky looked bluer than usual, as if the sun approved of my plan to make Ruth the new Mrs. Moskowitz. I found myself singing along to "Hey Paula" on the radio as I drove.

Eddie found me by the bakery counter, eyeing the babkas. I didn't want to think about what Ruth would put in one if she made it, but her mention had sparked a craving. And a well-made babka would be a perfect celebration tonight when the date went well.

"What's the occasion?" he asked, leaning an elbow on the counter to face me.

I smiled broadly. "I'm getting rid of Ruth," I said.

"Barbara," Eddie said, feigning seriousness. "Murder is never the answer."

He cracked up as well when I laughed. "Noted. But no. She has a date tonight!"

"Really?" he asked, leaning back a little. "With who?"

"A widowed neighbor of mine."

Eddie closed his left eye to scrutinize me. "Wait. Not the one who came out of his house screaming at me when I parked down the street that one time?"

I shrugged. He hadn't told me about that. "Probably. He's the neighborhood grump."

"Ruth agreed to go out with *him*?"

"Well, kind of. I may have made up a reason for dinner. But *he* agreed. And you should have seen them together last week. She made him laugh. Mr. Moskowitz, laughing!"

"Well, she's funny. But, Barbara, setups don't work like that. I should know. Janet has set me up with enough people."

"Has she?" I asked. Strange that I didn't know that. "Either way, she'll be good for him."

"But will *he* be good for *her*? I obviously didn't know her husband, but Harry didn't have a grumpy bone in his body."

"He had a couple of grumpy bones," I said, but I couldn't quite meet Eddie's gaze.

I realized I didn't know what drew someone like Abe to Ruth. Had she been softer when she was young? Heaven knew I wasn't the same as I was when I had Harry. Or did opposites attract? A small niggle of doubt formed about my plan, but I tried to shrug it off. What I needed mattered too. And I needed Ruth out of my house.

"It's one date, Eddie," I said finally. "If she doesn't like him, I'll look for someone else."

"You know better than I do," he said. "What would an old bachelor know about matters of the heart?"

I looked at him sharply—that second sentence had a bite to it. But if anything, Eddie's face was a little sad. "Do you *want* to be set up?" I asked, genuinely curious. Janet's view of her brother certainly wasn't the same as mine. No, I didn't know anyone for him, but I'd be happy to keep my eyes open if he was looking. I started mentally going down the hospital nurses' relationship statuses.

"No," Eddie said firmly. "If I meet the right girl, I meet the right girl."

"If that changes—"

"You'll be the first person I ask," he assured me. "Wrap up the chocolate babka for Mrs. Feldman," he told the young man at the bakery counter, then turned back to me. "I have a feeling you may need it for when Ruth gets home."

Annoyed, I went home to put the groceries away, then stopped by Janet's house. Unlike Eddie, *Janet* would agree that this was a brilliant plan. After all, she had suggested it.

"Please," Janet said, pouring me a cup of coffee. "You think Eddie knows anything about love? I'm not sure he's even kissed a girl."

"I'm sure he's kissed plenty of girls."

"I'm not. You know, I've wondered if he—"

"Janet Weinstein, you stop that right now. There's absolutely nothing wrong with your brother."

"Who says it's wrong?" Janet shrugged. "He's my brother and I love him. I just wouldn't take matchmaking advice from him." She sipped her coffee, then added another sugar cube. "Of course, if your plan works out, you're hardly rid of her."

"I thought of that too late."

Janet laughed. "Let's find her a rich European. Put an ocean between you and her and get a nice, fat inheritance when she eventually kicks the bucket."

"Janet!"

She raised her coffee cup to mine. "To a mother-in-law–free home. With money for a pool."

This time, I laughed as I clinked my cup to hers. "You're incorrigible."

"A badge I wear proudly," she said. "Call me tonight and let me know how it went."

22

There was an unfamiliar car in my driveway when I arrived home, which I eyed warily. Ruth being home with any kind of worker had not gone well so far. But it was better than the fire department, I supposed.

Unless that was Mr. Waterman's car.

Ugh, I thought. *Hopefully just a solicitor. Ruth* is *the type who would let a Jehovah's Witness in. Granted, she'd wind up convincing him to convert to Judaism.*

With a sigh, I opened the front door and went inside, only to find Mrs. Kline inspecting every single item on my dining room sideboard as if she were in a museum where people were allowed to touch the exhibits.

"How curious," she said, picking up a gravy boat and examining it.

"How curious that Jews use gravy, just like gentiles?" I asked.

She jumped a mile, throwing the gravy boat into the air. Ruth caught it with a practiced ease that made me think this wasn't the first of my belongings to take flight this afternoon.

"Well, yes," she said, holding a hand to her heart. "You gave me quite a fright."

Why don't you go to the hospital about it? I thought. But I gave her a half smile, the most I could muster at finding her in my home.

"I'm sorry," I said. "I just didn't expect to find a patient inspecting my wedding china."

"I didn't know Jews used china." She quickly turned to Ruth. "Although yes, I know about your penchant for Chinese food. I suppose we *can* try that next week."

"We use silver too." She opened her mouth, but I cut her off. "To eat. Not to dismember Christian babies. That's called a blood libel. It's never been real."

She looked to Ruth, who nodded. "I've learned so much today. No holes in your sheets either."

My mouth dropped open at the idea that she had inspected my bed linens. "Now you—" I said, but Ruth stopped me by replacing the gravy boat and putting a hand on my arm.

"Louise was curious. But—" She looked at her wristwatch. "Oh dear. The children will be home from school soon. I'm afraid I need to send you home," she said to Mrs. Kline. "I'll call you about a bridge game, and we can go for Chinese next week. Wait until you try dim sum!"

"It's a date," Mrs. Kline said. She shook Ruth's hand and nodded at me. "Ruth. Mrs. Feldman."

Ruth walked her to the door, while I straightened the gravy boat, seething. As soon as I heard the door shut and Ruth's footsteps returning, I turned to face her. "How could you bring that woman into my house?"

Ruth crossed her arms. "That woman went from the most raging anti-Semite you've ever seen to being willing to eat at a Jewish deli. Give me a month, and she'll be donating to the United Jewish Appeal."

I closed my eyes and counted to ten. "I don't want strangers in my bedroom."

"She wasn't in your bedroom. I showed her the linen closet when she asked about holes in the sheets."

I shook my head and exhaled audibly. "I don't know *where* they get these insane ideas."

"Tzitzit," Ruth said, referring to a fringed, poncho-like garment that orthodox men wore under their shirts, with a hole cut out for the head. "That's what my mother said. Someone saw tzitzit hanging on a clothesline and thought that was a bedsheet for . . . relations."

For a moment, I stared at Ruth, not comprehending, and then I began to laugh.

"What's so funny?" she asked.

"The size of the hole," I said, then I clapped my hand over my mouth.

She waggled her eyebrows. "Well, that *would* explain why they hate us, then, if they think our men are that . . . well endowed."

I couldn't help it. I doubled over with laughter, Ruth joining in. "I'm going to go get the children," I said when I finally composed myself.

"Remind them to keep their horns covered in case Louise is driving by the school," Ruth called.

"Goodbye, Ruth." I shook my head, but I was still chuckling. And as much as I didn't want Mrs. Kline in my home, I did respect that Ruth had disarmed her so easily.

***

"No, no, no," I said as Ruth came downstairs wearing a dowdy suit. "That won't do."

"Why not?" she asked, holding out the fabric of the skirt. "It's a business meeting."

"It's a—well, O'Donnell's is a nice restaurant. You should wear a dress."

"I've been to O'Donnell's," Ruth said. "This is just fine."

"For lunch, maybe," I said. "When's the last time you went for dinner?" She looked uncertain.

"I have dresses," she said. "But I don't want Morty to get the wrong idea."

"Ruth," I said, putting an arm around her shoulder and guiding her toward the stairs. "It's 1963. Women can be just as powerful in a dress as in a suit. Look at Jackie Kennedy. No one takes her less seriously when she dresses for dinner. She didn't wear a suit when she had dinner at Buckingham Palace."

"I'm hardly Jackie Kennedy, and no one is confusing Morty Moskowitz for Prince Philip, Barbara."

I waved a hand in the air. "You know what I mean. Go on. Wearing a dress out to dinner won't kill you."

She reluctantly climbed the stairs, returning in a dress that was at least a decade old but flattering nonetheless. "Better?" she asked.

"Much," I said. Though if this date didn't work out, I was going to have to take her shopping—likely on my dime—for some clothes that were made during the Kennedy administration. "Actually, wait," I said, running up the stairs. I hadn't worn my new hat yet, but it was a perfect match for the trim on Ruth's dress and was just the touch needed to modernize her outfit. "Wear this with it," I said, handing her the hat.

Ruth examined it. "It still has a tag on it."

"Where do I have to go in a nice hat? You can borrow it for the evening."

She put it on her head and went to the mirror by the front door to examine her reflection. "It *is* flattering," she said. "Not everyone can wear this shade of pink."

I blinked, wondering if that was a dig at my skin tone, but shook it off. *I* knew the hat looked better on me, even if *she* didn't. I smiled tightly and removed the tag, hoping my new hat made it home in one piece.

At five forty on the dot, there was a knock at the door. Bobby went running to answer it, trailed by Pepper, stopping short and staring at Mr. Moskowitz before turning heel and running upstairs. "I didn't do it," he yelled down. "Whatever he's mad about, I didn't do it!" Pepper growled and barked at the intruder.

Mr. Moskowitz was holding a bouquet of grocery store carnations but looked irritated. "If that's what he says when he sees me, the young man is guilty of *something*." He looked down at Pepper. "Quiet, *pisher*."

"The only thing he's guilty of is being scared of you, with good reason," Ruth countered, and I suppressed a smile as she defended my son. She scooped Pepper up and handed her to me, whispering, "Dogs know a good one when they see one. And they can smell a rotten egg."

She turned back to Mr. Moskowitz. "Are those for me? Or do you just like holding them?"

He held them out. "They're for you," he said. "You look very nice, Ruth."

She took the flowers, handing them off to Susie and telling her to put them in water. "I suppose we should get this over with," she said. "Should I drive? I heard you're not—"

"Mr. Moskowitz is fine to drive," I said, cutting her off. If she let him know that I had said he wasn't comfortable driving at night, this evening was going to be over before it started.

"Shall we?" he asked, holding out an elbow. Ruth looked at it but didn't take it. Instead she picked up her handbag from the table in the hall and walked out before him.

"Is Grandma on a date?" Susie asked me, her eyes wide.

"She is," I said. "She just doesn't know it yet."

Susie made a face. "Couldn't she find someone better than Old Man Moskowitz?"

"Mr. Moskowitz," I corrected, even though I called him that in my head as well. "And you should have seen them the other day. They got on famously. Now go play with your brother while I make *our* dinner."

~

It was so nice having a meal with just my children. No one complained about the food or brought up atrocities that had been committed against the Jews of Europe. Just eating, talking about our days, and enjoying each other's company.

I let the kids go play in the backyard with Pepper after they finished eating, and I cleared the table and pulled out bowls to give them ice cream for dessert. The days were getting longer as spring progressed, and the simple joy of it still being light out at six thirty made me smile as I watched them from the kitchen window.

Then the front door opened, startling me as it slammed shut just as suddenly. It hadn't occurred to me to lock it. I snatched a frying pan off the stove, then went into the hall, prepared to fight off whatever invader had entered my home.

But it was Ruth, forcefully smashing her bag onto the hall table and kicking off her low heels.

I lowered the frying pan, and she looked up at me. "That—that—that cad!" she exclaimed as she removed my hat. "I have half a mind to fling every single dropping Pepper leaves from now on at his front door. The chutzpah of that shmuck!"

"What happened?" I asked, alarmed, but also pulling my hat from her trembling hands before she crushed it. Was he secretly a bottom pincher like Dr. Howe? Or worse?

"He couldn't care less about the Jewish community. He tried to kiss me, that's what! Me! A respectable widow!"

A wave of guilt rose and crested inside me. That was my fault. I lied to both of them about the setup. But neither would have gone if I hadn't. That wasn't a *lie* exactly. Was it?

"Then he took you home?"

Ruth shook her head and wiggled her right ankle at me. "No. I kicked him and got in a cab." She pointed a thumb over her shoulder. "The driver is still out there. You'd better go pay him."

"Me?"

"Barbara Feldman," she said in a tone that made me want to go hide under the bed like my kids did when I took the same tone with them. "Do you think I was born yesterday? I know he didn't want to talk about the JCC."

We stared at each other for what felt like a long time. Then finally, I moved toward the stairs. "I'll get my wallet."

23

"Mr. Moskowitz was a terrible plan anyway," Janet said on the phone later that week. "You don't want her three doors down from you."

"No, you're right. I know you're right. But who, then?"

Janet didn't have ideas but suggested I get Eddie in on looking. "He knows everyone who shops at the store."

I said I would ask him the next time I saw him, though I knew full well that Janet would be calling him as soon as she hung up with me.

On Wednesday the following week, I made the rounds at the hospital, taking food orders. It had been a busy night Tuesday, which most of the nurses attributed to a full moon, and the candy stripers, Ruth included, were occupied with patients.

And I never minded helping however I could, whether it was in my job description or not. At Harry's funeral, the rabbi explained that the Jewish custom of each mourner dropping a spade of dirt onto the coffin was a mitzvah of the highest order, because it was one that could never be repaid. The nurses' whole job was that kind of mitzvah. Emulating them was the closest I would ever be able to come to repaying them.

The patient in room 213 had just been released by the surgical team. I glanced at the chart hanging outside his door—emergency appendectomy.

"Good morning, Mr. Goldberg," I said as I walked in. A handsome older man looked up at me, with silver hair and brilliant blue eyes.

"Good morning," he said, sitting up straighter, then wincing and pressing his hand to the right side of his abdomen.

"No sudden movements," I said, crossing to check and make sure he didn't need a bandage change. "How bad is the pain?"

But he smiled up at me with perfect white teeth. "All better. Well, mostly. Just need to remember to go slow."

"At least until your stitches are out," I said, returning his smile. I found my eyes traveling to his left hand, which rested next to him on the bed. No ring. Then again, they would have removed it for the surgery, I chided myself. And as an actual hospital employee, I needed to stay professional. "Now," I said, back to business, "let's get you all set up for lunch so you can get better and go home."

But after I left his room, I made a pit stop at the chalkboard by the nurses' station and switched the side of the hall that Ruth was assigned to. If sparks flew between a volunteer and a patient, well . . . it wouldn't be the first time a candy striper found love on the ward.

Though it might be the first time said candy striper was pushing sixty.

~

When it was time to clock out, Ruth was nowhere to be found. I grabbed Gloria's arm as she went past. "Have you seen my mother-in-law?"

Gloria laughed. "Oh, you don't know?"

"Don't know what?"

She grinned wryly. "Sounds like she caught the fish in 213, but you didn't hear that from me. She's been in there for the last hour."

I couldn't stop myself from smiling.

I *might* have taken a second look at his chart. He was single. Three years younger than Ruth, but I didn't see that mattering at their age.

I went down the hall and paused outside the room. But all I heard coming from inside was low voices and the occasional laugh. *Maybe I should let them have more time,* I thought, checking my watch. If I called Janet, she'd be happy to take the kids to her house for an hour or two.

I shook my head, remembering my own long-ago single days. It was better to leave them wanting more. So I rapped on the doorframe with the back of my hand before walking in. Ruth was sitting on Mr. Goldberg's bed and apparently neither of them heard my knock. ". . . and the next thing I know, I hear a siren," she was saying.

"The popcorn!" Mr. Goldberg said, laughing.

"Meanwhile, I'm trying to get the puppy to do her business and have no idea the house is burning down. I smelled smoke and went around the front to see whose house was on fire. Imagine my surprise when it was mine."

Mr. Goldberg looked up and saw me, then cleared his throat.

"Well," Ruth said, turning around. "I suppose it was *her* house. Barbara, darling, have you forgiven me for the kitchen yet?"

No, I thought. "The fire? Of course. That could have happened to anyone." I looked from her to him. "Well, anyone who stored popcorn in the oven." Mr. Goldberg chuckled. "The wallpaper, on the other hand . . ."

Ruth turned back to Mr. Goldberg. "You should see the wallpaper I picked out. It's so festive. Barbara here was going to paint the kitchen yellow, which is fine, of course, but so bland. Cooking, especially for people you love, is too fun for bland."

"Fun" was one way to describe Ruth's cooking. "Terrifying" was another. But I couldn't exactly throw a zinger at her in front of the man who I hoped would be my savior by removing her from my house.

"I'm just teasing," I said. "The kids love it."

"Barbara is a *wonderful* mother," Ruth said. "They're the two best-behaved children in the entire world. Truly."

I eyed her carefully, but there was no sarcasm in her voice. Likely she was just acting the part of the perfect mother-in-law to curry favor with the handsome man whose bed she was sitting on, but I'd take it.

"Speaking of which," I said. "It's time to head home so I'm not late picking them up from school. But if you're not ready, I can—"

Ruth stood up and smoothed her pinafore. "No, of course. I lost track of time." She smiled beatifically at Mr. Goldberg, and I was once again struck by how pretty she was when she bestowed a smile on someone. "We'll continue this conversation tomorrow."

"I look forward to it," Mr. Goldberg said. Then he turned to me. "You've got quite the mother-in-law."

"Don't I know it," I said. "Have a good night, Mr. Goldberg. The nursing staff here is fantastic. They'll take good care of you."

"Sam," he said.

"At work, I'm afraid you're Mr. Goldberg," I said. "But candy stripers have different rules."

On the drive home, Ruth was uncharacteristically chatty about her new friend. "So handsome," she said. "And a widower—but he's been alone for fifteen years now. No children. And a great sense of humor. He just needs someone to take care of him. Imagine—he could have died if he hadn't been able to call for an ambulance himself."

"Thank goodness for small miracles," I murmured, but I was practically vibrating with the potential here. I had never seen Ruth so giddy before.

No, that wasn't true. She was when we told her I was pregnant with Susie. And again when Bobby was born. But certainly not since Harry had died. I couldn't wait to tell Janet.

∼

The following day, Ruth told me she was just going to pop in and check on Mr. Goldberg before doing her rounds. "Go," I said, shooing her with my hands. "It's a light day. You spend as much time with him as you—as *he* needs."

Ruth patted my arm. "This is why you're so good at this job. You care about people."

I could get used to the smitten version of my mother-in-law. I wouldn't even mind visits with her if she was this pleasant and full of praise.

One volunteer down, I was on my feet for the full five hours of my shift, taking only a minute break to gulp down a cup of coffee and have a bite of a doughnut at noon before I was needed again. But I hardly noticed being hungry or overextended. I was about to be free. I just knew it.

As I clocked out and went to get Ruth, Dr. Worlitzer was in Mr. Goldberg's room. ". . . looks right on track for us to discharge you tomorrow morning."

"Wonderful," Mr. Goldberg said, then shot a glance at Ruth. "I'll certainly miss the care here, however. Might have to fake an injury to come back."

"Nonsense," Ruth said, putting a hand on top of his. She was on his bed again. Had she been a young girl, I would have scolded her for sitting so close. "Why don't you come for dinner tomorrow night? A good home-cooked meal is exactly what you need to recover fully."

Mr. Goldberg glanced up at me and grinned. "And is that okay with the mistress of the house? I don't want to impose—especially when children are involved."

I couldn't very well suggest that he take her out instead when the whole pretense for the meeting was a home-cooked meal. But Ruth's cooking was likely to sour the match. I would have to convince Ruth to let me make the meal—and all subsequent ones until there was a ring on her finger.

"The mistress of the house thinks it's perfectly fine to come for dinner," I said. "Ruth can write down our address in case we don't see you tomorrow morning."

"Oh, I already gave him our number," Ruth said, smiling at Mr. Goldberg. "I'm not letting this one get away that easy."

24

Not that Ruth had any intention of giving up the cooking. "I'm not going to the hospital today," she declared Friday morning.

I eyed her suspiciously.

She either didn't notice or pretended not to. "I'll need to go to the store for dinner for tonight. I'm making a brisket."

This would require a delicate hand. "Ruth," I said. "Why don't you let me do the cooking? I don't mind. That way you can . . ." I tried to think of what would get her out of the house while I was gone. "Go to the beauty parlor. And maybe pick up a new dress. On me," I added hastily, knowing she would refuse to buy herself new clothes.

"How thoughtful," Ruth said. "Yes, a new dress would be perfect, wouldn't it? Are you sure you don't want to pick it out?"

"No," I said, putting a hand on Ruth's arm. "Whatever you pick will be lovely."

Ruth pulled me in for a hug, which I accepted stiffly. "I'm so excited for this," she said. "I just have such a good feeling about him."

"Me too," I said, patting her shoulder.

∼

I left work half an hour early and stopped by Greene's. I agreed that brisket was the way to go, but I was going to be the one to cook it.

Eddie looked surprised to see me. "Did Ruth forget something?"

A little warning bell went off in my head. "What do you mean?"

Eddie chewed his lower lip. "Um. Ruth was here. A couple hours ago. She got a brisket for . . . She said she had a 'gentleman caller' coming tonight."

I rolled my eyes. "I'd say that was an overly dramatic way to put it, but then again, living with her *does* feel like something out of a Tennessee Williams play."

"It's not that neighbor, is it?"

"No. You were right about him. That date ended with a swift kick from Ruth and me paying for a cab ride home." Eddie gave a half smile. "It's a patient from the hospital. The two of them seemed to really hit it off."

"And she knows it's a date this time?"

I put a hand over my heart. "All aboveboard this time, officer. *She* invited him over. For a home-cooked meal." Then I realized we had a problem. "Oh no. If she came in, she's already cooking."

"Her cooking can't be *that* bad."

"Eddie Greene, if you don't believe me, then *you* come for dinner one night. Just don't blame me when she manages to ruin brisket for you. Forever."

He grinned. "I'm up for the challenge."

"Let me get through this dinner, and then we'll set something up. If her cooking scares him off, I'm going to need your help finding someone else."

"Aw, Barbara, I don't think—"

I held up a hand to stop him. "Hopefully it doesn't come to that. But Janet already volunteered you to help if it does."

"I swear—"

"Don't be mad. You know how she is when she loves someone."

"Yeah," he said tightly. "I do. Speaking of which, are you going to be at Paula's birthday party next weekend?"

"Of course," I said, realizing I still had to buy a gift.

"Good," Eddie said, his smile genuine. "You can tell me all the details about the 'gentleman caller' then."

"I so hope she calls him that to his face. I mean, I don't. I want it to work. But I'd love to see it anyway."

Eddie shook his head. "That was always why you and Janet were so dangerous together. She's fearless, and you love to egg people on."

He wasn't wrong, though it had been a long time since the two of us had actually caused any trouble. Ten years ago, we would have gone after Old Man Moskowitz for trying to force himself on Ruth.

Which was how Harry and I met. One of his and George's fraternity brothers unceremoniously dumped our friend Charlene for another girl. And after a few drinks, Janet and I decided we were going to paint "Henry Goldman sleeps with goats" on the fraternity house lawn. Harry caught us and was going to call campus police, but when I told him *why* we were defacing his lawn, that twinkle in his eye started sparkling. He got George, who helped him keep watch, and they took us out to a local diner for pancakes afterward. It turned out they weren't Henry fans either, but boy did they like us for having "bigger balls than Henry did."

Honestly, Janet would probably still be up for a good prank if I asked her. I was the one who was no fun anymore.

"You okay?" Eddie asked.

"I'm sorry," I said. "Just . . . remembering the trouble we used to get into."

"My mother used to worry the two of you would get expelled."

I chuckled. "She didn't need to worry. We both graduated." I looked down at the meat counter. "Well, I suppose I'm not buying a brisket. Although if I were smart, I would, just for when Ruth destroys the one she bought."

Eddie shook his head. "Unless you're planning to go cook for this man every night, he's going to have to learn to love her, bad cooking and all."

"Think her sparkling personality will be enough?"

Eddie shrugged good-naturedly. "As long as he likes dogs, you've got a shot." One of the cashiers called over the loudspeaker for Mr. Greene. "Duty calls," Eddie said, then he sighed as he started toward the registers. "I'll see you Monday?."

"See you Monday." I found myself smiling as I walked away.

25

I could smell the brisket before I even opened the front door. And it actually didn't smell bad. Of course, it was only three—she had plenty of time to burn it to a crisp before Mr. Goldberg arrived. But if I could nudge her out of the kitchen, maybe I could prevent that.

Music emanated into the hall, Ruth's voice rising off key to sing along to the Chiffons. She was standing at the stove, her hair newly chopped into a Jackie Kennedy bob, along with fresh color—no more streaks of gray. It suited her. And I felt my heart lift, really for the first time since she moved in. She clearly liked this man. And what better deed could I do than find real happiness for Harry's mother? It wasn't even me being selfish anymore. I was excited for her—for the possibility of a new beginning and a more fulfilling life for her.

"You get on out of here," Ruth said, gesturing toward the door with a wooden spoon and dispelling the mood. "I've got this all under control. Just get the kids, and then I'll watch them so you can relax and get dressed for tonight. I got you a new dress too. And that new Marilyn Kleinman novel that everyone at the hospital is talking about—you never take the chance to put your feet up, and that's just what the doctor ordered this afternoon."

I didn't want to admit that I hadn't read the first Marilyn Kleinman novel yet—especially because I knew her cousin, Beverly.

And as much as I wanted to take over the cooking to make sure tonight went smoothly, I had to admit Eddie was right. Better

Mr. Goldberg learn what he was in for now. Besides, I hadn't seen Ruth this excited in a long time. It gave me such hope that I found myself agreeing with her.

"You're the boss," I said. "I'll bring Pepper with me to get the kids . . . and maybe go the long way to leave a little present on Old Man Moskowitz's lawn."

She pointed a finger at me with a grin. "Now *that's* a plan I can get behind."

～

I supervised homework when the kids got home, then let them go out in the backyard to play with Pepper. And I took Ruth's advice, sitting on the chaise lounge on the patio and opening the book she'd brought me. Before I even knew it, an hour had passed and I needed to get myself and the kids ready for Ruth's date.

The dress Ruth had picked for me was shockingly stylish. A sleeveless sheath dress with a slim silhouette, as opposed to the crinoline-lined skirts Ruth still favored, in a shade of light blue that made my eyes pop. As I fluffed my hair and applied a coat of lipstick, I found myself admiring my reflection. I couldn't remember the last time I *really* looked in a mirror, because, quite honestly, who cared what I looked like anymore?

I think I had been afraid to look too closely since losing Harry. I was scared that instead of the laugh lines that had been beginning to form, I would see lines of sadness. A permanent reminder of what I had lost.

But I saw neither as I studied the woman in the mirror. Just me. I winked, and she winked back at me. My heart was a crisscrossed mess of scar tissue, but on the outside I looked just as I always had. The laugh lines would have deepened if Harry were here. My mother would consider that a plus. I looked skyward. "I miss you, you big lug," I said quietly.

A knock at the door pulled me from my thoughts, and I called to the children as I went down the stairs. "Best behavior tonight."

"Yes, Mama," Susie replied. She elbowed Bobby, and he echoed her.

Ruth came down the stairs behind me, wearing a new dress, with capped sleeves and a flared skirt, belted to show off her slim waistline. "Do you want to get it?" I asked her.

"No, no," she said. "I should check the brisket. You go."

She's nervous, I thought. It was strangely adorable . . . not a term I ever thought I would use about my mother-in-law. But I smiled as I reached for the doorknob, then opened the door to see Mr. Goldberg on my front step, wearing a sport coat and tie and holding a bouquet of colorful Gerbera daisies—my favorite flowers.

"Mrs. Feldman," he said, holding out the flowers.

"Barbara," I corrected with a welcoming smile. "I'm not your patient liaison anymore."

"Is that your job title?" he asked.

"It is."

"It suits you," he replied. "And please, call me Sam." He gestured with the flowers. "For you. Thank you for having me over tonight."

"So thoughtful," I said, taking the flowers. "Please do come in. I'll bring these to Ruth."

I led him to the living room, while the children gawked awkwardly. "Bobby, Susie, this is Mr. Goldberg. Your grandmother invited him for dinner tonight." Bobby looked unsure, while Susie dropped a curtsey. We were going to have to work on their manners with guests if Ruth was going to be dating.

Sam smiled and took a seat on the sofa.

"Can I get you a drink before dinner?"

"Scotch, if you have it."

"It may be a few years old, but I believe we do." I grinned at him sheepishly. "We haven't exactly entertained much since Harry—my husband . . ."

"Anything you've got is fine," Sam assured me.

I took the flowers to the kitchen and showed Ruth before pulling out a vase to put them in. "Quite the gentleman," I said, managing not to add *caller* at the end. "You should go say hello."

"I'm about to," Ruth said, pulling off her apron and draping it over the back of a kitchen chair. "But, Barbara? Tell him you made dinner."

"Me? Why?"

"I want him to be impressed."

It was a rare vulnerable moment from her. And my heart expanded at the knowledge that she wanted me to pretend to be the inferior cook, entirely so he would be awed by her. *She must really like him*, I thought. I wondered if she had shown this much interest in any man since Abe passed—I doubted it. As much as Harry always said he wished she would find someone, he didn't think she would actually be willing to try. I glanced up and nodded. I would do this for her. For Harry.

"Of course." Ruth turned and thanked me. I smiled in return, then took down a highball glass and reached for the liquor cabinet.

Ruth was in the chair across from him when I brought the drink. "Please let me know if it's . . . turned . . . or whatever scotch does. We have a bottle of bourbon that I can vouch for."

"I'm sure it'll be fine," Sam said, crossing one leg over the other. "Scotch is better aged."

I chuckled. "I believe that means in a barrel, not in a half-drunk bottle in a widow's liquor cabinet for nearly three years. But don't feel obliged to drink—or eat—anything that isn't to your liking." Ruth shot me a warning look.

"You can always have a peanut butter sandwich if you don't like dinner," Bobby offered. "That's the rule."

Sam leaned forward. "Now that sounds like a nice rule."

Bobby nodded sagely. "You just have to make it yourself."

Susie came to help me, and the two of us made short work of transferring all the food to the dining room, where Ruth had set the table with Shabbat candles and a covered, store-bought challah. I stopped short at the sight of the candles. We hadn't done a proper

Shabbat dinner in years. I insisted when the kids were little, but then we lost Harry and . . . well, the tradition fell by the wayside. But maybe we should start again. Susie *should* grow up knowing the blessings for when she had her own family.

"Go tell everyone we're ready," I told Susie as I pulled a matchbook from the sideboard. Ruth led Sam in, Bobby trailing behind them, and there was a mildly awkward moment as I realized Ruth had set the table so that Sam was at the head—Harry's spot. I blinked rapidly several times, swallowing the desire to tell him he couldn't sit there. That we'd move his place setting to the empty spot at the other end of the table. But Harry's voice whispered in my head: *It's okay. It's for her.* So I swallowed thickly, then told Sam to have a seat. Ruth sat at his side, across from me, at his other side, and I brought Susie to me to do the blessing over the candles.

"We haven't done a proper Shabbat in a while," I said. "Excuse me if we're a bit rusty."

I reminded Susie to cover her eyes and helped her with the gesturing over the candles, leading her as she recited the end of every other word with me from memory. *"Baruch atah Adonai, eloheinu melach ha'olom asher kidshanu b'mitzvatov v'zivanu l'hadlik ner shel Shabbat."*

"Amen," Sam and Ruth replied, Bobby chiming in after them.

Sam smiled. "We did this every week of my childhood," he said. "I love to see the children being raised traditionally. Is the challah from scratch too?"

"Barbara makes wonderful challahs," Ruth said. She had called my last one too dense and dry. "But she had to work today, so I'm afraid this one came from the store."

"More's the pity," Sam said. "As good as you are at your job, I'm sure you miss the freedom to be home, taking care of the children."

"Quite the opposite, actually. I started working because the kids were in school, and I was going stir crazy. I began volunteering, and before long, the hospital hired me. I can set my own hours, take off when I need to, and I'm helping people. It's much more freedom than being tethered to the house."

"I suppose that's well and good while you're not married," he said, helping himself to a portion of brisket. "But once you settle down"—he glanced at the children—"again, your husband will expect you to stay home because he'll provide for you."

Well, this man was certainly perfect for Ruth, because boy did he know how to ruffle my feathers in a hurry. Harry would have had no problem with me working outside the house if it was what I wanted. And he *had* provided for us, even now.

I took a sip of water before replying, as measuredly as I could. "I'm afraid I'm not a naive twenty-one-year-old anymore. I don't see the need to 'settle down' with someone who doesn't recognize that I have the autonomy to make decisions for myself."

Ruth shot me a warning look and I dropped it, reminding the children that they needed vegetables, not just meat and challah for dinner.

I cut a small piece of the brisket and sniffed it discreetly before taking a bite. It smelled fine, but chewing was as herculean an effort as consuming a piece of tire rubber would be.

"Barbara is a wonderful cook, isn't she?" Ruth asked, then took a bite of brisket herself. I worried she'd lose a crown on the tough meat, and the date would end with an emergency visit to a dentist. Why wouldn't she just let me actually cook? He could learn she was awful at it *after* she had hooked him.

Sam finally swallowed the piece he had spent an abnormally long time working on. "Quite," he said, reaching for his water. He glanced at me before attempting a brussels sprout that I couldn't quite recommend based on the appearance. "So, Barbara, do you want more children?"

I choked on my brisket. "Excuse me," I said, after gulping some water. "I—I haven't—I don't—" I looked to Ruth, who shrugged at me. "Ruth is—uh—just wonderful as a grandmother," I said, reaching for anything to redirect the conversation to her. "I think, at my age, unless I met the right guy tomorrow . . ."

"Or today," Ruth said, inclining her head toward Sam.

"You're not too old at all," Sam said. "Twenty-eight, right?" He turned to Ruth.

I blinked heavily at Ruth, and she smiled pointedly back at me. And suddenly I realized—

"Ruth. Kitchen. Now. Please." I stood, put my napkin on the table, and left the room.

Ruth joined me a moment later. "You're being so rude," she whispered loudly. "He's going to lose interest."

"In *you*?"

She looked confused. "Why would he be interested in me?"

"You asked him here. On a date."

"A date for you."

I pinched the bridge of my nose, a headache coming on suddenly. "Why?"

"Well, he's handsome and single and Jewish. I thought he'd be a good fit."

"He's your age!"

"So? His parents are both still alive. He could outlive you."

I closed my eyes and counted to ten. Twice. "Ruth," I said warningly.

"Well, he's not here for me. So you might as well go be polite and give him a chance."

I was willing to make concessions to make Ruth happy. But not by marrying a fifty-seven-year-old man who thought my place was in the kitchen. *That* was a step too far.

"I am not even a little interested in that man," I said slowly. She started to argue, but I held up a hand to stop her. "At the risk of sounding like one of Bobby's Dr. Seuss books, that man is a louse. And there's no room for a louse in my house."

"No one is going to be Harry," Ruth said quietly. "I understand that. But you don't get any points for being a martyr."

I wanted to stomp my foot and call her a hypocrite. She *was* a hypocrite! She wasn't out here trying to replace Abe even after more than twenty years. How *dare* she call me a martyr for not wanting to remarry just *two* years after losing Harry?

But if I let myself say anything to her right then, it was going to cause irreparable harm. And the children were likely to hear it. And even in my deepest, darkest, most explosive rage, they mattered more than anything I wanted to say to this impossible woman before me.

So I pushed past her back to the dining room and took my seat at Sam's right. "I'm terribly sorry," I said, my voice trembling with the effort to contain my anger. "But I'm afraid there's been a misunderstanding in inviting you here tonight. I thought Ruth asked you here as her date."

"*Her* date?" Sam asked, confused. "Why would I want to date an older woman?"

Yes, I was seeing red because of Ruth. But I was starting to get even more angry at him. "She's only three years older than you."

"Which is too old to have children," Sam said. "I'm in my prime. You're a little past yours, but I'm willing to overlook that."

I stood suddenly, bumping my knees on the table and knocking over a water glass in the process. "Don't you dare overlook a single thing about me. I love my job. I even love that horrible woman in there." I turned and saw her standing in the doorway. "And most of all, I love these kids, who are *never* going to have someone like you in their life. Now, I'm going to have to ask you to please leave my house."

He stared at me for a moment. "Smooth your feathers," he said. "Your cooking is terrible, but I'm not going to throw the baby out with the bathwater over that. You can learn."

I glanced back at Ruth, whose brows had met in the middle. "I'm afraid I agree with Barbara," she said. "Dinner is over. Goodbye, Mr. Goldberg."

He looked from her to me, and back to her, then stood, throwing his napkin onto his plate. "You deserve each other," he said. "Crazier than loons, the two of you. The hospital is going to hear about this. I doubt they want people like you working there."

"I recommend you go to a different hospital next time," I warned him. "Because I guarantee, I will still be working there. And *if* I choose to remarry, it will be to someone who appreciates my interests and supports my decisions. Good night, Mr. Goldberg."

He left, grumbling about rubbery brisket and stale scotch.

"I think this is Grandma's best brisket yet," Bobby said.

"Thank you, sweetheart," Ruth said, hugging his head to her chest.

"It's like chewing gum. I love chewing gum."

She pushed him playfully away. "Eat your gum," she said. Then she looked at me. "He wasn't a gentleman."

I shook my head, still pretty angry, and started clearing the table.

26

Ruth, the kids, and I went to Janet's house an hour before the party started on Sunday to help set up.

Susie and Bobby ran right upstairs to play with Janet's older kids, Jeanie and Kevin. I led Ruth through the house to the backyard, where Janet was smoking a cigarette on the back patio.

"I swear, the things I do that this child will never remember," she said by way of greeting, while stubbing her cigarette out violently in an ashtray. "Why is there a pony in my backyard right now? I couldn't tell you. If that thing craps on my azaleas, it's going to be glue by tomorrow."

"But it's such good fertilizer," Ruth said, completely unfazed.

"Until one of these brats tracks it all over my carpets," Janet said, picking up a glass that should have held water at that time of day but was full of a darker liquid instead. "This just isn't worth the stress. You're lucky your kids have summer birthdays. Just throw them in a pool and be done."

"How can we help?" I asked as the pony lifted his tail and left a deposit in the middle of the lawn.

"Hey!" Janet yelled at the trainer. "You need to clean that up!"

"Yes, ma'am," the poor man said.

"I wouldn't do that job for a million dollars," Janet said. She checked her watch. "I suppose we can start putting out food. And pin the tail on the donkey."

"Please tell me you have a paper donkey and aren't going to let kids stick pins in the pony," I said.

"It's a thought," she said, glowering at the creature. "But no. It's on the dining room table ready to be tacked to a tree."

"I'll take care of that," I said. "Ruth, could you help with the food?"

"One of the benefits of having a brother who owns a grocery store," Janet said. "Eddie brought over platters this morning. If I had to make a thousand sandwiches, I was going to lose my mind." A blood-curdling shriek came from an open window upstairs and Janet turned toward it. "They're probably fine, right?"

"I'm sure they are," I said, patting her arm. But as Ruth and I went back into the house, I said I would handle the food and asked her to go check on the kids instead.

I watched Ruth go up the stairs, then went to the kitchen to make sure we had everything we needed.

Eddie, George, and Janet and Eddie's father, Mr. Greene, were all at the kitchen table with bottles of beer. I caught Eddie's eye and pointedly looked at my watch. He had the good grace to look mildly ashamed.

"It's Sunday," he said with a shrug. "And Janet has been throwing fits all day."

George clinked his glass to Eddie's, and I tried not to smile. "Hi, Mr. Greene," I said to his father. Then I turned back to Eddie. "You know how she is with parties. Once the guests arrive, she'll be just fine." Then I pointed to him and George. "But for now, I'm putting the two of you to work. These trays of food need to go out on the patio table." I looked around the kitchen and spied a blue Coleman cooler in the corner. "Does that have ice in it yet?"

"It does," Eddie said. "And Cokes."

"Probably would have been smarter to fill it outside," I said as I attempted to lug it across the floor.

"I've got it," George said. He stood and finished his beer, then deposited the bottle in the trash can and carefully covered it with a napkin to hide the evidence from Janet.

"Here," I said, reaching into my handbag and pulling out a roll of Wint-O-Green Life Savers. I offered it to the three men, who each took one. "I don't think Janet will actually care—she's got a drink of her own right now—but if you don't want her to smell it on your breath . . ."

"You're a doll, Barbara," George said gratefully.

"As long as you help set up," I warned.

Footsteps came down the stairs, and Eddie and Mr. Greene hurried to dispose of their bottles as well. But it was Ruth who entered the kitchen.

"George, Mr. Greene, I'd like you to meet my mother-in—"

"Mrs. Feldman!" Mr. Greene exclaimed, a note of genuine pleasure in his voice.

Ruth's lips parted slightly as she tried to place the man in front of her, and then she shook her head in surprise. "Mr. Greene," she said. "Eddie said he was your son, but it didn't occur to me that you would be here."

"You two know each other?" George asked.

Mr. Greene smiled broadly. "My favorite customer from the days down on O Street. No one could pick a melon like she could."

"No one *had* melons like you did back then."

Eddie and I made eye contact and then quickly looked away from each other to avoid laughing.

"We'll let you two catch up then," Eddie said, picking up a tray of sandwiches. "Let me know if you need help with that cooler, George."

George tried the handles. "I need help with the cooler."

I took the tray from Eddie. "You two grab that, then come back for the rest. I'll take this out and then get the plates."

"What's Janet doing?" Eddie asked.

I raised my eyebrows at him. "You know those fits you said she was having? She planned the party, invited everyone, and rented a pony. You leave her be for now."

"Okay, okay," Eddie said, grunting slightly as he lifted his half of the cooler. "You were right. Should have filled it outside."

"I usually am," I said with a smile. "Now come on."

Everything was set up with ten minutes to spare before guests were due to arrive, and Paula woke up from her nap just in time. Susie and Jeanie took over the small children, directing them to line up for the pony rides, while Bobby and Kevin declared themselves too big for "baby parties" and went to hide out in the treehouse, allowing only other boys over five to join them. Beyond that, it looked like a dance before the band started playing, husbands on one side of the yard, sneakily passing around drinks, and the wives ostensibly supervising the children from the patio while chain-smoking cigarettes and complaining about their husbands.

It was nice to see the friends who had been a lot more scarce in the last two years. But I could have lived without all of them opening with "How *are* you?" I didn't have a terminal disease. And I didn't want to talk about (or be reminded of) the loss of Harry at a child's birthday party.

Evelyn Gold was the only one who didn't ask, and I appreciated her for it. Though she had her hands full with her eldest trailing after Susie and Jeanie, her middle daughter monopolizing the pony, and her one-year-old, who wasn't walking yet, on her hip. "I know he'll walk when he's good and ready," she said, "but if he gets any heavier, he's going to have to be ready when I say he is."

I smiled at his chubby cheeks. "May I?" I asked, reaching for him.

"Please," she said. "You can keep him." The baby came to me willingly and scowled at his mother.

"Oh, stop with the face," she said. "I'm only teasing, Richie." Joanie began to cry when she didn't get to stay on the pony, and Evelyn asked if I was good with him for a few minutes. I said of course, and Evelyn rushed off.

"You're not so heavy," I told him, inhaling the sweet scent of his hair as a tinge of sadness washed over me. I probably would have had a third if Harry were still here. I sighed and attempted to put the thought out of my head. There was no use in dwelling. "But let's see if we can't help your mama out, huh?"

I stood Richie up on the patio, holding his hands as I had done with Susie and Bobby and coaxed him into taking some steps with me. "You're fooling everyone, aren't you?" I asked him. "I bet you can walk if you want to."

I extricated one hand from his and moved in front of him, gently removing my other hand and making sure he was steady on his feet. He wobbled a little but didn't fall, though his face started to crumble. "It's okay," I said, crouching down as he reached for me. "Just take a couple of steps. I'm right here."

Richie shook his head, tears welling up in his eyes.

"You can do it," I said soothingly. "And your mama will be *so* happy." For a few seconds, nothing happened. Then Richie lifted one foot, moving it a half inch in front of where it had been. "That's it!" I said. "You're doing it!" Buoyed by my enthusiasm, he did the same with the other foot. "Again," I said. And he did. Six tiny baby steps until he collapsed into my waiting arms.

Evelyn rushed over and took him from me. "You're a miracle worker!" she exclaimed. Then she turned to Richie. "And you, you little stinker! You couldn't do that for Mama?"

"I bet he will," I said. "Here, give him back to me, and you stay right there."

Richie came back to me and nestled into my shoulder, but I put him back on the ground in his little white shoes. "Show your mama what you can do," I said. Evelyn held out her arms, and Richie stepped tentatively toward her.

Evelyn embraced him, then called to her husband. "Fred!" she said, gesturing wildly for him to come over. "Richie can walk!"

Fred guiltily handed the flask in his hand back to Linda Stein's husband, and came toward us. "That's wonderful, Evie," he said.

Evelyn turned back to me. "Can I take you to lunch soon? It's been too long, and we'll be in Hereford again for the summer."

"If a Monday works. It's my day off from the hospital."

"Sure," Evelyn said. "I'll find a sitter for this little guy."

"That'll be my Susie and your Anna before you know it."

She looked toward the girls and smiled. "Such little mothers already. They grow up so fast." Then she glanced toward her middle child and sighed. "Joanie, on the other hand . . . Do you know I caught her 'punishing' her baby doll by smacking it on the table the other day? I'm not so sure she's cut out for kids."

I laughed. "She's four, Evelyn. She'll grow into it." I saw Janet light another cigarette and then go scold the pony trainer for some unseen travesty. "Or not."

Joanie tried to cut the line to get another pony ride amid the chaos of Janet's wrath, and Evelyn rushed over as the girl pulled another child out of the line by her hair.

I checked the food trays and made sure nothing needed a refill, then realized I hadn't seen Ruth in—I checked my watch—the hour since the party started. I scanned the yard, but she was nowhere to be seen. Knowing Ruth, she was probably reorganizing Janet's closet and donating half of her favorite clothes.

I went into the house to make sure she wasn't causing too much trouble, only to find her and Mr. Greene sitting at the kitchen table, deep in conversation. Neither of them saw me, so I stayed in the doorway for a minute.

"—wasn't easy," Ruth said. "But it never is, is it?"

Mr. Greene shook his head. "No. It never is. I still remember wondering how you did it when your husband passed."

"I've never forgotten how kind you were to send food for his shivah."

"I came to the funeral, you know."

She looked at him in surprise. "You did?"

He nodded. "I didn't want to impose by coming to the shivah—"

"You wouldn't have been imposing."

Mr. Greene shifted uncomfortably. "I didn't really know you. I just . . ." He shook his head again. "I wanted to make sure you had people there."

Ruth smiled. "You didn't need to worry about that, did you?"

"No," he said, returning her smile. "I've never seen such a full house."

"Abe was . . . Abe was something special. Everyone who knew him felt it."

Mr. Greene nodded. "That much was clear from the eulogy, even ignoring the size of the crowd."

"I wish you'd told me you were there."

"It felt . . . too intimate. I don't know. I didn't want you to think—"

Ruth put a hand on top of his. "I wouldn't attribute an ill motive to you in a hundred years," she said. "And that son of yours is a mensch, just like his father."

"He certainly is," Mr. Greene agreed. "I just wish he'd settle down already."

"Do you think he—?"

I cleared my throat to announce my presence.

"Barbara," Ruth said, removing her hand from his quickly. Too quickly. "Joseph and I were just catching up."

Joseph, I thought, struggling to keep from raising my eyebrows. Now *that* was an interesting development. I looked from her to him, and his eyes were fixed on Ruth in a way that I recognized. A *very* interesting development indeed.

"You two keep catching up," I said, waving a hand at them. "I was just going to start setting up the cake." It was a *little* early for that, but it was on the counter and provided the perfect excuse.

"Oh, we should go out for that," Ruth said, beginning to rise from her seat.

"No, no, you stay," I said. "I'll come get you when we're actually ready."

I picked up the box containing the cake and made my way to the back door. Eddie was on his way in and opened the door, then offered to take the cake from me. "I've got it," I said. "But, Eddie!"

He turned to look at me and brushed back a stray lock of my hair that had fallen over one eye while I held the cake. I felt an unfamiliar jolt of electricity at the intimacy of the gesture. "What?" he asked.

"I—" What was that flutter in my stomach? Had the sandwiches turned? "I think your father and Ruth are flirting with each other!"

"My—what?"

I nodded. "She was patting his hand. And did you know that he went to Abe's funeral?"

"Who's Abe? I'm lost."

"Ruth's husband. They seem like they were a lot closer at the O Street Market than Ruth let on."

Eddie's eyebrows went up, and his jaw went slack in horror. "You don't think that they—?"

"No, no, no," I said quickly. There was no chance there had been anyone else for Ruth. Before or since Abe. And Mr. Greene had been crazy about Eddie's mother. I knew that much. "But now . . ."

Eddie shook his head. "You need to stop this yenta business. I don't want to risk my father's heart in your plans."

"What plans? Go see for yourself. This wasn't me!"

"Barbara—"

"Eddie Greene," I said, removing one hand from the cake box to put it on my hip. "I swear—"

A child went barreling past us, shrieking, "Potty!" and I almost dropped the cake, but Eddie caught my arm and the cake, steadying us both.

"If you drop that, Janet is going to be furious at me," he said.

"Won't she be mad at me?"

"No," he said. "She needs you too much."

"She needs you too," I said, moving toward the table and setting the cake safely down. "Who else is going to bring prepared food for birthday parties?"

Eddie straightened the cake, then turned toward me, his back to the table. "She could always hire someone for that. She can't hire a best—"

The little girl who had run past us, now identifiable as Evelyn's daughter Joanie, came scrambling back out, screaming, "My turn on the pony!" Her eyes were fixed on the poor creature, and she never even saw Eddie as she rammed him full force into the table behind him. The table broke his fall, but the seat of his pants landed squarely on top of the cake box, which was now crushed beneath him.

"Ooh, cake," Joanie said, grabbing a fistful of smushed cake that had oozed out the side, before running back to the pony.

Eddie and I looked at each other, eyes round as Janet stormed toward us.

"Save me," Eddie whispered.

I grinned. "I'll throw Joanie under the bus. But you may have to run to the store for another cake."

"Deal," he said as I held Janet off by explaining about Evelyn's daughter.

27

I was absolutely dying to ask Ruth about the sparks I had seen between her and Mr. Greene, but I forced myself to wait until the kids were in bed.

I told myself not to say anything and to let it unfold organically. But once Susie and Bobby were down, I just couldn't help it.

Ruth was watching Ed Sullivan when I came down the stairs, and I managed to wait until he went to commercial after Judy Garland finished singing "Smile" before I turned to her.

"You and Mr. Greene certainly seemed to hit it off," I said, watching her for a reaction.

She brushed a piece of hair (which hadn't been out of place) behind her ear, which I gleefully took as a victory. Women in love played with their hair. Women who weren't interested did nothing of the sort.

"Joseph? Well, we knew each other a long time ago, when he was at the O Street Market. You knew that."

"Yes, but I couldn't tell you the name of a single person at a market where I shopped before Eddie took over Greene's."

"Maybe you're just not friendly enough," Ruth said, her eyes drifting back toward the television, where a disembodied voice told us that people who think young, say Pepsi please.

"I've known Mr. Greene since I was in college," I said. "I've never seen him light up like when he saw you."

She touched her hair again. "Haven't you ever run into an old friend?"

"Is that what he was?"

She snapped her attention back to me. "What are you implying? We were both married—happily married—when we knew each other."

"I'm not implying anything. I just think it was an awfully . . . happy . . . reunion for a grocer and a shopper."

"And what about you and Eddie? I've seen the way he looks at you."

That took an unexpected turn. "I—what? Eddie's my best friend's brother. Of course we're friendly with each other."

"Mmhmm," Ruth said knowingly. "I had a best friend too. Her brother never did more than pull on my braids. He certainly didn't come fix my wall when Abe passed."

I ran a hand through my hair. She was impossible. "Oh, did you blow up your own oven and need him to? Or did your mother-in-law start a fire?"

"Cute," Ruth said, then something in her demeanor softened. "You don't understand what it was like," she said slowly, looking off into the distance. "Abe did his best, but the Depression . . ." She shook her head. "Joseph was kind. He understood the hardship of feeding a family back then. And he was good about helping to stretch a dollar to its fullest. Not everyone at the market cared if your family went hungry. And when Abe died . . . Let's just say Harry learned a valuable lesson from that. There was some insurance, but not nearly enough. I took in boarders, and I worked at a drugstore while Harry was in school." She glanced back at me and shook her head. "Harry never knew that. I never wanted him to know how tight money was." She lowered her head, studying her hands. "A woman working back then . . . But Joseph used to slip extra food into my basket. He knew somehow. You can't understand how much that helped when everything looked bleak."

I swallowed the lump that was rising in my throat. I understood all too well. No, money wasn't tight—Harry knew more than she realized, based on the sizable insurance policy he had hidden from me. But those extra treats that Eddie sent for the children. The way he always seemed to know the best small gifts for them. The way he looked after us in ways that I didn't even know I needed until he showed up to patch a wall, shovel a walkway, or bring dog supplies. I understood exactly how much that support meant when life without Harry got too overwhelming.

I put a hand on top of Ruth's. "He sounds like an even more wonderful man than I knew," I said quietly.

She pulled her hand from mine. "Yes, well . . . it was nice to see him."

I didn't tell her what I had overheard, about the funeral. About how he didn't want to overstep by coming to the shivah. I couldn't remember if Eddie was at Harry's funeral. I only knew that he arranged the shivah platters because Janet told me later. That whole period was a dark blur of tears, when simply forcing myself to take the next breath consumed my existence. I could still feel the weight of that sorrow—something physical, like when the summer humidity of DC felt like it was pressing you to the earth and not allowing you to breathe—whenever I thought about the funeral or shivah.

But I also wasn't giving up on this one. That awful man whom she invited to dinner last week was all wrong. So was Mr. Moskowitz. But this? This had real potential. Even if Janet—and Eddie—might not love it. But then again . . . Would they really deny their father the happiness that *I* saw on his face while talking to Ruth?

Okay, Janet would.

But Eddie would absolutely come around and help Janet to as well. I hoped.

"We should invite him for dinner," I said, thinking aloud.

"No," Ruth said immediately.

I looked at her, curious. "Why not? If he's a friend."

She pointed a finger at me. "Now don't you go getting ideas," she said. "It was nice to catch up with him. That's all." Her lips curled up into a coy grin. "Unless you're interested in him, that is. In which case, I'd be happy to invite him."

"Ruth!"

She chuckled. "That's what I thought. Now hush. The show is back on. Ed said it's going to be a really big one."

"You know he says that every single week, right?"

"Has he been wrong yet?"

She did have a point.

28

Ruth declined to go grocery shopping with me the following day. "I'm taking Louise to lunch and the JCC today."

I shook my head. "You'll have her converting before you know it."

"That one? She'd get all out of sorts the first time a rabbi said no. But if we can cure her main ailment, loneliness, I would think the anti-Semitism will die down too." Ruth grinned at me. "Then we'll start tackling her issues with other groups."

To her credit, Ruth was one of the few of her generation who didn't suffer from the xenophobia that was leading to the mass exodus of Jews from the corridor of Washington, DC, that they had spent the last fifty years inhabiting.

Not that my hometown of Philadelphia didn't have the same issues. The moment the first family with darker skin moved into Oxford Circle, people started selling. And once Ada Heller, the area's Jewish matchmaker who set up my own parents, was gone, well . . . synagogues were popping up in the suburbs of the city now.

Louise Kline, however, had pitched just as much of a fit over hospital maids as she had over Jewish doctors and nurses. So Ruth had her work cut out for her there.

"Have fun," I said, thinking that afternoon sounded like anything but.

"It's not about fun," Ruth said with a sigh. "It's about *tikkun olam*."

"About what?"

"Making the world a better place," Ruth said, her head cocked in surprise that I didn't know the term. "My father was a rabbi. Before we came here. Here he opened a laundry."

I studied her. "I never knew that. I thought you lived on a farm."

"We did—it was from my mother's family. A wedding gift. But it's why they came for us first. They knew attacking a rabbi's family would make others leave."

I tried to imagine being forced out of my childhood home. Not just my home—my whole country. Taking only what I could carry. It was unfathomable. More so now that I was a mother myself.

"Do you hate them?" I asked.

"Who?"

"The Russians. Soviets now, I suppose."

Ruth shook her head. "Life is too short to hate. I told Louise that. Besides, everything happens for a reason. I never would have met Abe if we had stayed. Or had Harry. Or Susie and Bobby." She looked up at me. "Or you."

I chuckled mirthlessly. "I would assume you'd consider that a bonus."

Her expression turned curious. "Would I be here if that were the case?"

I didn't have an answer. Yes, she had said all along that she was there to help. That I didn't realize I needed it. But I took her words to mean she didn't trust me to raise the kids properly on my own. Was it possible she actually really just wanted to help?

No. The fireman and Sam from the hospital. She was here to meddle. But as long as she was going out and not destroying my house, I could enjoy a trip to the store on my own.

～

Mr. Greene was at the grocery store when I arrived, restacking the entire display of apples, while Eddie looked on, appearing every bit as annoyed as he did when Janet tried to manage his life for him.

"What's going on?" I asked quietly.

He startled, having not noticed me until I said something. "Apparently the produce isn't stacked correctly," Eddie said, shaking his head. "Taking over the family business has its downsides."

My mother was a housewife and my father worked as an accountant. "No danger of that for me."

Eddie glanced over at me. "Where's Ruth?"

"Going to lunch to convert an anti-Semite and fix the world."

"Huh?"

"It's a long story."

Eddie inclined his head toward his father. "Then I'm putting up with this for nothing."

It was my turn to look confused. "I don't understand."

"That's why he's here. He asked me what day you two did your shopping."

I watched as Mr. Greene placed a perfect ripe apple at the top of the pyramid he had constructed. One careless shopper taking one from the middle and the whole thing was going to topple into the aisle. "He wanted to see Ruth?"

"Seems pretty keen on her if you ask me."

I chewed the inside of my cheek. I agreed, based on what I had seen at Paula's party, quite honestly. And Ruth's protestations aside, I thought she felt the same.

"That's an . . . interesting . . . development," I said, thinking out loud.

Eddie turned to me. "Don't you be getting any ideas," he said sternly as his father started on the pears. "My father isn't your ticket to getting rid of Ruth."

"Is that what you think of me?" I asked, genuinely hurt.

"No," Eddie said quickly. "But you *did* say it."

"That was before. Eddie, you should have seen them together in the kitchen yesterday. I actually asked Ruth if he was *really* just a friend from how cozy they seemed."

Eddie colored slightly and opened his mouth, but nothing came out.

"She got offended, don't worry. Nothing happened while . . . Nothing happened," I finished quickly. Saying *while his mother was alive* wouldn't end well for anyone, and I didn't feel like prying my foot out of my own mouth. "I just think there was a connection. And the fact that he's here to see her . . . ," I trailed off.

"How old does someone have to be before a Jewish mother stops trying to fix them up?"

"Dead," I said, then laughed.

Eddie shook his head, his annoyance visibly evaporating as he tried and failed to contain his own laugh.

Mr. Greene looked over at the sound. He replaced the pears he had started on willy-nilly and came over. "Barbara," he said with a nod, then looked around. "Is your mother-in-law with you?"

"She isn't." I honestly felt as disappointed as he looked. "She had a lunch date with a friend."

His shoulders drooped, and I felt an innate urge to make him feel better by inviting him to dinner with her. But both Eddie and Ruth had said no. And as frustrating as Ruth had been between Sam Goldberg and that fireman, I wasn't going to stoop to her level. Again, that is. I definitely didn't want her kicking Mr. Greene the way she had Mr. Moskowitz.

But he had such a hangdog look that I couldn't resist feeding him some crumbs. "I'll try to get her shopping with me next week though."

He perked right up. "You should 'forget' something today, so you need to come back this week."

"Pop," Eddie said warningly.

"What? I'm an old man. Who knows how long I have left?"

"You're sixty-one," Eddie said. "You're hardly at death's door."

"Your mother was forty-nine."

"And you don't have breast cancer."

"On that note," I said brightly, "I'm going to do my shopping. But I'll try to come up with something else we need when I'm home."

As I pushed my cart down the produce aisle, I could hear them arguing behind me. By the time I was done shopping, Mr. Greene was nowhere to be found, but Eddie was waiting by the registers.

"You know he's coming in every day now, right?"

I cringed. "Oops."

"Yeah. Oops."

"Tell him I said I'll call you if I'm bringing her, so he doesn't need to wait at the store."

"Have you met my father?" he asked. "He's like a dog with a bone. When he wants something, nothing gets in his way."

"Oh, speaking of which, I need more Milk-Bones for Pepper." I grinned at Eddie. "Almost got me back here this week already."

Eddie pointed to the aisle with dog food. "Go get them, and I'll start ringing you up, so you don't have to wait in line."

I leaned up and kissed his cheek before walking past, leaving my cart with him. "By the way," I called over my shoulder. "I don't buy that gruff act for a second, just so you know."

He didn't reply, but when I peeked back at him, I felt a small knot of satisfaction to see he was as red as the tomatoes in my cart.

~

The phone was ringing when I got home. I left the bags in the front hall and dashed to the kitchen to get it, hoping it was Janet, not a sick child at school.

But it was Shirley, one of the nurses from the hospital.

"Barb," she said. "You need to get down here."

I looked at the clock and sighed. "I can pop in, but I can't stay. I have to get the kids. What's wrong?"

"It's your mother-in-law. She just got admitted. They're examining her now. Just come as fast as you can."

29

I didn't even put the milk away before I got back in the car and peeled out of the driveway and raced down the street, tires screeching as I took the turn at the end.

This is my fault, I thought. *I wanted her gone.* I reached a red light and drummed my fingers on the steering wheel, willing it to change. Then I quickly said, "*Kinehora,*" rolled down the window, and spit three times. Okay, I didn't *really* spit. What if someone saw me? But I did the *yiddishe* mama *pu pu pu* to ward off the evil eye. Did that work when it was your own eye that produced the evil? I didn't know. Ruth would.

I swore loudly, and the woman in the car next to me put her hand to her mouth in shock. Normally I would apologize, but the light turned green and off I went. If a police officer turned on his lights behind me, well, then I'd have an escort, because I wasn't stopping.

The kids. Oh no. They couldn't deal with another loss. I—well, I'd feel guilty forever, but I could take whatever was thrown at me. Losing Harry proved that. Then I spit three more times and repeated *kinehora*. No. I couldn't handle losing a son like Ruth had. I was jinxing myself with this whole line of thought.

But the kids needed stability. And they loved Ruth to bits. Of course they knew we'd lose her someday—beyond her moving out—but not *today*. I couldn't remember the prayer for healing, so I just thought over and over again, *Let her be okay. I'll be so much nicer to her. She can live with us forever. Just let her be okay. Don't put the kids through that.*

Let her be okay. Her only other family is in Boston. I'll have to plan the funeral. STOP IT, BARBARA.

This was definitely my fault.

The rational voice in my head said I didn't know that. It could have been a car accident, or Mrs. Kline might have stabbed her with a silver stake. But I couldn't push aside the superstitious voice that blamed me.

I whispered an apology to Harry as I parked the car at a skewed angle, then ran inside.

Gloria was at the front door, waiting for me, and immediately whisked me up to a room on the second floor. "She's stable," she said. "They're still running tests."

"What happened?"

Gloria shook her head. "I don't know. They just told me to get you."

"Is she—"

Gloria pulled the chart from the door as I went in. "You go see her. I'll find out what I can."

Ruth lay in the bed, the sheet pulled up to her neck, her face pale and devoid of the red lipstick I was constantly wiping off the children's faces. Her eyes were closed, and her face was twisted in pain.

"Ruth," I said. "It's Barbara. I'm here."

Her face contorted, and she let out a small moan, but she gripped the hand I slipped into hers tightly.

"Barbara," she croaked in a hoarse whisper. "Where's my Harry?"

My eyes widened. *Oh no.*

"There he is," she said, opening her eyes and pointing shakily toward the corner with her other hand.

I looked, but there was nothing there.

"Ruth," I said more insistently. "You're in the hospital. What happened?"

She turned to squint at me. "It's my time," she said, her face contorting again. "That's why Harry is here."

"No, Ruth. The doctors here are so good. They'll help you." I glanced over my shoulder. Where *was* a doctor? I wanted to go flag someone down to help her, but she squeezed my hand tighter. I couldn't leave her alone like this.

If someone didn't come soon, I'd have to at least poke my head into the hall. She was in pain. And even if they could do nothing else, they could alleviate that. I looked at her arms. No IV. What on earth were they doing?

I started to take my hand back. She needed care. But then I heard footsteps in the hall, not the clacking of a nurse's heels, but the heavy soles of a doctor.

I looked up and felt my nostrils flare involuntarily at the sight of Dr. Howe. But, as much as I detested him as a human, he *was* the best doctor we had. Of course they had assigned him for my mother-in-law.

"Dr. Howe," I said, making sure to keep the distaste out of my voice. "How is she? What happened?"

"I'm afraid it's quite serious," he said. "She may not have much time left at all."

Ruth moaned again, and I felt my heart sink. What would I tell the children? Janet would have to pick them up today, but the idea of telling them we had lost their grandmother . . . My mom would have to move back in. I closed my eyes and took a deep breath.

"Doctor," Ruth whispered. "Come."

He came to her bedside, and she took his hand with her free hand, placing it on top of mine. "Take care of my Barbara. Promise me."

Dr. Howe glanced at me before returning his eyes to Ruth. "Of course, Mrs. Feldman," he said.

"She thinks—she thinks she doesn't need help. But she needs someone strong like you." Then she turned her gaze to me. "You give him a chance," she said. "That's my dying wish. My grandchildren need a father figure."

I would rather eat shards of glass, but I couldn't deny a dying woman—especially not Harry's mother—her dying wish. Especially when it was for the benefit of my children. Although I wished she would pick literally any other man on the planet. Sam Goldberg and Mr. Moskowitz included.

"I will," I said.

"Promise me," she said, closing her eyes.

"I promise."

"Wonderful," Ruth said, sitting up suddenly. "Dr. Howe gets off at four today—he'll pick you up at six. He's taking you downtown to a fancy restaurant."

"What—?"

"Wear something slinky," Dr. Howe said. "I've been dying to get you out of those matronly dresses for a year now."

Ruth had gotten out of the bed, fully dressed, and was pulling lipstick and a compact from her purse.

I looked from her, to him, and back to her, then pulled my hand free from his. "You tricked me?"

"Nudged," Ruth said. "But you promised to give him a chance."

"I'm not giving him the time of day!"

"A promise is a promise," Dr. Howe said. "And honestly, half of the time I was misbehaving with the nurses, it was just so you would come give me a stern talking-to. I did always like a strict schoolteacher."

"Leave," I said to him, utterly furious. "Or I'm going to throw up. And I'm not using a bedpan. Ruth, this is—"

"You did promise," she said. "And what if I get into a car accident on the way home? Then you really *did* go against my dying wish."

"If you get hit by a car," I said through gritted teeth, "and die, *then* I will *consider* letting that man buy me a meal. But no more than that. And not before you're in the ground."

"Tsk-tsk," Ruth said, shaking her head. She looked to Dr. Howe. "I did tell you I didn't think she'd go for it."

"I honestly don't know which is worse," I said. "You doing this to me at all, or the fact that you colluded with the worst person I have ever met to do it."

"Not the *worst*," Dr. Howe said. "There's still Mrs. Kline."

"I would marry Mrs. Kline's son and have her as a mother-in-law before I would get in a car with you," I said. I picked up my purse where I had dropped it on the floor to get to Ruth's bedside, and swept out of the room, trying to slam the door behind me, but it was stuck on a doorstop, and I couldn't get it to budge. I let out a growl of frustration and walked swiftly down the hall, rounding a corner and bumping square into Gloria, knocking us both down.

"I didn't know," Gloria said immediately, holding up her hands from the floor. "I was running up to tell you."

"SHE is the most impossible woman who has ever been born," I said, still absolutely seething with rage as I stood up, taking Gloria's elbow to help her. "Dr. Howe of all people! I'd as soon kiss a pig. With warts!"

"Wait, kiss? I just know they were trying to convince you to do something."

"Yes. To go on a date with Dr. Howe." I shuddered. "That was the first step. She told me she was dying and her dying wish was for me to let him take care of me."

Gloria gagged slightly. "I don't care if it's a dying wish. I will go object to any wedding that he's in."

"They don't ask for objections at Jewish weddings."

She scrunched up her face. "Clearly they should start."

I chuckled, the tension lifting slightly. "That woman is going to drive me to drink."

"I think there's a bottle in the nurses' lounge if you need it."

I did. My heart still hadn't regulated itself from the shock of seeing her looking like death in that bed. But I checked my watch, and I didn't want to drink before going to get the kids. "I can't. But once I get home tonight, it's a different story." I took a few steadying breaths, my heart finally starting to slow down. "There's an old joke," I said. "Why do Jewish men die before their wives?"

"Why?"

"Because they want to," I said. "I never thought it was funny—especially after Harry—but damned if I don't think it was true in her husband's case."

Gloria laughed, then covered her mouth. "On the plus side," she said, looking hopeful. "If you go to Dr. Harper about this, maybe they'll finally get rid of Dr. Howe. Misuse of hospital resources or something?"

I raised my eyebrows. "Now *that* would be a public service." Then I shook my head. "How can such a horrible human being be such a good doctor though?"

"Because this is real life," Gloria said. "Prince Charming doesn't exist."

He did, I thought. *Complete with a wicked witch of a mother.* I smiled sadly at Gloria and told her I'd see her tomorrow. If I wasn't in jail for matri-in-law-cide.

"Get one woman with a difficult mother-in-law on that jury, and you'll walk free."

"Or a woman whose bottom has felt the wrath of Dr. Howe," I added.

Gloria raised her hand. "I'd take your side."

I patted her arm. "You're a good friend," I told her. "Now see if you can't hold Ruth up in some paperwork."

"You got it," Gloria said.

I left the hospital, looked up at the blue sky above me, and shook my head. But I could swear I almost heard Harry chuckling.

30

I got home, only to realize I needed to buy more milk and ice cream because I had left in such a rush, and what I had bought was now lukewarm, sitting in wet brown paper shopping bags in the hall.

Annoyed, I slammed cabinets and the refrigerator as I put away the items that could be salvaged.

But then . . .

The piece of paper where my mother had written her phone number on the refrigerator for the kids caught my eye. The long-distance part was harder for them to remember than local numbers.

Mother knows best, Ruth said in my head.

My eyes narrowed. *She* certainly didn't know best. But *my* mother on the other hand . . .

I glanced out the front window, making sure Ruth's car was nowhere in sight, then returned to the kitchen and picked up the phone.

My mother answered on the third ring. "Hello?" She sounded out of breath.

"Hi, Mom."

"Barbara!" she said warmly. I checked the date on the calendar on the refrigerator and counted backward in my head. It *had* been a little long between calls. "How are you? How are the kids? Do they miss me?"

"The kids are good," I said. "They miss you every day." They hadn't mentioned her all week. "And I—well, I need your help."

"What can I do, darling?"

"It's Ruth," I said bluntly. "I need you to come back down for a visit and convince her to either find her own place to live or go stay with her sister."

"Why can't you do that?"

"Mom. You don't understand how bad this has gotten. Please. She won't stay if you're here. And you're the only one I know who can make her as miserable as she's making me."

"I'm not certain that's a compliment. Just tell her she's overstayed her welcome, and it's time to go home."

"I tried that! The first week."

"Well, a week isn't a very long visit with grandchildren. How long has she been there now?"

I counted up weeks on the calendar, looking for the date I had circled as my first day on my own. "Five weeks."

"Well, considering I stayed two years, even five weeks doesn't quite feel like a real visit, does it?"

"Mom, could you have handled Bubbie Cohen for five weeks?"

There was a long pause. "No."

"Then you have to help me."

My mother sighed. "It's a bit complicated right now. Your father and I are going on a vacation next week."

"A vacation?" My parents went to Atlantic City for a week every single summer. That was it. Their entire vacation repertoire for the thirty-two years of my life, and the two years before I was born, if you didn't count their honeymoon in Niagara Falls. They didn't even go to the Catskills when my aunt invited them to stay with her.

"Yes," she said. "We booked a cruise."

"A cruise? But you hate boats!"

"This is a ship, Barbara, not a boat. It even has a pool on board."

"Great," I said sarcastically.

"Darling," she said, a warning tone in her voice. "Be happy for me. I just spent two years helping you raise your children. Which I don't begrudge you for a moment, but it took those two years for your father to realize he needed to expend more effort on me. And I don't intend to let that go to waste. I'm happy to come for a little visit after that, but you wanted to do this on your own. That includes dealing with Ruth."

I didn't reply, and my mother eventually sighed.

"What's she doing that's so terrible?" she asked. "Aside from the fire—you did tell me about that."

"I think she's trying to marry me off. Or scare me out of ever getting married again. I honestly can't tell with the creeps she's bringing around. Mom, she faked nearly dying today to try to force me into going out with the doctor who harasses every single woman—and some married ones—at the hospital. She never remarried and is fine. Why do I have to have a man to survive suddenly?"

There was a long pause.

"Maybe that wasn't by choice," she mused. "Maybe she doesn't want you to be as lonely as she is."

"Ruth isn't lonely. I tried setting her up and she kicked the poor man." Okay, calling Mr. Moskowitz "poor" was being hyperbolic. He likely deserved that and more. And that wasn't *entirely* truthful, considering why I had decided to fix her up in the first place. But I wasn't letting my mother talk me out of getting rid of Ruth. Not after what she had pulled today.

"Are *you* lonely?" she asked.

The question caught me off guard. "I haven't had time to be."

"That isn't what I mean, and you know it. You can be just as lonely with someone else in your house."

I hadn't let myself think about it because I didn't want to. But yes, I was. I missed Harry enough that I talked to the ceiling pretending he could hear me. I still rolled over in the night expecting to feel the warmth of his body next to mine, only to wake myself up when I realized he wasn't there. But it also wasn't the same. I had the kids, who filled my non-working hours, and work at the hospital to fill the holes while they were at school. And I had yet to go even twenty-four hours without a mother or mother-in-law occupying my house since he had died. But there was truth in what she said. I could be lonely without being alone.

"Yes," I whispered.

"I couldn't quite hear you," she trilled.

"Don't make me say it again."

She conceded the point.

"If you're lonely after two years, I don't care what Ruth says. She wouldn't be trying to fix you up if she didn't know something you don't about living your life as a widow."

This call wasn't going how I wanted it to at all.

"So maybe agree to date, but you get to pick the man. I think that would placate her."

"I don't *want* to pick a man," I said, realizing I sounded like a petulant teenager but unable to stop myself.

"Then I'm afraid you're stuck," she said. "Back to packing I go. I'll send you a postcard from the Bahamas. And if you want me to visit when we get back, I'm happy to. Though I won't be rude to Ruth for you. She can be frustrating, but she means well. Now tell me to have a nice trip."

"Have a nice trip," I said sullenly.

"Thank you, darling. I plan to. Ciao."

"Ciao?" I said out loud, even though she had already hung up. *Who was that person and what did she do with my mother?*

It wasn't quite time to go get the kids yet, but if Ruth came home and I was there alone with her, a fight was definitely going to erupt, so I scribbled a note telling her to go buy more milk and ice cream because she ruined mine, then slipped Pepper's leash on and walked to Janet's house, the cardinal from the backyard following us for a block while Pepper jumped and tried to fly after it.

"What did Ruth do to my father?" Janet asked by way of greeting.

"I have no idea. He's clearly losing his mind if he sees any redeeming qualities in her."

Janet peered at me, then pulled a pack of cigarettes and a lighter from a drawer. "Paula's still sleeping. Let's go out on the patio, so George doesn't get mad that I smoked in the house again."

To be fair, George thought Janet had quit, not just quit in the house. And he never questioned why she kept a bottle of perfume by the back door. Men.

"So," she asked around the cigarette as she lit it outside, "what happened?"

I plucked the cigarette from her mouth and took a long drag myself.

"Must be bad if you're smoking," Janet observed, starting to pull another from the pack. I had quit when Bobby was two.

"No, take this one back," I said, handing it to her. "I don't actually want it. Just needed that for fortification."

Janet raised her eyebrows but said nothing, and I launched into the whole hospital saga. When I had finished, Janet stubbed out the butt of her cigarette and lit another. "Wow," she said. "I've got to hand it to her. She's persistent. Is the doctor good-looking at least?"

"Sure. For a demon."

Janet shrugged. "Demons are good for keeping you warm at night."

"Janet!"

"Okay, okay. But I've got a toddler in my bed every night, so let me at least imagine a handsome doctor."

I'd take a toddler over no one, I thought. Then I shook my head suddenly. Where did that thought even come from?

"And then I called my mother, because I thought she would come and send Ruth packing, and do you know that woman convinced my father to go on a cruise?"

Janet's face darkened, but she took another drag of her cigarette and it passed. "Your father leaves his armchair?"

"Apparently now he does!"

"Wow," Janet said again. "Wonders never cease." She checked her watch, then stubbed out her cigarette and stood up. "I've got to get Paula so we can pick up the kids."

I stayed on the patio, deep in thought. Would Ruth even leave if I *did* get married? I had no desire to find someone new, though if it got rid of her it was worth considering. But if she was going to stay . . .

To hell with it, I thought. She had said no to dinner with Mr. Greene. Well, she was going to get a taste of her own medicine. If it worked, great. She could focus on him instead of me. If it didn't, then she was going to learn that I could play dirty too.

I just hoped she didn't try to foist him on me. The thought of Janet and Eddie's father in bed . . . That was the one image possibly worse than Dr. Howe.

A small figure came barreling out onto the patio. "Auntie Bawba! You bwing me cake?"

I shook my head and Paula pouted. But I opened my arms and she crawled onto my lap, snuggling in, her thumb in her mouth. "I'll bring cake next time, sweetheart. I promise."

Bobby and Susie were too big to climb onto my lap anymore. I breathed in the soft, baby scent of Paula's hair. I thought again about how if Harry were still here, we would have had a third baby.

And then there would be no spare bedroom for Ruth.

"What is that look on your face?" Janet asked.

I grinned. "Can I borrow Paula for a week or so?"

"Keep her," Janet deadpanned.

Paula's little face screwed up, and Janet plucked her from my lap, kissing her nose. "Mama's kidding, you silly goose. I would *never* give you away."

Comforted, Paula leaned into Janet, then wrinkled her nose. "I tell Daddy you smoke."

"Take her," Janet said, holding her out to me.

I laughed. I could always count on Janet to restore my good humor.

31

The drive to the hospital Tuesday morning was tense. Which would have been true even if Ruth *had* picked up milk. But she hadn't and instead used the last of what remained in her coffee, and I'd had to take mine black, which did nothing to improve my mood.

"Passover began last night," Ruth said mildly as we drove toward the hospital.

I cringed guiltily, the memory of Harry's rich baritone leading the story of our exodus from Egypt flooding my head. We hadn't held a seder since Harry died. The first year, we were only a couple of months past his death, and I think we forgot about Passover entirely. Last year, Janet invited us to join hers—one of the major tenets of Passover involved inviting in anyone who needed a place to be. But I worried it would just be too sad without Harry, and my mother surprised me by agreeing. So we swapped bread for matzo and called it good enough. While I was sure Janet would let us come this year if I asked her, it was too much on such short notice, and I didn't read Hebrew so I couldn't lead a seder of our own.

"I'll buy some matzo when I go get more milk," I said pointedly. I expected her to argue to uphold the tradition—her father had been a rabbi after all.

"Get some gefilte fish and horseradish too," she said. "We can tell the kids the gist of the story in English."

If I wasn't still so angry about Dr. Howe, I would have loved that idea and the simplicity of maintaining the custom without making it sad as we missed Harry. But a good idea coming from Ruth right now was enough to sour the whole concept. We rode the rest of the way in silence.

I pulled into a parking space, took a deep breath, and turned to look at her. "No more funny business—especially at my place of work."

Her hands were clasped over her handbag. "No," she said, a hint of contrition in her voice. "Nurse Ramirez dressed me down about him already."

Thank goodness for Gloria, I thought. I needed to thank her.

"He's a wonderful doctor," I said. "But truly one of the worst people I've met in my life."

"He couldn't have been kinder to me." I lowered my sunglasses to give her a look. "How was I to know?"

To be fair, we didn't assign young candy stripers to any rooms he would be in without supervision. We didn't discuss his indiscretions in front of patients or volunteers. And while I complained to Dr. Harper weekly about Dr. Howe's behavior, the nursing staff was careful about our reputation as a whole. He had never been inappropriate with a patient to any of our knowledge, and with the hospital unwilling to sanction him, it was his word against ours.

I sighed. "I suppose you weren't."

"Were men always such cads?" she asked.

She had met Abe at eighteen and was married by nineteen. And while yes, she spoke frequently of "the men" who had chased them from their home in Russia, I doubted she had ever been on a bad date prior to Mr. Moskowitz.

"Not all of them," I said lightly. "We both found ones who weren't."

"Were they the only two?"

If her choices for me were any evidence, that was a distinct possibility. "They may have just been the ones we were allotted," I said, my anger dissipating. "But, Ruth, if you pull something like that again, you'd better at least go replace the milk that spoiled."

"You really should have put that in the refrigerator before you came to the hospital."

"Yes, well, I figured the wasting of food would do you in if whatever put you in the hospital didn't," I grumbled. But there was no malice left in my tone. I supposed I was getting used to her shenanigans by now.

I still wrapped Gloria in a hug as soon as I saw her.

"Want her on bedpan duty today?" she asked.

"No," I said with a chuckle. "I think she got the message loud and clear."

"She might wind up on bedpan duty anyway," Gloria said. "Dr. Howe called out, and now we're short staffed."

I rolled my eyes. "Well, he *did* suffer a tremendous bruise to his ego yesterday. I'm sure he'll need to nurse that for the rest of the week. Then make my life miserable when he comes back."

"I wish we weren't considered expendable," Gloria said, shaking her head. "I'd love to see them try to run this hospital without us. But if we make *him* miserable, we're out. He's too important."

"Or at least he thinks he is." I patted her arm. "Don't you worry. I won't let him take it out on anyone else."

"I don't want him taking it out on *you* though."

I smiled at her. "I'm living with Ruth. I'm sure I've been through worse."

Someone called for Gloria, and she looked over her shoulder. "Duty calls," she said, shaking her head. "Gonna be a busy one."

"Like a full moon on the Fourth of July," I agreed. "Let me know if you need help—I can call some more candy stripers in."

"This is why you're the best," Gloria said as she hurried off.

Busy or not, I'd take a reprieve from having to face Dr. Howe after Ruth's stunt. Hopefully his ego was badly bruised enough that he wanted nothing to do with me, but a year of working with him didn't leave me hopeful on that front. I was paged over the hospital intercom and determined to put him out of my head. There wasn't room for him in there anyway.

32

Ruth said she should get straight home for Pepper after the hospital, so I dropped her off, then went back to the grocery store for milk, ice cream, and Passover supplies.

Mr. Greene was stacking a display of canned goods in a pyramid near the front of the store when I walked in. Eddie was behind the counter by the registers, leaning on his elbows, watching him with resigned irritation.

I observed Mr. Greene for a few seconds before turning my cart to where Eddie was.

"He's back?"

"You have to bring Ruth in," Eddie said. "I can't take much more of this."

"Funny. That's how I feel having her in my house."

We both watched as Mr. Greene started a new row.

"That thing is going to be taller than him before he's finished," Eddie said, shaking his head. "No one is going to be able to take a can without bringing it all down."

"Must be in our blood," I said. Eddie looked at me confused. "Jews building pyramids."

At first, his expression didn't change, then he barked out a *ha!* before peering into my empty cart. "What did you forget yesterday? You know you can call me when that happens, and I'll drop it off."

"I appreciate that," I said, patting his arm. "But I didn't forget anything. Ruth faked being at death's door to try to get me to promise I would go out with an absolute louse of a doctor."

He squinted his left eye at me. "She didn't."

"Oh, but she did."

"Is she all right?"

"Perfectly so. But when the hospital called me, I dropped everything to rush over there, so the milk spoiled."

Eddie shook his head. "She is something else."

"That's one way to put it."

"Meanwhile, that one is smitten and driving me insane." He pointed to his father just as a child came careening down the aisle that he was at the end of, pushing a half-full cart while his frantic mother chased after him in her heels.

"David, no!" she yelled as he headed straight for the pyramid of cans.

Eddie jumped over the counter with ease, and before any of us knew what was happening, he had a hand on the child's cart, slowing him to a stop inches from the cans, which would have likely toppled onto his father.

"Whoa there, buddy," Eddie said. The child grinned up at him and Eddie returned the look. "No running in the store, okay?"

"Sorry, Mr. Greene," he said, his face falling.

"No harm done," Eddie said as his mother caught up to him and took his arm forcefully. He nodded to the mother. "It's okay, Mrs. Jacobson." He knelt down to the boy. "When you get to the bakery counter, you go tell them that I said to give you a cookie, okay?"

David looked to his mother, who pursed her lips at him, then relented, ruffling his hair. "You're too easy on kids," she told Eddie.

He shrugged with a smile. "I was one."

"And a troublesome one at that," Mr. Greene added, but he too was smiling. Then he noticed me. "Back so soon?" he asked in absolute delight, looking around, I presumed for Ruth.

"She's not with me, I'm afraid," I said, and his shoulders sagged in defeat.

If he hadn't been there, I would have let it play out on its own. But Ruth deserved a little payback after yesterday's stunt.

"Why don't you come to dinner this week? Say, tomorrow night? I'm sure Ruth would love to have you," I said.

Eddie shook his head and mouthed *no* behind his father's back. I shrugged slightly, but Mr. Greene was already saying that he would love to.

"I should go get flowers," he said, starting toward the door. Then he stopped himself. "No. I should get them tomorrow so they'll be fresher," he said. Then he ran a hand over his head. "I'll go for a haircut though. And back for a shave tomorrow." And, talking to himself about how to prepare for dinner, he left the store.

"Barbara," Eddie said warningly.

"What's the harm?" I asked. "Worst case scenario, she's not interested, and he stops haunting the store waiting for her."

"I don't think that's how he works," Eddie said ominously. "Did you ever hear the story of how he and my mother met?"

"No?"

Eddie sighed. "She wasn't interested either. He spent two years wearing her down."

My eyes widened. He'd better not take two years to wear Ruth down. I needed her out of my house *now*.

No, that wasn't worth contemplating. They were such a good fit for each other. "There was a spark there on Sunday," I said. "I know it when I see it."

"I just don't think this ends well."

"Eddie, look. They like each other. They're both lonely." Eddie started to interrupt, but I didn't let him. "Janet says he is. And I think you know she's right. And I don't think for a second that Ruth would be living in my guest room if she wasn't also. It's . . . it's hard having someone and then suddenly not."

He looked at me carefully. "Are you lonely?"

I twisted a lock of my hair around a finger and pulled lightly. *Why is everyone asking me that lately?*

"Yes," I said, feeling vulnerable as soon as it came out of my mouth. I didn't want Eddie to feel bad for me or see me as some pathetic charity case who needed companionship. "And no. I have the kids. And a mother-in-law who won't let me be alone. Ever. Literally, her first day with me, she came barging into my shower. Opened the curtain and everything. Just to ask where the spatulas were."

Eddie chuckled. "And that's what you want to inflict on my poor father. Hasn't the man suffered enough?"

I pointed a thumb over my shoulder toward the door. "That guy? The one who practically ran out of here to get a haircut before coming to dinner tomorrow night?"

"Some people are just gluttons for punishment, I suppose."

"That's the only explanation I have," I agreed. "Say, why don't you come too? You'll see what I mean about them. And it makes it less like a date, more like a friendly family dinner."

He huffed good-naturedly. "Just what I wanted to do. Chaperone my father and your mother-in-law on a date."

"Well, Eddie," I said with mock seriousness, "if we don't chaperone them, the neighborhood will all be abuzz that they ate a meal together. In front of the children no less! The scandal! Oh, the scandal of it all!"

Eddie nudged me playfully with his shoulder. "I'll do it to keep gossip down."

"You're a good man, Eddie Greene," I said. "I won't even make you bring platters." Then I thought about it. "Actually, if Ruth insists on cooking, I may change my mind on that one."

"Oh no you don't," Eddie said. "I want to experience this cooking for myself. What doesn't kill me makes me stronger."

"Ruth's cooking may very well kill you."

He shrugged but was back to smiling. "You can put *Death by Knish* on my tombstone."

I laughed.

33

I was planning to tell Ruth that Mr. Greene was coming to dinner. I really was. But then she would want to cook because she didn't think I could pull off a decent meal. I wondered if that year of boiled cabbage she talked about had permanently damaged her taste buds, but if I wanted this to work, the element of surprise was my best option.

So when the two of us returned from the hospital on Wednesday, I asked Ruth if she wanted to pick the kids up from school.

She looked at me warily. "Why?"

"I just thought you might like to."

"What are you trying to get me out of the house for?"

I threw up my hands. "Fine, I'll go get them. I just thought you might like to for once."

Ruth picked up Pepper's leash and slipped it onto her collar. "No," she said. "I'll go."

"Enjoy," I told her. "It's a beautiful day."

She shot me one more look of distrust, then left with the dog. I watched from the window as she went up the street, and then I put on an apron and got to work.

By the time she got home with the kids, the brisket was already browned and had just gone into the oven, and I was peeling potatoes.

"Ooh, Mommy's cooking," Bobby said, running into the kitchen to hug me. Then he looked at the potatoes. "How are you cooking those?" he asked, eyeing me with suspicion. Ruth's "french fries" that were basically quartered baked potatoes, still cold in the center and sprinkled with a dash of salt, hadn't gone over well, nor apparently been forgotten.

"Chopped up in the frying pan," I promised. "The exact way that you like them."

"No onions?" he asked. Ruth had been on a mission to get him to appreciate onions and was slipping them into everything from chicken dishes to one disastrous batch of pancakes.

"Not in yours," I promised, ruffling his hair.

"What's the occasion?" Ruth asked.

"No occasion," I lied with a shrug.

"That's too many potatoes for the four of us," she pointed out, then opened the oven door. "And much too large a brisket."

"Leftovers," I said, refusing to make eye contact.

"Barbara," Ruth said.

I turned to her and crossed my arms. "Okay, when I went to the grocery store yesterday, Mr. Greene was there building the world's largest canned food pyramid. And it turns out, he was there hoping to see you. And I know you said not to invite him to dinner, but he looked so sad that you hadn't come with me, and it just slipped out. Eddie is coming too. It's fine. Just a friendly dinner. Among friends. A normal thing that friends do."

"Why are you saying *friends* so much?" Susie asked. "It sounds weird when you keep saying it."

"Your mother is a terrible liar," Ruth said, pursing her lips.

"Who's lying?" I asked. But it came out shrill, and everyone could hear it. "I didn't *lie*. I just didn't tell you."

"You said that's still lying when I do it," Bobby pointed out, ever so helpfully.

I sighed. "Like I said, Eddie is coming too. There's nothing sinister going on. I promise."

Ruth shook her head, then opened the oven door and sniffed at the cooking meat. "You should have let me cook," she said.

"And spoil the surprise?"

The look she shot me could have cut glass. But she was worried about the meal being impressive and I took that as a small victory.

~

At six on the dot, there was a rap at the door. Pepper started barking immediately, trusting strangers less since the intrusions of Mr. Moskowitz and Sam Goldberg. "Hush," I said, scooping her up. "You love Eddie."

I opened the door and at first saw no people because of the gigantic floral arrangement that threatened not to fit through my front door.

"Um . . . ," I said, craning my neck to make sure the Greene men were behind it and this wasn't a variation of the plant from *The Little Shop of Horrors* come to feast on my family.

Eddie emerged from behind the display first. "I'm sorry," he whispered. "He couldn't be talked out of it."

He attempted to take the flowers from his father to get them into the house as Ruth came down the stairs.

"What on earth?"

"For you," Mr. Greene's voice floated through the pungent arrangement.

"Did I die?" Ruth asked, and I smothered a laugh. This was definitely a funeral spray—and a massive one at that—not a bouquet for a date.

Eddie succeeded in wrestling them away, revealing a bewildered Mr. Greene. "Are they too much?"

Ruth looked to me for help.

"They're lovely," I said firmly. "Eddie, will you bring them into . . ." There were no discernable stems for a vase, and they were going to take over the entire kitchen, but I had no better answers. "The . . . kitchen . . . and I'll find something to put them . . . on?"

Eddie shook his head but took the colossal arrangement, which dragged on the floor behind him like a pungent train, and followed me into the kitchen.

"You don't have anything that will fit these," he said.

"I have a bathtub," I volunteered. Then I realized inviting Eddie up to my bathtub wasn't quite where I intended this evening to go. "I mean . . . let's . . ." I looked around the room. The kitchen table had the food that was ready to go on the dining room table on it and the counters weren't big enough. "Let's just put them in the corner for now," I said, gesturing toward an open area. "And I'll deal with them later."

Eddie wrangled them over there, then came back to me. "His last date was in 1928," Eddie said. "He has no idea what he's doing."

"Honestly, hers—if you don't count my neighbor who she kicked for being fresh—was earlier than that. They're likely on the same page." I glanced at the pile of flowers that came up to my waist. "Though he may be a little more . . . enthusiastic . . . about it than she is."

"That's what I'm worried about," Eddie said, his face twisted in concern. "He's just gotten more like himself in the last year or so. I don't want him getting his heart broken again."

It hadn't actually occurred to me that there were two invested parties here. In my mind, if I found Ruth someone she liked, that was that.

What if this didn't work? Janet would recover. But could I lose Eddie over this? Would he forgive me if Ruth wasn't up for finding someone new? Or worse, if she was, and Mr. Greene just wasn't him?

I put a hand on Eddie's arm. "Eddie—"

He looked at me, and I didn't know how to finish the sentence. But Eddie gave me a tight smile. "We'll figure this out somehow."

I nodded, reassured by his use of *we*. "Drinks," I said. "Let's start with drinks. What does your father like?"

"Besides Manischewitz?"

I laughed. "I think I could dig out a bottle if that's his poison of choice."

"Where do you keep the liquor?" he asked, and I directed him to the cabinet.

"Not a great selection," I said. "I don't really drink—well, I do more with Ruth here. The night she started a fire, I poured myself a big glass of bourbon."

Eddie finally smiled for real, and I felt the knot in my chest dissipate. "That one was earned." He turned back to the cabinet and pulled out the bourbon bottle. "If this worked for you, it'll work for him."

"Can you get the sherry for Ruth too?" Eddie obliged, and I got glasses that he poured into. "Anything for you?"

He shook his head, and I put the glasses onto a serving tray and brought it into the living room, where Susie was showing off a picture she had painted at school. "This is the cardinal that lives in our backyard," she said, pointing to the red bird in the center of the page. "Grandma says they're a message from someone who's gone."

"That's what my Gertrude always said too," Mr. Greene said.

I passed the drinks to Ruth and Mr. Greene, stopping to admire Susie's picture. "That's really good," I told her. "We should frame it." She beamed up at me, and I said dinner would be ready shortly.

"I would have cooked," Ruth said to Mr. Greene. "But my daughter-in-law didn't tell me you were coming until she had already begun."

He smiled at her. "I don't care at all what we eat. I'm glad you didn't have to work harder on my behalf."

"Wait until you taste it to say that," she murmured. I shook my head. Maybe if I served her boiled cabbage for a week or so it would reset her taste buds.

I returned to the kitchen and may have sawed into the brisket with a little more force than I normally would have used. But soon enough, everything was ready, and I started transferring food to the dining room table.

"Can I help?" Eddie asked, jumping up from the love seat.

"Sure," I said, gesturing over my shoulder toward the kitchen. "Grab the potatoes and put them on that trivet by the head of the table?"

I put the brisket on its trivet, and then returned to the kitchen to find Eddie running a finger under the faucet.

"Oh no," I said, rushing to his side. "I should have warned you. It's hot."

"I do know that now."

I took his hand and examined the red spot on his index finger. "Not too bad," I said. "It likely won't blister. But hang on. Butter is better than cold water according to Heloise."

"Of course—I forgot that," Eddie said as I went to the refrigerator and grabbed the real butter, not the margarine that I had on the table to go with the meat-based dinner.

I cut a pat of it and placed it on Eddie's finger. "You know Hints from Heloise?"

Eddie smiled wryly. "She has useful tips for bachelors too. I don't have anyone to get stains out for me."

"I'm sure Janet would."

He shrugged. "She's got her own family to worry about. I don't want to bother her when it's something I can do myself."

"Well, then bother me next time. It's the least I can do after everything you've done for me."

Eddie's smile turned much more genuine, and I realized I was still holding his hand—something I hadn't done with a man since Harry passed. I dropped it quickly. "I should get the rest of the food out there before it all gets cold. You keep that butter on until it melts, you hear?" I busied myself, grabbing the offending potatoes with a potholder.

"Is that okay? Don't you keep a kosher house?"

I looked at him over my shoulder. "Not *that* kosher. Just don't smear it on the brisket and you're fine."

Eddie mimed crossing his heart, and I carried the potatoes, calling to the family and Mr. Greene that dinner was served.

I wanted Ruth and Mr. Greene to sit next to each other, so I sat Eddie in Harry's place, at the head of the table. Putting Sam Goldberg there had felt criminal, but Eddie was like family, and his presence in the spot of honor didn't offend. Ruth and Mr. Greene sat to his left, the children to his right, and me at the other end of the table, closest to the kitchen so I could get anything we might need.

"Shall we say the *motzi*?" Mr. Greene asked, referring to the traditional prayer before eating. Even when we held Shabbat dinners, Harry and I typically skipped that step, opting for blessings over the candles and challah as our cultural touchstones.

"Do you say it for every meal?" Ruth asked.

"No," he admitted. "But I know you went to shul every week back when . . . Back then."

A slight cloud crossed Ruth's face, but she shook her head to dispel it. I remembered Harry saying that she brought him to say the mourner's Kaddish every Saturday for the first year after his father died. He had hated it and wanted to be outside with the other children instead of being forced to remember that his life would never again be like theirs. The thought had crossed my mind to do the same with Susie and Bobby, but Harry's childhood disdain talked me out of it. Instead, we focused on lighting the *yahrtzeit* candle at home on the anniversary of his death, talking about the significance of the candle and our memories of Harry.

"Why not?" Ruth said. "It's good for the children."

"Do we join hands?" Susie asked.

"Join hands?"

"Like they do on TV? When they say grace?"

I smiled at her. "No, sweetheart. Our people don't."

As Mr. Greene recited the prayer, I looked at Susie's sweet face, so pleased that she felt confident enough to ask that question. That there was no one in her world to chastise her for asking a question instead of knowing the answer. My brave little girl had been knocked down two years ago, but she was okay. We all were, I thought, looking around the table. Eddie caught my eye and smiled, and I returned it, thinking how natural he and his father felt at my table.

I could see weekly dinners once he and Ruth were married. We could add the leaves to the table and have Janet and her family there as well. She and I would finally be the sisters we had wished to be since that first year of living together in college. Marrying two best friends was the closest we had come before. And, well, we wouldn't *exactly* be related, but closer.

Then I realized everyone was looking at me, waiting for me to serve the brisket. The prayer had ended as I lost myself in my little fantasy of entwining our two families.

"Sorry," I said, gesturing for Mr. Greene to pass me his plate. "Head in the clouds today."

Ruth and Mr. Greene reminisced about the O Street Market, Eddie chiming in from time to time with what he remembered from being a child and helping his father when he didn't have school. Mr. Greene watched Ruth with rapt fascination each time she spoke. She snuck peeks at him but would flush when she caught him staring at her and turn her attention back to her plate or the children.

As the plates emptied, the children asked to be excused, but I had them sit a couple more minutes.

"This was a wonderful dinner," Mr. Greene said. "Thank you, Barbara."

"Yes," Ruth said. "The brisket wasn't nearly as dry this time."

My brisket was never dry. But I refrained from saying that, shooting a pointed look at Eddie and managing a thank you.

"And the company," Mr. Greene said, turning to Ruth and taking her hand. "This is the happiest I've been in years."

Ruth looked uncomfortable. "Joseph," she said. "I—"

"Joe," he replied, gazing at her adoringly.

"Joe," she repeated. "I—"

"Or Joey." He placed his other hand on top of hers, stroking it with his thumb.

"*Joseph!*" she exclaimed, extracting her hand.

A snort erupted, which I realized, as I glanced around the table to see everyone staring at me, was mine as I tried to hold in a laugh.

"Mommy!" Bobby said. "What was *that*?"

And then I started laughing. I couldn't help myself. Eddie joined me, and then the children.

Mr. Greene (I would never be able to look at him without thinking *Joey* again) was still looking at Ruth as if she was dessert. But it was Ruth's face that sobered me. I had never seen her look so flustered as she did right then. Even when we lost Harry, she had been devastated but never so adrift as this.

He tried to take her hand again, but Ruth stood from the table so suddenly that she knocked over a water glass. She righted it, and I sprang into action, applying a napkin to the tablecloth.

"Pepper needs a walk," she said, her voice shrill. "I'll take her."

"The kids can take her in the backyard," I said.

"No, no, no. I'll take her," Ruth said, practically running toward the small table where we kept the leash, Pepper hot on her heels.

"I'll come with you," Mr. Greene said, pushing his chair back.

"No!" Ruth said, her eyes wild. "I—you—eat dessert. I need some air." She clipped the leash onto Pepper's collar and the door was shut behind her before any of us even realized she was gone.

"I—I should go after her," I said, dropping the wet napkin onto the table.

"I'll go," Mr. Greene said, clearly not understanding that he was the source of her distress.

"No, I need to make sure she's okay." Then I looked at Bobby and Susie, who were staring at me with eyes as wide as saucers. I couldn't leave them to go chase after Ruth. But she had looked so pale. Visions of Harry's last moments flashed through my mind, and I gripped the back of my chair so tightly that my knuckles turned white.

"Go," Eddie said. "I'll clear up and get dessert out."

I swallowed. "Are you sure?"

"Go."

"It's—it's an apple crumble," I said. "Heat it at—"

"Barbara!"

"I'm going, I'm going!" And I took off after Ruth.

The days were growing longer, and while the streetlights had come on, I could still see enough in the fading light to catch her form walking briskly up the street toward the school. I chased after her as fast as my heels would allow, until I was close enough for her to hear me. "Ruth!" I called out.

She didn't turn around, but she slowed and then stopped. I finally reached her, my breath fast from exertion, her chest rising and falling rapidly though she was no longer walking.

"Are you all right?" I asked.

She didn't respond, and my mouth went dry.

"Ruth. Talk to me. If you need to go to the hospital—"

She shook her head. "I'm not sick," she said, her voice barely a whisper.

"Then what?"

"I—I don't want this."

"Don't want what?"

She closed her eyes and swallowed thickly. "Don't invite him over again," she said. "Please."

"I thought—"

"Please."

"Okay," I said, nodding. "I won't."

She took another deep breath and then opened her eyes. "Thank you."

I wanted to ask why—I had seen sparks in Janet's kitchen. I knew I had. And her touching her hair when she talked about him. What changed? But her demeanor told me I was better off waiting than demanding answers.

"Do you want me to get rid of them before you come home?"

"No," Ruth said. "I don't want you to be rude. But I may say I have a headache if that's all right with you."

"I'll tell them you do. You can go straight upstairs."

She smiled thinly and thanked me again. I took her arm, and we walked home together in companionable silence.

34

But Eddie was right about his father's persistence.

The flowers, Ruth couldn't have cared less about. "Does he think we have a greenhouse?" she asked as more arrived, gesturing to the ornate display still sitting in the corner of my kitchen. I honestly didn't even know how we were going to dispose of them all—it was too large for a trash bag, and I wasn't sure that the county would take them if we lugged them to the curb as they were.

I poked my head out the door and peered down the street, certain we would see him somewhere as he would want to know her reaction to the flowers. But if he was hiding, he was doing a fine job of it.

I came back into the kitchen just in time to see Ruth pocketing the note, which she hadn't read out to me. *Interesting,* I thought. But I said nothing, deciding to let this unfold on its own.

The following day, a deliveryman arrived with a box of chocolates that could barely fit through the front door.

"A crate of chocolates, more like," Ruth grumbled. "We'll have no waistlines left if we eat these."

"We can take them to the hospital," I said, eyeing the box. It *might* fit in my trunk. If not, we would have to take Ruth's car. "The nursing staff does love when I bring in sweets."

"True," Ruth said. "Though we should save some for the children." The last thing they needed was more sweets. Ruth had taken to buying them candy whenever she went shopping, claiming it was a grandmother's job to spoil her grandchildren. But I chose to believe that was a desire to keep some of the gift.

"It's simply too much," Ruth said, as she tossed chocolates into a large Tupperware container. "Why is he doing this?"

"Ruth." She turned to look at me. "What did Abe do when you met him?"

She crossed her arms. "This isn't the same at all."

"How did you two meet? I asked Harry once, and he said it was something about a cousin?" I had asked if that meant Ruth and Abe were cousins, to which Harry replied by laughing merrily.

Ruth took a seat at the kitchen table, then selected a chocolate for herself and took a bite. "They *are* quite good," she conceded. Then she sighed. "I came down from Boston—my father opened a laundry there. From a rabbi to a launderer." She shook her head at the injustice the world had forced upon him.

"Why wasn't he a rabbi here?"

"There were so many already. We had no money left, no congregation, nothing. He gave it all up for us." She finished the chocolate. "He made a good living—as good as he could have at the time."

I knew what she meant from my parents' stories about their childhoods. Even my own youth had a different tinge to it in my memories. Not for us the sepia-toned nostalgia of an easier time; instead much more worry about what the situation in Europe meant for our place in the world. After the war, things had gotten better.

"But I came to visit my friend Miriam. She had come from the same shtetl, and we kept in touch. Her family had relatives in Washington, so they settled down here. When she came to meet my train, her cousin drove her to pick me up." She smiled, looking over my shoulder at a faraway past. "He was so handsome, but Miriam told me he was engaged, so I looked out the window for the entire drive. Meanwhile, Miriam told me later that he nearly crashed the car turning his head to look at me. He called off the engagement that night, then came to Miriam's house for dinner—unannounced, I might add."

"You little home-wrecker," I said with a laugh.

"I am no such thing," Ruth said, reaching for another chocolate. But she looked amused. "I certainly did nothing to encourage him."

"I'm seeing a pattern here," I said, gesturing to the chocolates and flowers.

She shrugged. "I can't help it if men are naturally drawn to me."

I did try not to laugh. I really did. But it came barreling out of my throat in a giant guffaw. Ruth looked mildly insulted, then shrugged again and pursed her lips. "You should have seen me back then," she said. "I was a looker."

I reached over and patted her hand. "You still are," I assured her, genuinely. "Tell me what happened next."

Ruth shook her head, but her smile had returned. "Miriam and I didn't get a moment alone together until we went to bed. He was there until bedtime and back again for breakfast the next morning. Finally, his mother came over and told me if I didn't agree to go out with him, he'd lose his job, and then where would they be?"

"Had he asked you out?"

"Not in so many words. But I told him I'd have dinner with him—just the two of us—if he would go to work. He did and picked me up that evening."

"What did he do?"

"He ran a dry goods store with his father."

I arched an eyebrow. "So he wasn't actually in danger of losing his job?"

"He might have been. His father was a difficult man. But he kept working, and we were married less than a year later."

"Then you lived with his parents?"

She made a sour face. "You think *I'm* bad? You should have met Abe's mother." She shook her head.

"You're not so bad," I said, reaching out to put my hand back on hers. I was surprised to find I meant it.

She shook her head with a half smile, eyes looking into the past again. "There were times when I thought I'd have been better off with the Russians." She looked back at me. "I squirreled away every penny that I could to save up so we could move out."

Whether she was used to men pursuing her or not, it was the singing telegram that put her over the edge. The knock on the door on a Saturday was unexpected, and I was behind the sofa, Susie sitting on the back of it, as I muddled through attempting to French-braid her thick, curly locks before she left for a birthday party. I was definitely not cut out for hairdressing, and her complaints every time I tugged too hard made me want to call my mother and apologize for the hassle doing my hair had been. Then again, I no longer had any pain sensation in my scalp from my mother tearing a brush through my own curls.

Ruth picked Pepper up and said she would get it, which I appreciated.

"Ruth Feldman?" A man's voice asked from the doorway.

"Yes," she said, hesitantly.

The sound of a harmonica caused me to look toward the doorway, Susie almost falling off the couch in the process, as the man in a red-and-white pinstripe suit and a straw hat began to sing.

"Your Joseph misses you," the man sang. "Your Joseph misses you. He's wondering what did he do? What did that poor man do? Can't catch a break. He wants a date. Your Joseph really likes you. So call him please, or send one of these. A message in a bottle would do too."

The man finished, removing his hat and bowing with a flourish. Both kids clapped, and Bobby yelled, "Bravo!"

I held a hand to my mouth to hold in a laugh.

"Did you know about this?" Ruth asked, turning around to look at me.

"Not at all," I said, miming crossing my heart. "I swear."

The singer still stood there expectantly, and Ruth, with a sigh, took a few steps to the console table where her purse rested, and pulled out a dime, which she dropped in his hat. The man looked at it, clearly hoping for more, then thanked Ruth and pocketed the coin as she shut the door in his face.

Ruth shook her head, visibly annoyed, when there was another rap at the door. "These people," she muttered, opening it. "Now listen, I gave you a tip, that means I'm done with—oh—"

Mr. Greene stood on the doorstep, hat in one hand, a much more appropriately sized bouquet of flowers in the other.

"Ruth," he said with a nod, then extended the flowers. She looked at them as time stood still, then eventually took them.

"Joseph," she said quietly.

"I—I do hope that wasn't too much."

"Joseph—" Ruth said.

"Joe."

She held up a hand. "Please don't start all that again." She sighed. "You're not going to stop until I have dinner with you, are you?"

He shook his head, but grinned, and I saw so much of Eddie in him when he did. "When I know what I want, I don't like to waste time." The unspoken part, that he wanted her, hung in the air.

For a long time she said nothing. "If I go to dinner with you, and then say I'm not interested, will you leave me be?"

"I hope that isn't the conclusion you reach," he said, running a hand through his gray hair. "But if it is, then yes. Tonight?"

"I suppose," Ruth said. "You can pick me up at six."

Mr. Greene looked so giddy that I honestly thought he might jump up and click his heels together. "You tell me where you want to go, and I'll get us a table."

"I don't care," Ruth said. "You decide."

Mr. Greene nodded. "I will. I'll ask Janet for recommendations. It's been so long since I took a woman out."

"I'll see you tonight," Ruth said, gently ending the conversation.

He plucked the hand that didn't have the flowers from the doorframe and kissed it. "Until tonight," he said gallantly.

She shut the door, and I caught her eye as she turned around.

"Don't you say a word," she warned me. "I'm just doing this so our house isn't overrun with flowers."

I didn't even flinch at her calling the house "ours." "I'll try to find a vase for those," I said. We had pruned down the casket spray into all available vases, so it was likely to be a water glass. But it was the thought that mattered.

Ruth sneezed. "He'd do better sticking to the chocolates," she said, holding the offending flowers away from her. "My allergies may never recover from that man's affections."

35

After Susie was securely deposited at her birthday party, I dropped Bobby off to play at Janet's house. Janet looked noticeably frazzled. "Are you sure you're okay?" I asked her as the two boys scampered off to play.

"I'm fine," she said, waving me away. "You need the break more than I do."

I offered to take Paula for a few hours on Monday to give her a break as well, which she gratefully accepted. "I don't even remember the last time I got my hair done," Janet admitted. "That would be wonderful. Thank you."

"All you ever have to do is ask," I reminded her. "You know that."

She looked at me, but her usual wry face was gone, and a naked honesty shone in her eyes. "I never want to ask. Especially not you."

"Janet," I said. "You can always ask me."

She smiled grimly. "I just know how much you have on your plate."

I wrapped my arms around her in a hug. For a moment, she hung there limply, then hugged me back fiercely. "I am never too busy for you. I couldn't have gotten through those early days if you hadn't been there forcing me out of bed. Promise you'll lean on me when you need to?"

"I promise," Janet said. She pulled out of the hug, visibly fortified by it. There was a small crash followed by a yelp from upstairs. "Now get out of here. I'll go deal with that." She went thundering up the stairs. "Nothing better be broken, and that includes you two," she called ahead of her. I shook my head as I left.

Then I went home and told Ruth we were going shopping.

"I don't want to run into Joseph at the store," she said.

"Not *food* shopping. We're buying you a dress for tonight."

"No."

"My treat."

Pepper's ears perked up and I could have sworn Ruth's did the same. "I suppose I can look good while convincing him that I'm not interested."

Or while you discover that you are, I thought. "Exactly. Now come on. We'll go to Woodies."

"Fine," Ruth said, rising with a sigh. "Let me just get my pocketbook."

~

Outfitted in a flattering new dress (which took me and no fewer than four salesgirls to convince her was the current style and that no, a crinoline would ruin the svelte silhouette), Ruth came down the stairs shortly before Mr. Greene was due to arrive.

"How do I look?" she asked the children, turning around for their benefit.

"Beautiful," Susie said, walking around her appreciatively in a circle.

"Like you're younger!" Bobby chimed in. I swatted playfully at him, but Ruth laughed.

"Maybe I should change, then. I don't want Joseph getting the wrong idea."

"No," I said quickly. "It's perfect. Right, Bobby?"

"Right," he said. "That's what I meant."

There was a knock at the door, and Ruth reached for her handbag, but I stopped her. "It just needs one thing." I reached into my pocket and pulled out a tube of Revlon's Snow Peach. "This," I said, uncapping the lipstick. I applied it to her bottom lip before she took the tube from me and studied it.

"It's a little . . . pink . . ."

"It looks really good on you," I assured her. "And *Vogue* says this is the hottest new color."

"Whatever happened to classic red?"

"I heard Jackie Kennedy is wearing this shade now."

"Fine," Ruth said, crossing to the mirror and running a finger under her bottom lip to catch any that I had gone astray with. I hadn't, but she still had to make sure.

There was another knock at the door.

"Will someone let him in?" she asked before pressing her lips together.

I started toward the door, but Bobby beat me to it. He flung the door open, then looked disappointed.

"Where are your flowers?" he asked.

"Bobby!" I said, restraining myself from clapping a hand over his mouth. "He was here this morning with flowers!"

"Don't worry, young man," he said with a wink. "I didn't come empty handed." He pulled the top of a long jewelry box out of his jacket pocket.

At least it isn't a ring box, I thought. But oh my. Jewelry was a bit much for a first date.

Ruth eyed him warily from behind us. "Joseph," she said warningly.

"It's not what you think," he said, removing the box. "I promise." He opened it to reveal an ornate hatpin.

"A hatpin?"

"No hat required," he said. "I know you're not as keen as I am—yet. And Eddie said I've been coming on a bit too strong. When I met Gertrude, she carried a hatpin in case any men got fresh. I know it's been a long time since . . . well, a long time, and I thought, this way, maybe you'll feel a little more comfortable going out with me."

Ruth looked from the hatpin to him, back to the pin, then back to him. "That's—"

Bizarre, I finished in my head.

"Extremely thoughtful," she said. I looked at her in surprise. "My father gave me a hatpin—a much plainer one—when I was a young girl for much the same reason." Then she peered around him. "There are flowers in the car though, aren't there?"

"Well, yes," Mr. Greene said sheepishly.

Ruth started to laugh, then slipped a hand into the crook of his elbow. "Don't wait up," she called to us over her shoulder.

I picked my jaw up off the ground and looked at the children. "I . . . didn't see that coming."

Bobby looked up at me hopefully. "Does Grandma being gone mean we can have pancakes for dinner?"

"Sure," I said, shaking my head. "This day is upside down as it is."

"Yay!" both kids cried, scampering off as I tried to process the unexpected success of a hatpin—designed for stabbing an overzealous suitor—as a gift before a date. The best conclusion I could come to was that the generation that spawned me was simply inexplicably strange. I wondered if my own children would someday feel the same about me.

36

As I slid the last batch of pancakes onto the children's plates, there was a knock at the door.

I glanced at the Kit-Cat Klock on the wall, its tail swinging. They hadn't even been gone half an hour, and I sincerely hoped Ruth hadn't used that hatpin while Mr. Greene was driving.

"Is that Grandma?" Susie asked.

I wiped my hands on my apron and moved toward the door, asking her with a levity I didn't feel, "She doesn't exactly knock, does she?"

But when I pulled the door open, I saw Eddie on the doorstep instead, hat in hand.

"Eddie," I said, smiling, then I took in his look of concern. Maybe Ruth *had* used that hatpin after all. "What's wrong?"

He ran a hand through his hair. "Nothing. Sorry. I shouldn't have come."

He turned away, and I reached out, putting a hand on his arm to stop him. "Nonsense," I said. "The kids wanted pancakes for dinner. Can I offer you pancakes? Or I can whip up something else if you're hungry?"

"No, I don't want to be a bother."

I shook my head but was smiling. "You're the opposite of a bother. Come in." I pulled him gently inside.

"The pancakes *do* smell delicious," he conceded.

"I'll start the next batch. The kids and I are always happy to see you."

He stopped walking. "I didn't bring them anything."

I leaned in conspiratorially. "They'll live." Then, when he still wasn't smiling, I really looked at him. "What happened?"

He sighed. "Nothing. I just—my father is SO excited, and Ruth seems less so—"

I put my hand back on his arm. "I know," I said. "I felt terrible that I suggested we get them together and then . . . this. But honestly, he made her laugh before they left. I think—maybe—it could be good for both of them. She did tell me not to wait up."

"She did? You don't think they . . . ?"

I mimed a gag. "I'd rather not think about either of them like that."

"Me neither," Eddie agreed. "Sorry. It's strange to worry about your father going on a date. He just hasn't shown any interest in meeting anyone, and then he saw Ruth, and it was like the light that burned out when my mother died suddenly turned back on."

I couldn't imagine my own father ever moving on if my mother went first. Then again, he didn't seem all that interested in my mother either. Although maybe her absence had made the heart grow fonder these two years. My mother, on the other hand, would be on a date before his body was cold. She had been urging me to start thinking about dating before she left. Some people could be alone, and some couldn't. And I was learning I was the former, though I had never wanted to be.

"I don't want to jinx anything," I said. "But as long as she doesn't use that hatpin, I think this could work."

"Hatpin?"

I grinned. "Go sit down. I'll let the kids tell you all about it while I make up some more pancakes."

The children squealed with delight at the sight of him, and I didn't mind mixing more batter. Having Eddie at the table just felt right.

Eddie said he should be going when I announced that it was bedtime for Susie and Bobby, but I told him he was welcome to stay. Bobby had started letting me leave before he was asleep in the last couple of weeks, so I would be back down within half an hour.

"Can Eddie read me a bedtime story?" Bobby asked.

I shrugged and raised my eyebrows at Eddie. "That's up to him," I said.

"Please?" Bobby asked. "Mommy never does the boy voices right."

I chuckled, cuffing him playfully on the head. "Imagine that. I don't sound like a Hardy Boy."

Eddie smiled broadly. "I loved the Hardy Boys as a kid." He knelt down to Bobby's height. "It would be an honor, sir."

As Bobby and Eddie went up the stairs, Pepper hot on their heels, I swear I felt my heart growing larger, just as Ruth had said it would. The grief of losing Harry would always be there. But there was so much room for happiness in our lives too. And I realized, as I peeked into Bobby's room as Eddie read aloud about Frank and Joe's adventures as they worked to solve a mystery that the grown-ups couldn't, that Bobby was going to be just fine. Eddie and George would help with the masculine tasks that I couldn't. And besides, if I could shave my ankles without bleeding out, I could figure out how to teach him to shave his face eventually.

Even if Ruth never left. We were okay. I picked Pepper up and took her downstairs to let her outside, then as I stood in the living room, looking out the back door as she did her business, I turned my face skyward. "We'll never stop missing you," I said quietly. "But we're going to be okay." And for the first time in over two years, I felt something, like a small kiss on my forehead. The type Harry used to plant there when I was worried about something.

Then I felt it again.

And again.

I looked more carefully at the ceiling, and a drop of water plunked onto my face right between my eyes. Not a kiss from my departed husband, but a leak from the bathroom above us.

Oh no. "Eddie!" I yelled. "Help!"

An hour and a set of wrenches later, the problem seemed to have been resolved, and the children were finally in bed.

"You got lucky," Eddie said, replacing the wrenches in the toolbox and taking it to the basement, while I showed him where it went. "That could have been a much harder fix."

"I was lucky you were here," I said gratefully. "What do I do about the living room ceiling?"

"I can redo that for you this week. I don't think too much water got in, but you don't want mold."

He turned to face me in the dim light of the basement, and I suddenly realized how close we were in the nook at the base of the stairs, where Harry had kept his tools. It felt intimate in a way I hadn't experienced in years, and I found my eyes drifting to his mouth. What would it be like to kiss Eddie? I felt a flurry in my stomach that I couldn't blame on a meal this time. My eyes returned to his and my breath hitched slightly. He leaned forward and I . . . shook my head suddenly and brushed past him to go up the stairs.

I looked over my shoulder and saw him still standing there, squinting with his bad left eye. "What?" I asked as if I hadn't just been thinking . . . well, thoughts that I had no business thinking.

"Nothing," he said, then he gestured to the room behind him. "You know, it wouldn't take that much work to make the basement into a playroom for the kids."

I peered at what I could see of it from the top of the stairs. Harry and I had talked about that as a someday project. "It wouldn't?"

"Not much at all. A little drywall, some paint, and either linoleum or carpet on the floors. Better lighting."

"Maybe I'll get a quote on that," I said as Eddie climbed the stairs.

"I can do it," Eddie said. "I like projects like that. And helping you."

I shook my head. "You do too much for us already." Had I moved closer to him? Or had he moved closer to me? I hadn't noticed the flecks of green in his eyes before.

He raised a hand and brushed a lock of hair from my face, and I felt my lips part. "Barbara," he said softly, and I moved an inch closer, my breathing rapid as I realized what was about to happen. What I actually *wanted* to happen. This was crazy. It was *Eddie*! But all I knew was that every fiber of my being felt this was right.

My head tilted slightly, and then—

The front door opened, and we jumped apart.

"Good night," Ruth called from the doorway, shutting the door behind her and then leaning on it and closing her eyes for a moment, a fresh bouquet of flowers clasped in her left hand. Then she opened her eyes and saw the two of us standing guiltily, looking at her. "Oh my," she said. "What excitement did I miss tonight?"

"I—uh—well," I stammered. Of all the times for her to come home!

"The upstairs tub was leaking," Eddie said quickly. "Just a loose connector. I fixed it right up."

She looked from me to Eddie and back to me. "How fortuitous," she said with a smirk.

Amazing how just two words could make me want to throttle her. Admittedly, it was the implication in her tone more than the words. But still. No one got under my skin the way she did.

"And how was your date?" I asked icily. "Do I need to hire a lawyer to defend you for assaulting him with a hatpin?"

"It's hardly assault when he gave me the pin," Ruth said. "But no. It was . . . nice . . . actually."

Nice, I thought. Better than ending in a hatpin-stabbing incident, but "nice" wasn't exactly the same as smitten and willing to marry him and leave me to raise my children in peace.

Then again, I wasn't getting any details with Eddie in the room. I snuck a look at him, but he was studying the floor. The expansion I had felt in my chest earlier contracted slightly. It was just the late hour and proximity. Maybe there hadn't even been any tension, and I had imagined it all. I fought to keep my face neutral. Poor, pitiful me. Two years without a man so much as looking at me and the first one who shows me a modicum of kindness, I practically jump on. I wanted Eddie to leave so I could wallow in my embarrassment. What had I been thinking?

"That's . . . wonderful," I said. "Isn't it, Eddie?"

"Yes," he said dully. "Wonderful."

Ruth's eyes narrowed as they flitted between us again. "I sense I'm interrupting something. Don't mind me. I'm just going to put these in water—if we have anything left resembling a vase at this point—and then go on up to bed. You two just go back to . . . whatever it was that you were doing."

"Eddie was just leaving," I said quickly.

His head turned in my direction, but he didn't meet my eyes. "Yes," he said slowly. "I'll be back later in the week to patch up the ceiling."

"I can hire someone to do that," I said, then bit the inside of my cheek at the wounded look on his face.

He finally made brief eye contact with me, then nodded. "Whatever you want to do," he said. "Have a good night, Barbara. Ruth."

Ruth moved toward the kitchen, and Eddie left without looking back.

"Well, well, well," Ruth said over her shoulder. "Lovers' spat?"

"Eddie? A lover? No."

She tilted her head, lips pressed together, but didn't push the issue. "I'm afraid I'm going to have to resort to a drinking glass for these," she said, looking through the cabinets for a vase.

"I think I have one more in the basement," I said. "I'll go get it."

But as soon as I was down the stairs, where I had first noticed how close we were standing, I felt tears prickling at my eyes, threatening to spill out. I was an absolute fool. And Eddie had run out of there so quickly, there was no pretending that I hadn't just ruined our friendship by almost kissing him. And for what? It wasn't like I was ready to move on.

I looked at the hanging lightbulb and fanned briefly at my eyes, willing the tears back into my body. I would apologize. Tell him I'd had a glass of sherry after Ruth left and wasn't myself. And hope that was enough.

I plucked the lone remaining vase—a wedding gift that I hadn't liked much but couldn't bring myself to get rid of—from the shelf and went back upstairs. "We're either going to need to buy more vases or get rid of the older flowers," I said, sounding cheerful though feeling far from it.

"Hmm," Ruth said, taking the vase from me and crossing to the kitchen sink to fill it with water. "We should bring whatever still looks nice to the hospital. Not everyone gets visitors."

I looked at her back as she arranged the flowers in the vase. It was a lovely idea.

"Maybe not the funeral spray though," she said as she turned around, looking for a spot to put the vase. "That could send the wrong message."

And despite myself, I laughed at the idea of walking into a patient's room with a display of flowers for a casket. If Mrs. Kline were still coming in, it would have been worth it.

37

I scooped Paula out of her stroller after my own children walked into school Monday morning. "Are you ready for an Auntie Barbara day?" I asked, spinning her around in the air.

"Yay!" Paula squealed. Then her little eyes narrowed. "I get ice-skeem lunch."

"You do *not*, you little fibber," Janet said.

I smiled at Janet over Paula's head. "I've got two of my own," I reminded her. Then I whispered in Paula's ear, "Ice cream *dessert*." Paula put her tiny hands on either side of my face and pulled me in close, kissing my nose.

"You my best fwend, Auntie Bawba."

"And you're mine, darling. Now come on. Let's let Mama go get even more gorgeous."

Janet shook her head. "She's going to be even more spoiled than usual when I pick her up, isn't she?"

I shrugged playfully. "It's entirely possible. Now go have fun. My little best friend and I have a date."

Janet faked a glower. "First she ruins my figure, then she steals my best friend. It's a good thing you're cute, kiddo."

Paula blew a raspberry and Janet laughed, kissed me on the cheek, and then left.

"Now," I said, "what do you think about going to visit Uncle Eddie at his store?"

"Yay!" she said again. "Unka Eddie AWAYS give me candy." Then she turned serious. "You no tell Mama."

I mimed crossing my heart. "I won't tell a soul," I said.

But secretly, I was relieved to have Paula with me while seeing Eddie for the first time since . . . well, since nothing actually happened Saturday night. She would ensure a sense of normalcy. And he would see that there was nothing untoward and we could remain friends.

I hoped.

We arrived at the store, and I held Paula's hand through the parking lot, matching my steps to hers before settling her in the seat of a shopping cart, taking a deep breath, and going inside.

Eddie was at the front of the store, looking at his watch when we walked in. "Unka Eddie!" Paula screeched. "Auntie Bawba bwing me today!"

I felt my cheeks grow warm at the use of *Uncle* and *Auntie* together, but if Eddie noticed anything amiss, he didn't let on. "That was sweet of her," Eddie said. "What's Janet up to?"

"Hair appointment," I said. "And I wanted a little Paula time."

"You're a good friend," Eddie said, and I wanted to confess that I hadn't been a good enough friend if Janet felt she couldn't ask me for help. He was the one person I could have said that to. But not in front of Paula. And it was too heavy a conversation for a Monday morning at the store.

I looked around him. "Your father didn't come in today?"

Eddie raised his eyebrows in amusement. "Oh, you don't know?"

"Don't know what?"

"Come on," he said, taking the cart from me, pushing Paula as I followed.

We wound up at the back of the store, watching from a few aisles over as Mr. Greene stood at the deli counter sampling a platter of meats, a gigantic wicker basket on the floor next to him. I looked at Eddie questioningly.

"He's taking Ruth on a picnic today."

"A picnic? At their age?"

Eddie looked at me, amused. "Are you ever too old for a picnic?"

"Well, no, but how will they stand up once they're on the ground? Someone is going to need to call the fire department."

Eddie laughed and Mr. Greene looked over.

"Barbara, thank goodness. Which does Ruth prefer? Tongue or corned beef."

"Please say tongue," Eddie whispered, then laughed again.

"Corned beef," I called back, elbowing him. "I'm not getting stuck with her for life over your father's lack of taste in meats," I whispered.

"So I'm going to be stuck with her, then?"

I grinned. "Having a stepmother isn't so bad. It worked out for Cinderella—in the end that is."

He tried to glare at me but couldn't hold it, and I felt relief wash through my body. Eddie wasn't going anywhere. It had just been the hour and the close space the other night. We were fine. Even if I *did* feel like there was some kind of strange static electricity in the space between us now.

I took control of the cart and pushed it over to the deli counter. "Come on," I told Mr. Greene. "I'll help you pick out other things she likes." I peered into the picnic basket to see what he had already gathered, while he kissed Paula on the forehead.

"You know, I knew her order by heart twenty years ago, but now . . ."

I smiled at him. "Did you know all your customers' orders? Or just the pretty widows'?"

His chest puffed up. "I'll have you know, I'd never do anything inappropriate—"

"Of course you wouldn't," I said, putting a hand on his arm. "I meant because it helped her."

He settled. "I wished I could have done more, honestly. I always liked her. And now that I know what it's like to . . ." He shook his head. "Do you believe in *bashert*?"

I froze. Did I? It was the Yiddish concept of things being meant to be, specifically in terms of soulmates. Of course Harry had been mine. But did that mean I was now destined to be alone for the rest of my life?

"I think it was *bashert* that she came back into my life, now," he confided. My eyes drifted toward Eddie, who was straightening a display of jars at the end of an aisle near us. "It's not good for people to be alone for too long."

"Pop," Eddie warned without turning around.

"What?" he asked. "Your mother's greatest wish was for you to find someone too. But even she didn't want me to be alone."

"She didn't?" he asked.

"What kind of love is that?" Mr. Greene asked. "Where you want someone to be miserable after you're gone? No. We talked about that."

Harry and I had too, of course. And he'd said the same. But there was a big difference between the hypothetical situation and the reality of losing a spouse. Then again, there was a big difference between being alone for two years like I had and being alone for over twenty like Ruth.

"Ruth loves olives," I blurted out to stop my racing thoughts. "You should bring olives."

"Olives it is, then," Mr. Greene said. "What else?"

"Pickles—but no cabbage."

"I yike yoyipops," Paula said hopefully.

Eddie reached into his pocket and pulled one out for her. "I always keep one on me for my best girl."

I leaned in and mock-whispered. "I'm telling Susie you said that."

Eddie chuckled and reached back into his pocket, pulling out another lollipop, which he offered to me. "I'm not above bribes."

I plucked the candy from his hand and winked. "What Susie doesn't know won't hurt her."

"How does Ruth feel about herring with kichel?" Mr. Greene called from down by the fish counter.

"What kind of picnic is he packing?" I asked Eddie, thoroughly disgusted at the thought of herring in the hot sun.

Eddie shrugged. "I don't pretend to understand their generation."

"Everything in that basket is going to smell like fish," I said, groaning. "Which Ruth might not mind, with the way she cooks, but that's terrible."

I pushed Paula down toward her grandfather. "Simpler is probably better for a picnic," I warned. "Why don't we go look at some fruit? Ruth always talks about your eye for produce." I picked up his already-heavy picnic basket and set it in my shopping cart to make it easier for him.

"Such a good daughter-in-law," he said. "Shame about the cooking, but that's nothing compared to the kindness you show."

I counted to five in my head. "Thank you," I said through marginally gritted teeth. That woman was going to be the death of me if this relationship didn't pan out.

38

Ruth and I walked into the hospital on Tuesday loaded with flowers.

"Dr. Harper wants to see you," Gloria said, taking the flowers from my arms.

I reached into my handbag for my car keys. "Be a dear and bring in the rest of the flowers, will you?" I asked her. "Ruth's new boyfriend is a little overzealous, and we thought these could cheer up some lonely patients."

Ruth bristled at the term *boyfriend*, but Gloria hesitated. "Of course," she said slowly. "But, Barbara . . . something seemed . . . off . . . with Dr. Harper."

I noticed a worried crease between her eyebrows. "Off how?"

Gloria shook her head and crossed herself. "I don't know. But there was something ominous in how he said to send you to him."

Ominous, I thought. *The nurses must be actually threatening to quit over Dr. Howe this time.* "Don't worry," I said, patting her arm comfortingly. "I'll take care of it."

As I walked down the hall, I heard Ruth saying, "He's not my *boyfriend*. Good heavens, he's a grown man with gray hair."

I reached Dr. Harper's office on the third floor and knocked on the door.

"Come in," he said through the heavy oak door.

I opened it, and Dr. Harper stood.

"Gloria said you wanted to see me?"

"Yes," Dr. Harper said, gesturing for me to take the seat across from his desk. Then he sat back down and steepled his fingers. I sat in the seat he had indicated and crossed my ankles, waiting for him to speak, which took him a few moments, as he opened his mouth and closed it, looking strangely like a fish.

When he still hadn't gotten words out, I gently asked, "Is something the matter?"

He swallowed and then said, "Yes, Mrs. Feldman, I'm afraid something is the matter."

He had called me Barbara since I made the move from volunteer to employee. He wasn't meeting my eye either. And a little warning bell went off in my head.

"I understand there was an . . . altercation . . . between you and one of our doctors a little over a week ago."

"An altercation?" I repeated. Had I overstepped somewhere?

"With . . . Dr. Howe," he said and pressed his lips together.

I raised my eyebrows. "That's certainly one way to put it."

"I know that the two of you have had some . . . friction . . . in the past . . ."

He would like there to be a whole lot more "friction," I thought. But I couldn't say that to Dr. Harper. "Dr. Harper," I said measuredly. "I have spent half of my time at this hospital protecting nurses from his attention. I was naturally shocked to find that he had convinced my mother-in-law to help turn that attention to me."

A brief look of confusion crossed Dr. Harper's face, but he set it resolutely. "Mrs. Feldman, a hospital runs on a tight budget. And pretending your mother-in-law is ill to get time alone with a doctor, whose services are desperately in demand, is a grave offense indeed."

"I agree wholeheart—wait, what did you just say?"

"While I know that doctors and nurses sometimes find love at work, I really thought that your status as a widow would have prevented such lapses in judgment."

"Lapses in—I'm sorry, are you saying that *I* tried to seduce *him*?"

Dr. Harper swallowed again and then nodded.

"Dr. Harper, how many times have I sat in this very office complaining about him to you? He is the absolute last man—no, *cad*—on the planet whom I would agree to have dinner with, let alone anything else."

He cleared his throat. "Dr. Howe said that he has been rebuffing your advances for some time. Mrs. Feldman, you've been invaluable in your work here, but I cannot have my doctors feeling harassed. And Dr. Howe was too uncomfortable to return to work last week. He wasn't going to come in this week either unless I . . . handled . . . the situation."

What I wouldn't have said to both of them if I were a man. A man could have asked them to step outside over such accusations. But as it was, I had to sit there, silently fuming in a polyurethane chair while these two doctors dragged my good name through the mud entirely because I was a woman and therefore disposable.

I counted to ten inside my head and then through gritted teeth said, "So I've been disciplined, then. Now if you'll excuse me, I have work to do." I stood from the chair and turned to leave.

"Actually," Dr. Harper said, the scraping sound of his chair against the linoleum floor telling me he had risen as well. "I'm sorry. He's refusing to work here if *you* do."

My knees threatened to buckle, and I gripped the back of the chair for support. Once I was sure I could stand on my own, I squared my shoulders without turning around. "That's it, then?"

Dr. Harper came around his desk and put his hand on top of mine. "I'm sorry, Barbara. I am. I know—"

I shook his hand off. "Please don't patronize me further," I said with as much dignity as I could muster. And I forced myself out of his office without looking back.

Several nurses tried to talk to me, but I couldn't. Ruth was in the lobby, placing a bouquet of flowers at the intake desk, and I almost walked past her without seeing her until she called my name.

"Barbara," she repeated. But I couldn't talk to her either. She had done this. Dr. Howe would never have done such a thing without her encouragement. And no one else in the hospital would have helped him. She followed me out the main entrance and to the car. "What's wrong? Is it one of the children?"

Finally I looked at her. "He *fired* me," I said, my rage threatening to boil into ugly tears. "Dr. Howe lied and said I used you to get *him* to go out with *me*."

She processed this for a moment. "Well, that's just a misunderstanding, then," she said resolutely. "I'll go talk to him and—"

I shook my head, a fat tear spilling out of my eye and down my right cheek. "You don't understand," I said. "It doesn't matter. It was Dr. Howe or me. And they don't need me like they need him."

"But—"

I opened the car door. "I'm going home. I've had enough humiliation for one day. You can come with me, or you can stay. Gloria can call you a taxi home."

She opened the passenger door and got in without a word. I wiped at my eyes angrily as she handed me a Kleenex.

"I'll figure out how to fix this," she said, her mouth set in a firm line.

"You did enough," I said, and we rode home in silence except for an occasional sniffle as I fought back the flood of tears that threatened to wash me away.

39

I composed myself before the kids came home. This wasn't their burden to carry, and their childhoods had already been so heavy.

As they sat at the kitchen table doing their homework, a snack of apple slices spread with peanut butter on a plate between them, I thought maybe this was for the best. I would be home more. They deserved a mother who focused solely on them.

But was that all I would ever be now? An empty vessel of a mother whose only adult interactions came from the mother-in-law who refused to leave and the occasional chitchat at school drop-off or the park?

Just a couple of years earlier, being a mom was enough. But then I'd had Harry. And Bobby wasn't in school yet. Now, my job gave me such purpose. I couldn't imagine a life in which waxing the floor was the highlight of my day until the kids came home from school.

"Mama?" Susie asked.

I shook my head to clear it. "I'm sorry, honey. What do you need?"

"Is this right?" she asked, turning her page toward me.

I went through the long division, carrying the two. "Yes, sweetheart, you got it." I leaned down to kiss the top of her head.

It would have to be enough. I had tried making a difference outside the home and failed. But unlike Icarus, who also flew too close to the sun, I was still here. And I could make a difference to my children, even if learning that I couldn't soar because a man would always be capable of melting my wings was a difficult pill to swallow.

"What would you like for dinner tonight?" I asked, blinking away the tears that pricked at my eyes. "I'll make whatever you want."

⁓

When the kids went into school the next morning, Janet looked me up and down, taking in my pants and blouse. "Not going to the hospital today?"

I shook my head. "Not anymore. Unless one of us gets injured. Though I suppose I'd have to go someplace else for treatment even now."

Janet gripped my elbow tightly. "Explain."

I gave the short version, and Janet was positively fuming by the time I had finished. She let out an expletive-laced stream about what Dr. Howe could go do to himself, his mother, and a two-ton rhinoceros.

"I tell Dada you said the *fupping* word again," Paula said.

"Glad she hasn't mastered her *k* sounds yet," Janet said quietly to me, then knelt down to Paula in the stroller. "Mama said, 'Ducking.'"

"Nuh uh."

"Yuh huh," Janet said.

"Nuh uh. I tell Dada."

"And when I tell Dada what that man did to Auntie Barbara, he's going to march down to that hospital and say even worse words to him, so drop it, short stack," Janet said. Then she rose and turned to me. "He doesn't get away with this."

My shoulders sagged. "He already did. It's over. Dr. Harper knows the truth, but he can't run the hospital without doctors. And Dr. Howe *is* a really gifted doctor even if he's the worst human on the planet." I could see the gears turning in Janet's head, but I put a hand on her shoulder. "I'm okay."

She looked at me for a long moment, then acquiesced. "You've always been okay," she said. "I'd have crumbled if I'd gone through half of what you have."

I desperately wanted to tell her that I wasn't actually okay. I wanted her to see it. To know it was a veneer thinner than the finest china. But I was too good at hiding it, even from her. And to admit I wasn't all right would be to open a floodgate that would include what hadn't happened with Eddie a couple of nights earlier, and I was terrified that our friendship couldn't withstand that one truth.

Or maybe that I just couldn't bear to let that one out.

"Listen, I hate to do this after you just took her Monday, but do you think you could take Paula for another couple of hours today? Now that you don't have work."

I nodded, and Janet was gone practically before she could say goodbye. I wondered if she was in the middle of her own crisis. Something I hadn't seen because I had been too wrapped up in my own problems for the last two years. She *had* been awfully despondent when I was there last. And this running off as soon as she could unload Paula. The chain-smoking outside. She had said with Paula insisting on her sleeping in her room, there was nothing going on with George, but was there something with someone else?

No. Janet would never cheat. Would she?

My shoulders slumped. I didn't know anymore. I didn't know anyone.

Paula sneezed, and I said "Bless you" automatically. Then I mentally shook myself by the shoulders. "Come on, little one," I said, faking a cheerfulness I couldn't imagine feeling. "Let's go to the park."

We stayed until Paula started to yawn, me pushing her in the swing and sitting in the sandbox with her as she happily dug and built castles that she immediately squashed. Then I brought her to my house, fed her lunch, and laid her down on my bed to nap. I had no idea when Janet would be back.

"You're being maudlin," I told myself out loud. Then I realized Ruth wasn't home either. I didn't think she had told me she was going out. No, I didn't *really* want to talk to her. But this was why I went to work in the first place. The quiet when I was home alone left too much room to mourn.

As I tidied up the already-clean kitchen, I told myself Dr. Howe was not going to defeat me. I could volunteer at the Hebrew Home. The elderly weren't my specialty, but it was certainly a mitzvah to brighten their days. And after living with Ruth, I wasn't going to foist myself on my own children later in life. Maybe I could earn some good cosmic grace by working there now before I ended up living there myself.

Okay, that thought was too depressing for words.

Children were much more my cup of tea. But the ancient secretary at the elementary school made volunteering there equally unappealing. I knew a few women, primarily divorcées, who had gone to work either in retail or secretarial jobs. And while I wasn't above either option, I loved the feeling of being most useful to people who needed it at the hospital. I had *been* one of those people. I knew firsthand what a difference I could make there.

There was always the library. I had a degree in English literature going unused. I thought guiltily of the Marilyn Kleinman novel sitting still unfinished on my nightstand. That's what I should do with my newfound free time—engage my brain instead of sitting and wallowing.

Later, that was. If I went back into my room for the book, I'd wake Paula.

Instead I poured myself a cup of coffee and took Pepper into the backyard so she wouldn't bark in the house, and sat on the chaise lounge, wishing the best-laid plans of mice and men hadn't gone so far astray.

40

Ruth told me she had errands to run on Thursday. "Will you be all right?" she asked.

I looked at her, wondering if she was secretly sneaking back to the hospital to volunteer and afraid to tell me. She had been cagey about answering where she was the day before, though truth be told, I was too down and still too angry to press her on it. "Yes. I'll be perfectly fine in my own home," I said, a bit more tartly than I intended. But really, why shouldn't she volunteer if she wanted to? I certainly understood the appeal. And it was better than her blowing up or redecorating my house.

That was an idea, I thought as I looked around my oppressively bright kitchen. I could peel the wallpaper off. I picked at a corner, but it had been applied too well to do it myself without a steamer. I did look in the basement before remembering I had loaned my steamer to Janet. The wallpaper would live to see another day after all.

I grabbed a hammer and nail and hung Susie's painting of a cardinal in the hall, started a load of laundry, and re-vacuumed the carpets, which still had track marks on them from the last time. And then, when the noise of the vacuum cleaner could no longer properly drown out my thoughts, I picked up the Marilyn Kleinman book and went out back to read in the sunshine. I debated going to the park, but I was sure to see other mothers I knew there, and I just wasn't up to the small talk yet.

The book proved just the distraction I needed, following the adventures of a girl with her aunt, who followed no one's rules, not even her own, and I found myself laughing by the third page.

I was engrossed in chapter six when the main character ran inside to answer the ringing phone, only to be startled by how vivid the writing was. I swore I could hear the phone ringing as well.

Wait. No. That was actually my house phone. I jumped up from the chaise lounge, Pepper on my heels, as I dashed inside to answer it.

"Hello?" I said, panting slightly.

"Barbara? It's Donna Swanson."

I sighed. Donna was the head nurse. She had to know I didn't work there anymore. "Hi, Donna. Listen, I—"

"Your mother-in-law is here," Donna said.

"She's still volunteering, then?"

There was a long pause. "She's in a room, but hasn't been seen by a doctor yet."

For a moment, I thought this was a trick again. But there was no way she would do that to me a second time. Not even Ruth. Not after costing me my job. Would she? "What did she come in for?"

"They're evaluating that now. But I think you need to come down here."

"This is real?"

Donna didn't hesitate this time. "I wouldn't have called if I didn't think you needed to be here."

Shirley calling was one thing. But Donna meant business. I glanced at the clock. There was still plenty of time before the kids got out of school, so I'd call Janet from the hospital if I wouldn't be out on time. "Let me just grab my purse," I said. "I'll be right there."

I drove quickly, trying not to think the worst. But I was also still angry at her for the last time I was called to the hospital and its disastrous outcome. So as awful as it was to wish for her to actually be ill, I would take that over some harebrained scheme to get my job back.

I was there in under fifteen minutes, but as I pulled onto the hospital campus, I raised my sunglasses onto my head to make sure I was seeing what I thought I was seeing.

Dozens of women, most in white, some in red-and-white striped pinafores, completely blocked the main entrance to the building with large signs on sticks. Another woman in a vivid pink suit and matching pillbox hat stood on a soapbox with a megaphone at her mouth.

"—unacceptable work environment," she was saying to cheers. "No one should have to worry that they'll be harassed at work—especially in a profession where you've dedicated your lives to helping others."

"Bring Barbara back!" Someone yelled from the crowd, and the rest of the women took up the chant. My eyes widened, and I pulled quickly into a parking spot. I had to stop this. It wasn't appropriate at all.

I stepped out of the car and made my way toward the crowd, noting doctors and patients hanging out of windows, watching the commotion. But it looked like nearly every woman who worked at the hospital, including service staff, was out in front.

"There she is!" a voice called, and suddenly I found myself in the middle of a swarm of women embracing me and welcoming me back. I tried to extricate myself, only to find Gloria taking my arm and attempting to pull me through the throng.

"Come on," she said.

"What is this?" I asked twice because she didn't hear me over the chanting at first. "Where's Ruth? Is she okay?"

"Ruth is fine," Gloria yelled back at me. I was too stunned to even be mad that I had fallen for a trick about her health twice now. "We're not letting you go without a fight."

When I reached the front of the crowd, Janet emerged and hugged me tightly. "You did this?" I asked.

"Ruth and I did," she said. "As soon as you told me, I went to talk to her, and then we called Beverly."

I looked over her shoulder at the woman in the suit—I knew her from synagogue. Beverly Diamond had taken the community by storm last year when she threw her campaign manager husband out for cheating, only to become the campaign manager herself for the opposing candidate. Now she wrote a politics column for women in *The Washington Post*. I had always liked her, but I hadn't been around a lot in the last two years.

"Barbara," she said warmly, wrapping an arm around my shoulder. "So glad you could make it."

"What is all this?" I asked again.

Beverly smiled warmly. "This," she said gesturing toward the crowd, "is a strike."

"A strike? But what about the patients?"

"The doctors are on duty until the nurses' demands are met."

"There's a skeleton crew inside still," Gloria said. "For the critical care patients and emergencies."

I felt a lot less certain than Beverly looked. "But what if the hospital just fires them all?" There were a lot of women here whose families depended on them for these jobs. I would never sleep again if I cost them their jobs, even though I didn't organize any of this.

"They won't," Beverly said confidently. "That's why they have a union."

I was so confused. "But you're not a nurse or in their union," I said. "What are you doing here?"

She smiled again. "Representing you."

"Are you a lawyer now?"

"No," she said, pointing a thumb over her shoulder at a very grumpy-looking man who stood behind her. "But he is. Barbara Feldman, meet Stuart Friedman."

The name rang a bell. "Wasn't he—?"

"He's Senator Landau's chief of staff," Beverly said smoothly. "And he's here as a personal favor to me, so don't you worry about money. Right, Stuart?"

The grumpy man nodded, which somehow made him look even more cross. But he held out a hand, and I shook it. "Nice to meet you," I said.

"Likewise," he said. Then he checked his watch. "Let's get this over with. I need to get back to the office."

"Michael can function without you for an afternoon," Beverly said, completely unfazed by his attitude. "But yes, let's take care of this so that the patients can get back to getting the care they deserve. Shall we?" She gestured toward the front door of the hospital.

"Shall we what?" I asked, my anxiety rising as I looked at the entrance. I was back to dreading walking into that building.

"Get you your job back," Beverly said gently.

"I don't think—"

"We're not going back to work without you," Donna said, appearing at my shoulder. "Any of us."

I looked at her. "Why?"

"You stood up for us," Gloria said. "We're just returning the favor."

"Dr. Howe has terrorized the nurses long enough," Donna said. "That ends today. One way or another."

"There's only one way," Beverly said firmly. "The only person Stuart here has ever lost to was me. And I haven't lost yet."

Buoyed by Gloria on one side and Janet on the other, I followed Beverly and Stuart through the doors of the hospital, across the lobby, into the elevator, and eventually across the hall to Dr. Harper's office, where Ruth and Mrs. Kline stood in front of the door, their arms crossed in matching stances of determination.

"What—?"

"Making sure he doesn't sneak out," Ruth said, embracing me quickly but fiercely. "I'm sorry, Barbara. I never meant for this to happen. But we're going to fix it."

I stared at the indomitable woman in front of me, humbled by her admission of guilt. "It's okay," I said slowly. "Even if this doesn't work. I know you meant well."

She patted my arm and started to say something else, but Mrs. Kline spoke first. "I was never kind to you," she said. "But you made sure I was treated fairly every time. When Ruth told me what happened, I wanted to be here."

Mrs. Kline coming to my defense. Clearly I was downstairs in a coma because I would have assumed I would marry Dr. Howe before that would happen.

"Thank you," I stammered.

"Are you ready?" Beverly asked me.

"No," I said honestly. "I'm still pretty blindsided by all this."

"That's okay," she said. "It's actually better that you didn't call me or start the strike yourself." She squared her shoulders. "Come on, Stuart. Time to do an honest day's work."

The irritable expression disappeared. "After you," he said, grinning. "I do love watching you eviscerate people—*other* people, that is."

She elbowed him with a playfulness that surprised me. They were clearly close. I remembered gossip from the campaign, when people said Beverly was completely at odds with Michael Landau's childhood best friend who was running his campaign until she came barreling into their lives.

Beverly rapped firmly on the door. A moment later, Dr. Harper's head emerged. He saw Ruth and Mrs. Kline and started to retreat again, but Stuart put a foot in the doorway.

"Dr. Harper," Beverly said, sticking out her hand. "Beverly *Gelman* Diamond." She stressed her maiden name because her father had been a prominent congressman for years. "My associate"—she pointed to Stuart—"and I are here today to talk to you about the wrongful termination of Barbara Feldman."

Dr. Harper looked at me plaintively. "Barbara," he said. "Please call this off. I did what I had to do."

"Mrs. Feldman had nothing to do with the strike," Beverly said. "The nurses called that on their own and are refusing to return unless their demands are met. May we come in? I think we would all like to see this resolved today."

Stuart glowered menacingly, and Dr. Harper opened his office door. Beverly gestured for me to take one of the seats across from his desk, and she settled herself in the other. "Chairs?" she asked Stuart.

He rolled his eyes but complied, going to a nearby waiting area to procure seats for himself, Ruth, and Donna, who had followed us inside. Beverly asked Gloria, Janet, and Mrs. Kline to wait in the hall.

"Now," Beverly said, when everyone was settled. "After speaking at great length with Nurse Swanson, Nurse Ramirez, and the elder Mrs. Feldman, I believe you have two problems that need to be addressed in order for this strike to end."

"Two?" Dr. Harper asked, visibly distressed by the delegation in his office.

"First, Barbara Feldman needs to be reinstated. The situation that Dr. Howe presented to you is not an accurate representation of what occurred, and according to all parties who brought the matter to my attention, you already know that."

"I—but—no—" Dr. Harper sputtered.

"Second," Beverly continued, "you'll need to address the overall climate of harassment that you have allowed to continue for far too long from the aforementioned Dr. Howe. The nurses are unwilling to continue to work in such conditions, *especially* without a liaison like Mrs. Feldman who is comfortable bringing issues of harassment to your attention."

"I can't run a hospital without doctors," Dr. Harper said. "If we take every nurse's word over every doctor's, we'll never have anyone willing to work here."

"Can you run a hospital without nurses?" Beverly asked immediately. "Conditions seem a little . . . thin . . . today."

"We can hire more nurses," Dr. Harper said, but his voice was smaller than usual.

"You certainly could," Beverly said. "But they won't be from the Maryland Nurses Association, which likely means they won't be certified. Is that legal, Mr. Friedman?"

Stuart shook his head. "Maryland is a mandatory union state for nurses."

"And unfortunately for you, Dr. Harper, the MNA has pledged full support for the nurses at this hospital. So I *am* afraid you have a choice to make."

He was silent for a long moment, the only sound the ticking of the clock on the wall behind us. "I can discipline Dr. Howe," he said finally. "But I can't reinstate Mrs. Feldman."

"More the pity," Beverly said. "I'm afraid that's one of *their* conditions for returning to work. We also have a patient willing to testify that Mrs. Feldman was the one who ensured she was given fair treatment. I believe you know Mrs. Kline? And while, no, there is no current law on the books saying that Mrs. Feldman cannot be terminated for refusing the advances of a superior, I have firsthand knowledge that one is going to be introduced within the next year. However, if you'd like to try your luck in the courts, I have a feeling this case would go all the way to the top." She turned to Stuart. "Mr. Friedman, which way do you think the Supreme Court would go on this one?"

"Hard to say," he said. "But rulings of late have been trending more and more in favor of women."

"Would it be *Feldman v. Harper* or *Feldman v. Rock Creek Memorial*?" Beverly asked.

"Rock Creek Memorial," Stuart said. "Unless the hospital board chooses not to back Dr. Harper."

"Interesting," Beverly said, then turned back to Dr. Harper. "So if you'd like the case guaranteeing women cannot be fired for refusing sexual advances named after either you or your hospital, please, stand by your decision."

It was a struggle to keep my mouth closed, and it felt like an hour before anyone responded.

And when the silence was broken, at first none of us even heard what Dr. Harper said.

"Excuse me?" Beverly asked. "I didn't quite catch that."

"You win," he said, louder, raising his eyes, which hung above dark circles I had never seen on him before.

I still hadn't moved. But Beverly and Stuart stood, and Beverly extended her hand across the desk to Dr. Harper. "Thank you so much for your time today, Dr. Harper. I'll inform the nurses that they can return to their duties. Barbara will return to work on Monday."

"Tuesday," someone said, and I was surprised to hear the word coming out of my own mouth. "I don't work on Mondays."

Beverly smiled at me. "Tuesday it is, then. Good day, Dr. Harper."

41

Dazed, I walked out of Dr. Harper's office as Stuart held the door for us. "Aforementioned?" he said with a smirk as Beverly passed him.

"Well, it worked, didn't it?" she asked.

"The Supreme Court thing was good, I'll give you that. But Michael isn't going to like you talking about his civil rights bill before it's introduced."

There was a twinkle in Beverly's eye as she replied. "Who exactly do you think is tweaking the wording on that bill?"

Stuart shook his head. "I'm never going to be rid of you, am I?"

"No, darling," she said, patting his arm. "And you wouldn't want to be either."

He chuckled, and Janet took my hand.

I looked at her. "I—why did you do this? *How* did you do this?"

She squeezed my hand. "I know you think you want to do everything on your own, but you can't."

"No one can," Beverly said. "I couldn't have left home to work on the campaign last year without my mother and my best friend."

"And the nursing staff won't work without you," Donna said. "It's that simple."

I felt tears prickling at my eyes, but I willed them back down. "I don't know what to say. Does that mean I can never decide to retire?"

"Not anytime soon," Gloria said, smiling. "But there's a big difference between you choosing to leave and Dr. Howe forcing you out."

My heart sank at the mention of his name. "He's going to *hate* me. I don't know how much good I'll be able to do anyone if he's out to get me at every turn."

"If he tries to retaliate against you in any way, you call me," Beverly said firmly. "But my guess is that Dr. Harper makes him uncomfortable enough to leave. I don't think he wants another meeting with us."

"With you," Stuart said. "I think I said ten words."

"Yes, but your presence is menacing enough," Beverly said. They bickered like an old married couple. If they were characters in the novel I was reading, they would be in love by the end of the book. But this was real life, and if mom gossip was anything to go by—and it usually was—her affections lay elsewhere.

"Do you want to tell the nurses?" Donna asked me.

I shook my head. The idea of speaking into a megaphone in front of the crowd out front . . . My eyes drifted through the front door of the hospital, and I saw cameras. "Is the press here?" I asked.

Mrs. Kline grinned. "I may have called a newsroom or four."

"You did?" Ruth asked her.

"Well, I called them multiple times about my treatment at the hospital. This is just the first time they came."

"Because it's actually something this time," Ruth said. Mrs. Kline put her hand through Ruth's arm companionably—an act of friendship with someone of a different religion that could have knocked me over with a feather.

"Thank you," I said to the pair of them. Then I turned to Donna. "I don't want to speak to the press though."

"I'll handle the press," Beverly said. "Nurse Swanson, would you like to inform the staff, and then I'll give a statement to the press? Or would you like me to do both?"

"Call me Donna," she said. "And I'll tell my staff."

"Wonderful," Beverly said, bending to pick up the megaphone that had been left by the door. "Mrs. Feldman and Janet, wait here with Barbara. Donna, take this, and go tell them. I'll talk to the press immediately after you finish. While I do that"—she turned back to me—"the three of you walk around the other side of the crowd to Barbara's car. I'll be distraction enough to keep you out of the newspapers."

"Do you think that's wise?" Stuart asked quietly.

"Do you think this is my first time speaking to the press?" she asked, straightening her undented pillbox hat.

"Lead the way," he said, holding open the front door.

Donna squeezed my shoulder, then walked out first, smiling broadly to the assembled staff. She raised the megaphone to her lips as she reached the front. "We won," she said as a whooping cheer went up. "Mrs. Feldman returns to work on Tuesday. We return to work now." There was a lot of chatter in the crowd. "Come on," Donna said. "Chop-chop."

Buzzing, the nurses filed back into the building, most stopping to embrace me as they passed.

"Showtime," Beverly said.

"Beverly," I said, stopping her. "Thank you."

"Of course," she said simply, as if she did this every day. Then again, maybe she did. "As my mother says, never underestimate what determined women can do."

And then she was gone, walking confidently toward the photographers and reporters, Stuart on her heels.

"That's our cue," Janet said, linking arms with me. She glanced at her left wrist. "Besides, it's almost time to get the kids."

Gloria hugged me. "If anyone calls and tells me Ruth is in the hospital again, I'm not coming," I said.

"Fair," she said. "But would you have come if we told you the truth?"

"Absolutely not."

She grinned. "That's what I told Donna. I'll see you Tuesday."

Janet, Ruth, and I walked to our cars unmolested by the press, Mrs. Kline following behind us. "I don't know what to say."

"I've been thinking I want to do something like you did when Paula goes off to school," Janet said. "Not at a hospital though. I don't like blood. Or sick people."

"Paula! Who's watching her?"

Janet laughed. "She's fine. I made George take the day off work."

My jaw dropped. "George took the day off work to watch her?"

"Like I said, no one can do this alone. When I lost my mom, and then you lost Harry and I didn't feel like I could ask you for help, I thought I had to. And it was overwhelming."

"You always could ask me."

"I know that now," Janet said. "And that goes two ways." She nodded toward Ruth, who was talking to Mrs. Kline. "Three, honestly. I know having someone in your house is a lot. Hell, I don't want George there some days. But she's not so bad, that one."

"Even if she becomes your stepmother next?"

Janet pulled a cigarette from her purse, put it between her lips, and lit it. "Don't you start with that," she said. "Besides, that might mean my father moves in with you too."

I laughed. "What's it matter anymore? The more the merrier."

"Better you than me," Janet said, offering me the cigarette. I shook my head. "I'll see you at school. Unless you want me to grab your kids too?"

"No, I'll see you there."

She wrapped me in a quick embrace, then got into her car. "Get out of here before you wind up in the *Post*."

"Yes, ma'am."

"Louise drove me," Ruth said. "Do you mind if I ride home with you?"

"Climb in."

"I'll call you this weekend," Ruth said to Mrs. Kline.

"See that you do. Goodbye, Ruth. Goodbye, Barbara."

"Goodbye, Mrs. Kline," I said, still shocked that she had shown up for me. "And thank you."

Ruth closed her door, and I put the car in reverse to back out of the parking spot, checking in the rearview mirror that Beverly was still entertaining the press.

"This . . . ," I said, shaking my head. "What just happened?"

"I do try to clean up my messes," Ruth said.

"How about the wallpaper in my kitchen?"

"What about the wallpaper? It's lovely."

"It's awful."

"Well, I can't help it if you just don't have good taste," Ruth said.

I started to laugh. "Do you want to go home or come with me to pick up the kids?"

She hesitated. "I'd love to come with you. If that's all right."

I reached over and put a hand on top of hers, where it rested on the bench seat. "It's more than all right," I said. "Maybe we'll take them for ice cream too."

"Before dinner?"

I grinned wickedly. "The night before you arrived? Ice cream *was* dinner."

She made a *tsk-tsk* sound. "I see I came just in time, then."

I shrugged. "I can't help it if you just don't have good taste."

Ruth laughed. "I suppose I deserve that."

～

That night, after the children were asleep, I went down to the kitchen and poured myself a glass of brandy, then I went to the back door, flipped on the patio light, and went outside with my drink. I settled myself on the chaise lounge and looked up at the stars.

"Did you send her?" I asked Harry, thinking about how Janet had said none of us could do this alone. Maybe he did, to teach me that lesson. But Ruth seemingly *had* done it all alone. And look where she was now. Still alone. Maybe Harry knew that and didn't want it for either of us.

There was no answer, not that there ever really was.

But then—a star streaked across the sky, disappearing as it entered the atmosphere.

"I'm going to take that as a yes," I said, raising my glass in an imaginary toast. "I don't think I'll ever stop missing you. But if this was you, aggravating as she is, thank you."

42

With work settled, we fell into a routine that I wouldn't call uncomfortable. And before I knew it, it was the beginning of June. Ruth's two-week visit had stretched to three months, with no end in sight.

Then again, she never said two weeks.

I had.

I glanced back through the calendar on the refrigerator before fastening it on the new month. My circled first day on our own long abandoned. And I realized that I had resigned myself to her presence. She no longer redecorated or brought home animals or set fires—though I supposed I couldn't entirely rule that one out from happening again. She still complained about my cooking and tried to feed us inedible meals.

But life had calmed down.

Until she came home from a date with Mr. Greene, slamming the door behind her and storming upstairs to her room.

The children hadn't even finished dinner yet. I looked at the two of them.

"What was *that*?" Bobby asked.

"I'm not sure," I said, standing and putting my napkin on the table. I hadn't expected teenage behavior until Susie started dating in seven or eight years. "I'll go check on her."

I climbed the stairs, wondering if this was how my mother felt when I came home from a date with Donnie Goldblum after he tried to stick his hand up my blouse. Though I doubted Ruth would be as shocked as I had been. And she had the hatpin Mr. Greene had given her after all.

I knocked gently on the door. "Ruth?" I asked. "Is everything okay?"

"No," she said. The door remained shut. If one of my kids were inside, I would have opened it, but it felt wrong with Ruth, even in my house.

"Can I come in?"

I heard the lock turning, but the door stayed shut. I wasn't positive if she had locked it or unlocked it, but I tried the knob, and it opened. Ruth was sitting on the bed, facing the wall, her back to me.

"Are you okay?"

"The absolute nerve of that man," she huffed.

I scanned her for blood. The hatpin had looked sharp. "You didn't use the hatpin, did you?" I asked. I really needed to call Janet immediately if she had.

"No," Ruth said.

"What happened?"

"He—he—he *proposed*."

"He *what*?"

"We've been seeing each other maybe a couple of months," she said. "The very idea that he would think . . . no . . . I'm not burying another husband. I'm not. I'm not doing it. I'm not. I—"

"Shh," I said, sitting on the bed next to her and putting an arm around her. "It's okay. You don't have to do anything you don't want to do." Her shoulders heaved as she breathed heavily. "You have a home here as long as you want it."

She looked at me in surprise. "I do?"

"You do."

"What about when I'm old and doddering and can't be of any help?"

"Ruth," I said, "you caused an explosion in my kitchen and got me fired. Do you really think you can do anything worse when you're older? Besides, once the kids go off to college, I don't want to be all alone."

"You could remarry."

"So could you. And sooner than me apparently."

She shuddered. "So we'll just be two lonely old widows alone in this house until I die, and then you become Susie's problem?"

I shrugged. "Or Bobby's. But we won't be lonely until then. We'll have each other. And I get the feeling you're not leaving us anytime soon."

Ruth shook her head. "If I've learned one thing in this life, it's that you never know when someone's time is up."

"How old were your parents?" I asked, genuinely curious. Harry had a few memories of them from his early childhood, but I was fuzzy on when—and how—they had died.

"Not that old. My mother was about my age. Cancer. When she was gone, my father simply gave up."

"Was that before . . . ?" I trailed off, not wanting to bring up Abe's death.

She nodded. "In five years, I lost both of my parents, my husband, and one sister. In ten, I had lost everyone except Harry and my sister Alice."

I tried to imagine being truly alone. But there was no way to imagine that without experiencing it. What would have happened to Harry had something happened to Ruth in those years?

A tear trickled out of the corner of my eye, and I wiped at it to keep her from seeing. I wished desperately that I had been better about bringing the children to see Ruth in the two years after Harry had died. How must she have felt, truly isolated, in that house?

"It's hard to move on," she said finally. "From that much loss."

The loss of Harry alone had nearly crushed me under its weight.

"I'm so sorry," I said. "I shouldn't have pushed you to go out with Mr. Greene. I thought . . ."

"You thought you were getting rid of me," she said flatly.

"I did," I admitted. "But I also thought I was helping two people find some happiness. The way you talked to each other at the birthday party . . . I thought—"

"I know," Ruth said. "I thought the same with those men for you."

"Maybe neither of us was cut out to be a matchmaker," I said. "Maybe it has to happen on its own. If at all."

"Matchmakers in 1963," Ruth said, a ghost of a smile on her face. "No. The world has moved on."

"The kids are still finishing dinner," I said. "Come down and eat with us?"

"I couldn't eat," she said.

"I'll be forced to throw out the leftovers if you don't."

She shook her head, but the mood had lifted. "Another knife to my heart. You're a cold woman, Barbara Feldman."

"You don't mean that."

"No," Ruth agreed, rising from the bed. "I don't. But if you throw those leftovers out, I'm redecorating the whole house again."

"Oh good," I said, and she looked up at me. "You're feeling better."

"A little. However, if he starts showing up with singing telegrams again, I'm going to use that hatpin."

"Just don't kill him," I warned. "I'd bet Beverly Diamond could argue you out of charges for assault, but murder is entirely different. And Janet and Eddie would be miffed."

"Marriage," she said, shaking her head again. "I need a husband like I need a *loch in kop*. The old fool."

I secretly disagreed—Mr. Greene was definitely preferable to a hole in the head—but I told myself to ask Eddie to tell his father to slow down. She might come around yet.

"They're good for opening pickle jars," I said.

"So is a whack with a spoon."

She had a point there. "Come on," I said. "I made apricot chicken. You'll love it."

"*Apricot* chicken? Oy."

"It was one of Harry's favorites. I haven't made it in a long time."

"Barbara," Ruth said, turning serious. "I have something to tell you that you may not like. But Harry grew up eating my food. He was being polite to you."

"Maybe so," I said, putting an arm around her shoulders and trying not to laugh thinking about Harry's description of the way his childhood dog used to waddle from all the inedible food he slipped her.

43

Dr. Howe took a job at another hospital, officially becoming someone else's problem. I *might* have picked up a cake from Eddie's store to celebrate the occasion. But Gloria provided the confetti.

And even Dr. Harper had a small piece of cake. "No hard feelings?" he asked me.

I hesitated briefly. There were some hard feelings. But my year of working for him combined with the genuine compassion he showed me when Harry died were enough to tell a white lie. He would never fully understand the reign of terror that Dr. Howe had held the nurses under because he had never experienced anything of the sort. And in the end, he did the right thing—even if Beverly Diamond had forced his hand. Besides, I would get over it. Eventually. If I could make peace with Ruth, there were few grudges that I would hold.

"Let's put it behind us," I said, extending a hand.

He set his piece of cake down on the counter in the nurses' lounge and took it.

"Barbara?" Donna asked, scanning the room for me.

"Duty calls," I told him, then went to Donna. "What's happening?"

"Um—your mother-in-law brought a . . . friend . . . to volunteer today."

Did Ruth have friends? Then it dawned on me. "You don't mean—?"

Donna nodded. "I'm at a loss here."

"Better than having her as a patient?" I asked uncertainly.

"She showed up for you last week," Donna said. "Maybe you can handle this one."

"What's she doing?"

"Bossing the nurses around like when she was a patient. Can you talk some sense into her?"

I grinned tightly and rolled my eyes. "I'm never going to get rid of her either now, am I?"

"It's looking that way."

"What floor is she on?"

"Two."

"I'll take care of it," I said. "Go have some cake. It's from Greene's."

Donna smiled. "Don't mind if I do." She started to walk away and then spotted Dr. Harper. "Dr. Harper, this is the nurses' lounge. You have your own space for doctors."

He looked at the floor. "Right. I'm sorry. I—"

"I'm teasing," Donna said as I walked away.

I hummed to myself as I took the stairs down a floor, feeling better than I had in a long time.

I found Mrs. Kline at the nurses' station, wearing a red-and-white striped pinafore.

"—absolutely needs an electrocardiogram. Now you put that in his chart and go get Dr. Lefkowitz and tell him he's performing one."

"Mrs. Kline," I said, putting a hand on her shoulder.

She jumped at my touch and turned around, looking relieved when she saw me. "Good. Barbara will agree with me. Tell them that Mr. Bellflower needs an electrocardiogram."

"Let's take a little walk," I said.

"A walk? A man is going to die if we don't help him."

"Maybe," I said. "But his care isn't up to us. Come on. I'll get you a cup of coffee."

"I don't need coffee," she said shrilly, and I realized that was likely true. She was practically vibrating as it was.

"Well, I do," I said. Especially if I had to deal with Mrs. Kline on a weekly basis. "And we need to have a little talk. So come with me. Please."

She leveled a glare at the nurse on duty. "I expect to see Dr. Lefkowitz in there when I get back," she said, then turned to walk with me. "Let's keep this quick. The standard of care is abysmal if I don't stay on them."

"My dear Mrs. Kline—it *is* Mrs., isn't it? You didn't go to medical school?"

A bony finger appeared in my face. "Don't you get smart with me."

"I wouldn't dream of it. But did you ever notice that every time I came to talk to you, it was to agree with what the doctors and nurses said?"

She made a sour face. "I did."

"That's because I'm neither a doctor nor a nurse. I started off as a volunteer, doing what the candy stripers do. If I noticed something amiss, I would bring it to a doctor's or nurse's attention, but it was never my job to diagnose or order tests."

"Well, after so much time here, I have a greater understanding—"

"Mrs. Kline," I interrupted gently. "We all have a role to play. And everyone appreciates that you want to help, especially after how . . . contentiously . . . you sometimes behaved as a patient. But to do so, you're going to need to trust the doctors and nurses to do their jobs."

"But they're not—"

"Did they miss a diagnosis on you?"

"No, but—"

"Like I said, if you have a concern, feel free to ask about it. But you *cannot* boss the doctors or nurses around if you want to volunteer here."

She looked at me for a long time, then opened her mouth to reply when the hospital's public address system cut her off. "Dr. Lefkowitz, you're needed on two immediately. Dr. Lefkowitz report to two immediately."

"See?" Mrs. Kline crowed. "I told you the patient needed an electro—"

The PA went off again. "Mrs. Barbara Feldman, report to the nurses' station on two immediately."

I swore softly. "We'll finish this later," I said, walking off as quickly as I could. I had only been paged three times—twice to deal with Mrs. Kline having a meltdown, and once when the school called to tell me that Bobby had fallen off the monkey bars and was bleeding from the head. With Mrs. Kline *not* currently hurling insults at the staff, the likelihood of it being the school calling went up dramatically.

Donna was standing at the nurses' station when I reached it. "Which kid?" I asked.

"I'm sorry?"

"The school. Which kid is hurt?" She looked confused. "Oh, just give me the phone."

"Sit," Donna said, pulling out a chair behind the desk.

I looked around and saw the phone still in the cradle, no lights blinking to indicate a hold. "Are they on their way in an ambulance?" I asked, fear locking my throat in a vise grip.

"It's not the kids," Donna said gently, pushing me down into the chair. She took a deep breath. "Ruth collapsed in a patient's room. Dr. Lefkowitz is with her right now. We think she's having a heart attack."

I looked at her, the tension draining from my shoulders. "What is she trying to trick me into doing now? Did she put you up to this? Or is it a Gloria prank?"

"Barbara—"

"I'm not falling for it a third time," I said, standing up. "Now if you'll excuse me, I want to finish my talk with Mrs. Kline and make sure she understood me loud and clear."

"Barbara!" Donna said, taking both of my arms at the elbow. "Ruth actually collapsed."

For a few seconds, her words didn't connect. And then I found myself back in the chair, the room spinning.

44

"Where is she?" I asked weakly, trying to stand up. "I have to go to her."

"She's with Dr. Lefkowitz now," Donna said soothingly. "Let him examine her first."

"No," I said, forcing myself out of the chair. "Harry was alone. I'm—" I choked on the words. "I'm not letting that happen again. Where is she?"

"Room 237," Donna said. "But I want you calm before you go in there."

"If this is a trick—"

"Barbara," Donna repeated. "Dr. Lefkowitz is the best. You've said it yourself a million times."

He didn't save Harry, I thought. Which was entirely unfair. Harry arrived too late, and I knew that. But rationality had gone out the window.

I took off down the hall toward room 237, Donna hot on my heels, talking, but I couldn't process it all.

". . . just next door," she was saying. "And she dropped. The patient called for a nurse. Should have caught it soon enough—"

I didn't knock or wait to be admitted. Instead I flung the door open to see Ruth in the bed, an oxygen mask on her face. Her dress was unbuttoned to her brassiere, and Dr. Lefkowitz stood with a transducer on her chest. Her eyes opened at the sound of my entrance, and I hurried to her side, taking her hand.

"Ruth, I—"

"Easy now," Dr. Lefkowitz said. "I don't want to have to redo this if we don't have to."

"Is she—?"

"She's stable," he said. "I don't think it was a heart attack, but I want to rule it out. Now, you can stay, as long as you can be quiet and calm," he said. Then he glanced down at Ruth. "And if the patient wants you here, of course."

Ruth nodded, and Dr. Lefkowitz gestured for me to pull up a chair and have a seat. I dropped Ruth's hand only long enough to do so, then sat at her bedside, gripping her hand in mine. I looked down and saw it was her left. I squeezed, and she didn't squeeze back. I had been working at the hospital long enough to know that wasn't a good sign despite what Dr. Lefkowitz had said.

Please, I thought, over and over again in an unorganized sort of prayer, too desperate to find other words.

It felt like an eternity before Dr. Lefkowitz replaced the transducer. "Everything looks good preliminarily," he said, removing his gloves. "I want to analyze these results and see what your blood work looks like before we officially say it isn't your heart, but all the valves seem to be functioning as they should. Is there any history of heart disease in your family?"

"Yes," Ruth said.

I shook my head. "No, he means your birth family," I said. "Her husband and son did," I told Dr. Lefkowitz.

"No, then," she said, her voice small. "I suppose not."

Dr. Lefkowitz looked sympathetic and glanced toward me with a small nod. He remembered. "Any new stress in your life?"

"No," Ruth said.

"Well . . . ," I said. Ruth turned to look at me. "The man she's been seeing proposed."

"Congratulations," Dr. Lefkowitz said.

I shook my head. "She turned him down."

"I see," Dr. Lefkowitz said. "Yes, that fits the bill."

"I told you dating him was a bad idea," Ruth said weakly. "He gave me a heart attack."

"Not quite," Dr. Lefkowitz said. "I believe he gave you an acute anxiety attack instead."

"Anxiety?" Ruth argued. "No, Doctor, this was real pain."

"Acute anxiety attacks are commonly confused for heart attacks," Dr. Lefkowitz assured her. "And I can promise you, they frequently manifest with physical symptoms like chest pain or pressure and struggling to breathe."

Ruth didn't reply.

"What—what does that mean for recovery?" I asked.

"Well, again, I want to see the blood work to completely rule out a heart issue, but if we can do that, management usually involves removing the source of stress and sometimes seeing a psychiatrist if the issue persists."

Ruth scoffed and tried to get out of the bed, but I put a hand on her arm. She shook me off and crossed her arms but stopped struggling. "I don't need my head examined."

"Shush," I said. "He said *sometimes* seeing a psychiatrist."

"Either way," Dr. Lefkowitz continued, "we'll keep you overnight for monitoring. And if my suspicions are correct, I'd like you to consider taking up a relaxing hobby, like knitting or gardening."

"I volunteer here," Ruth said. "That's my hobby."

I sighed. It wasn't a low-stress environment. I enjoyed that because it wasn't *my* stress, and I could help alleviate others'. But the number of times I had cried in my car after seeing heartbreak here . . . No, Ruth's days of volunteering were numbered. But—

"Actually," I said, "I have been meaning to talk to you about that." Ruth turned to look at me, her arms still crossed, a contentious look on her face. "School ends in just a couple of weeks. I was hoping you might be willing to watch the kids while I'm at work."

Her face softened. "You were?"

I hadn't given more than a fleeting thought to it, and when I had, it was with regret that she wasn't someone I could fully trust to do that, like I could with my own mother. But something had changed since the day she and Janet worked together to get my job back. And I found myself nodding.

"I'll be back in the fall, then," she said crisply.

"I think if you don't have any more incidents, we can certainly re-evaluate come September," Dr. Lefkowitz said. He glanced at his watch. "I'll be back to check on you in an hour or so. And I'll let you know as soon as we have the blood work results."

"Can you have a nurse call me with the results as well?" I asked.

A hint of a grin crossed the doctor's face. "As long as the patient consents to share her medical records with you."

"I blew up her stove," Ruth said bluntly. "It's the least I can do."

Dr. Lefkowitz looked confused, and I snorted out a laugh. Of all the times to bring that up.

"I'll leave you two to it, then," Dr. Lefkowitz said. "But get some rest. If you don't choose to, your body will make the choice for you, which is likely what happened today."

Ruth nodded. "I am tired. Thank you, Doctor."

"My pleasure," he said and left the room.

"Will you hand me the phone?" Ruth asked, gesturing to the one on the hospital nightstand behind me.

"Who are you calling?"

"Is that your business?"

"I have access to your medical records now, so yes."

She sighed. "Joseph."

"Maybe wait until you're home. Otherwise, he'll flood the hospital with flowers."

Ruth shook her head. "I'm ending things."

"Why?"

"You heard the doctor. I need to remove the source of stress."

"Ruth—"

"I've made up my mind."

"Please don't do anything rash."

She started to get up again, and I held up a hand, moving toward the phone. She settled and held out her hand. But instead of giving it to her, I unplugged the phone, crossed the room, and marched it down the hall to the nurses' station. "Don't you give this back to my mother-in-law," I said. "If she needs me, you call instead, understood?"

"Yes, ma'am," one of the younger nurses said, tucking the phone under the desk.

I returned to Ruth's room, where she was still in the bed, glaring at me. "You really are the most irritating woman," Ruth said.

"Don't you worry," I said. "You and I are neck and neck for that title."

Ruth lay back against the bed and closed her eyes. "I *am* awfully tired."

I glanced at my watch. "I need to go pick up the children. Do you want me to tell them you're back at your house for the evening instead of here?" They didn't need to worry about her heart.

She nodded. "Thank you."

I patted her hand. "I'll call to check on you."

One eye opened. "Will they let me have a phone for that?"

I grinned. "Maybe."

"Irritating woman," Ruth muttered.

I leaned over and kissed her forehead as her breathing slowed. Then I left to go pick up the kids.

45

I was nearly home, less than a block from the shopping center where Greene's was, when I heard a hiss followed by a loud *thwap thwap thwap* sound that repeated as the car veered to the right. I tried to steady the wheel, but it was no use, as I eventually pulled to a stop on the gravel shoulder.

After checking the mirror to make sure no cars were coming, I got out and quickly walked to the passenger side to see what had happened, only to discover my front right tire was completely flat.

I let out a small scream of frustration, kicking at the faulty tire, which only resulted in a shooting pain in my foot.

Suddenly, it was all too much. Harry. Ruth. Losing and then regaining my job. Everything. Now this. There was only so much one woman could take, and I'd had enough.

I sank down next to the car, ignoring the sharp gravel that tore my stockings, and wept for the life I had lost and the one I now had to live.

Three years ago, if I had gotten a flat tire, I would have walked to Greene's, called Harry, and he would have left work to come deal with my tire. Who did I have now?

Janet said no one could do it all alone, but I *was* alone. Ruth's parents had been her age when they died. What if Dr. Lefkowitz was wrong? What if she didn't make it through the night? How would I break the news to Susie and Bobby? How would they make it through one more loss so young? And what if something happened to me? What if it had been my left tire and I had veered into oncoming traffic? What then? I cried harder. I couldn't fix this. I couldn't fix *any* of this. Not for me. Not for the kids. My whole perfect little life had come crumbling down, and it didn't matter how much I tried to pretend I could do everything because the universe was just going to keep reminding me that Harry was gone, and any one of us could be next.

"Barbara?" I heard, eventually. My head was on my knees, but I knew the voice, which filled me with equal parts hope and despair right then. I felt someone crouch down beside me. "A customer came in and said there was a broken-down car and a woman crying," he said, settling next to me.

"Oh, Eddie," I sobbed.

He put an arm around me and let me continue to cry, smoothing my hair with his other hand. "It's okay," he said soothingly. "It's going to be okay."

"Nothing is okay," I said, picking up my head, not even caring what a mess I must be. "Nothing."

"It's just a flat tire," he said. "I can put your spare on, easy."

"It's not just a flat," I said. "It's everything. Ruth is in the hospital—you can't tell your father that—she's—"

"Is she all right?"

I nodded. "She thought it was a heart attack, but the cardiologist called it an . . ." I fumbled for the words he had used. "Acute . . . anxiety . . . something. Not serious. She can probably come home tomorrow, pending blood work. But I—I—" The tears started flowing too strongly to speak again.

"She'll be fine, then," he said. "We'll put the spare on. You can even take my car, and I'll go get you a new tire. Everything is going to be okay."

"Nothing is okay!" I said again. "What happens when you're not here next time?"

"You find a phone and you call me," he said. "And I will be there."

I shook my head. "I can't keep leaning on you. I'm not your sister. And I can't keep relying on the kindness of strangers."

"Easy there, Blanche," he said, and I could hear the hint of a smile in his voice even though I wasn't looking at him. "And we're hardly strangers. I've known you since you were eighteen."

"You know what I mean," I said mournfully.

"I'm here," Eddie said. "I'm not going anywhere. Let me help."

"But you will go someday. You'll get tired of helping the poor widow and her fatherless children, and what will I do then? Better you teach me to change the tire myself."

"I can do that if you want," he said lightly. "But not today. Not when you're this upset."

I took a deep breath, hiccuping slightly. "I'm okay," I said shakily, wiping at my eyes. I glanced down at my fingers, which came away black. "Oh no."

A piece of cloth came into my field of vision as Eddie handed me his handkerchief, which I used to try to wipe the mascara away. Then I looked up at Eddie and attempted a small smile of thanks.

"Do you want me to call Janet and have her pick Susie and Bobby up from school?" he asked.

I struggled to stand up. "What time is it?"

Eddie looked at his watch. "A couple of minutes past three."

"It's too late. She'll have already left. How long does it take to change a tire?"

"Take my car," Eddie said again. "I'll deal with all of this."

I looked down at myself. "My stockings are ruined," I said.

"Then take them off."

"What?"

"I'll turn around," he said. "Actually, I'll go get the jack out of your trunk while you take them off. You have one, right?"

"I have no idea."

"Well, that'll be lesson one when I teach you. Make sure you have a jack." Eddie stood up and walked around the back of the car to the driver's side. "I'm not looking, I promise."

"On the side of the road?"

"Sit in the passenger seat," Eddie said. "I'm just opening the trunk."

I did as he said, leaving the door open as I unclipped my stockings from their garters and rolled first the right, then the left down my legs and over my feet.

"Let me know when you're decent," Eddie called from behind the open trunk.

I pulled a compact out of my purse—my face was far from decent. I scrubbed under my eyes with Eddie's handkerchief, and then slipped my shoes back onto my now-bare feet. "I'm okay," I said.

"Probably better if you hop out," he said, offering me a hand, the jack in the other. "It's going to be a lot harder if the car is in the air." I took his hand and stood, then he reached into his pocket and pulled out his keys, which he passed to me. "I'll put the spare on, then take it over to Reed Brothers for a new tire. You know which car is mine, right? I can walk you over if not."

I looked at him for a long time. "Why are you so good to me?"

He held my eye for a moment, then looked down at the ground but didn't answer.

A tiny voice in my head told me to leave well enough alone. But the words came tumbling out of my mouth before I could stop them. "You're going to be a great husband someday when you meet the right girl."

"Not likely," he said, still looking at the ground.

"Why?" I asked. It came out as barely a whisper.

For a long moment he didn't reply. Then he lifted his eyes. "Because the right girl thinks of me like a brother."

I couldn't speak. I half wished he would take me in his arms, and half wished the ground would open up and swallow me whole right then and there.

Finally, I croaked out his name. "Eddie, I—"

"Don't," he said, turning back toward the car. "I already know. Just go pick up the kids so they're not worried."

"Eddie—"

"It's not a big deal," he said. "I'll bring your car back tonight. You can just leave the keys in mine if you don't want to see me."

I always want to see you, I thought. But the fear of what such a response would mean kept me frozen.

"Go on," he said. "You're going to be late."

I turned and ran toward the parking lot before the tears started to flow again in earnest.

46

Bobby didn't notice anything amiss, but Susie asked what was wrong, despite my sunglasses covering the mess that was my eye makeup. I sighed. Best to keep it simple. "Mommy got a flat tire on her way to get you. I cried a little."

"Why did you cry over a flat tire?" Bobby asked.

"Because she didn't know how to fix it, dummy," Susie said.

"Hey." I stopped walking, pulling them to a stop with me. "Don't call your brother a dummy."

"Then he shouldn't ask dumb questions," she grumbled.

I was going to be in for it when she was a teenager if she was starting the sass at eight.

"Mommy knows how to fix everything," Bobby said.

I ruffled his hair. "Not everything, sweetheart."

"Is that Eddie's car?" he asked, spying it on the street and breaking free to go look for him. "Eddie! Where are you?"

"He's getting my tire fixed," I said, wishing desperately that I hadn't had to bring his car to get the kids. I wasn't ready to have a conversation about Eddie. I wasn't sure I ever would be after what he had said. A lump rose up in my throat, but I shook it off. I would *not* cry in front of the kids again. They saw enough tears when Harry died. Today, I would be strong for them.

Especially because I had to navigate Ruth's absence as well.

I waited until they were in the car before warning them that Grandma wasn't at home. "Is she out shopping?" Susie asked.

"No, darling. She went back to her house for the night."

Both faces in the rearview mirror showed concern.

"But she's coming back, right?"

"She is," I said lightly. "She just had to take care of some things, and it was easier to stay there for the night. She'll probably be back tomorrow."

"Good," Susie said.

"I actually kind of like her crunchy lasagna," Bobby said. "I like the bones in it."

"Those aren't bones," Susie said. "She just doesn't cook the pasta as long as Mama does."

"That's what she tells *you*," Bobby said.

"I was thinking," I interrupted, before it resorted to name calling again, "how would you feel if I kept working my normal hours this summer and Grandma stayed with you? She could take you to the pool."

"That could work," Susie said cautiously. "But you'll still take us sometimes too, right?"

"Of course. And I don't work Mondays or afternoons. I just thought that could be a good way for me to keep working and you to spend more time with her."

The kids seemed amenable to this plan, and we went home. They did their homework, and I started dinner, all the while keeping an ear out to see when Eddie showed up. I left the keys in the car largely because I didn't want to confuse the kids, and we were going to have to address what he had said, but I half hoped he would knock anyway.

Once I had a chicken in the oven, I went to the front window, but Eddie's car was still there.

We eventually sat down to eat—a strangely somber meal without Ruth. I never expected to miss her presence, but I was jittery and nervous, jumping up at every stray sound. Both children asked what was wrong with me multiple times.

"It's just taking Eddie a while to get here with the car," I said. "I hope everything is okay."

The sound of a car came down our street, and Pepper's ears perked up (as did mine) when the noise stopped in front of our house. I wiped my mouth and placed my napkin on the table. "That'll be Eddie," I said, rising. "I'll just go thank him."

If the kids noticed me practically sprinting to the front door, they said nothing. I stopped at the mirror in the front hall and fluffed my hair. I was pale, but I had cleaned my face at least. It would have to do. If he implied I was the right girl when I was a complete mess . . . well, he wouldn't be put off by me now. Taking a deep breath, I flung the door open, and ran smack into Ruth, who was walking inside.

"Ruth!" I exclaimed in surprise. "What are you doing here?"

She shook her head. "That doctor said my blood work was perfect. The nerve. And that hospital food is somehow even worse than yours. So I told them I was going home."

"But Dr. Lefkowitz wanted you to stay overnight."

She waved a hand in the air. "I promised to check back with him in the morning."

"But I thought—"

"Barbara," she said warningly. "I'm fine. I don't need a psychologist either." She sniffed the air. "On second thought, maybe I should have just eaten the hospital food."

I let out an exasperated breath. "It's rosemary chicken. I'll fix you a plate."

"Oh," she said. "You need to pay the cabdriver first."

She walked past me to the dining room, where she held out her arms. "Grandma is back," she announced as the children jumped up to hug her as if she had been gone a year instead of a few hours.

I shook my head, holding up a finger at the waiting cabbie to indicate I needed to get my wallet. Then I went to my purse and got money to pay him. She was never going to change. And sometimes that was okay.

I was washing up from dinner when I heard a car door shut over the sound of running water. Wiping my hands on the dish towel, I went dashing back to the front window. Eddie was looking in his car to see if the keys were there. His shoulders drooped slightly, and he began to walk up the front steps, my keys in hand.

I opened the door and he startled. For what felt like a long time, neither of us said anything.

My mouth opened, and "Eddie! Barbara, aren't you going to invite him in?" came from somewhere.

Ruth stood behind me, a hand on her hip.

"I—would you like to come in?" I asked, not sure that either of us wanted that.

"I . . . uh . . . I should probably be going," he stammered out.

"Whatever is wrong with the two of you?" Ruth asked, just as Bobby came barreling past her.

"Eddie! Did you bring me anything?"

Eddie's face dropped even further. "I'm sorry, champ. I didn't tonight. Just your mom's car."

"That's okay," Bobby said. "We rode home in your car today."

"Curiouser and curiouser," Ruth said, suppressing a smile. "Are you sure you don't want to come in? I was just getting the kids their dessert." She leaned forward, whispering loudly. "They're still hungry. The chicken was awfully dry."

"Oh, for Pete's sake," I said. "It was *not* dry."

"Only a little," Bobby said.

I threw my hands up. "I give up," I said. "Eddie, would you like some dessert?"

"I should get back to the store before it closes," he said, looking as though he'd like to do anything but.

"I'll walk you to the car," I said.

"You don't have to."

"I'll just be a minute," I told Ruth and the kids. "Go eat your dessert." I pulled the door firmly shut behind me.

Then it was just the two of us facing each other in the spring twilight. "Thank you," I said. "For today. For every day, really."

He nodded. "I'm happy to help. I keep telling you that."

"Yes, but this was—" I was going to say "above and beyond." But the reality was that everything he had done in these last two years had been above and beyond. "Thank you."

Eddie swallowed. "If you don't want to see me when you do your grocery shopping, I can stay in the back while you're there Monday."

"Please don't."

He looked at me plaintively. "I don't want to make you feel awkward. I shouldn't have said anything earlier."

It did change everything—but only if we let it. I didn't know what I wanted—yes, I had felt . . . something more than friendship that night when he fixed the leaking bathtub. But was I capable of more? Did I even want to be?

I didn't know. And I hated not knowing. There wasn't much I wouldn't have done for Eddie. I loved him—I just didn't know if I loved him romantically. I didn't know if I could *ever* love anyone romantically again. My heart felt like a piece of Swiss cheese, and I worried that he would fall right through one of the holes.

All I did know was that I couldn't bear the thought of losing Eddie's friendship. So much so that I wasn't willing to risk it by attempting more. "I want—" I stopped. "I just." No. "I'm sorry," I said finally, regretting the words even as they came out of my mouth. "Can't we—can't we just pretend you didn't?"

"Yeah," Eddie said, and my heart splintered even further. How long had he been pretending he didn't feel that way? I thought of the way he looked at me that had made my knees go all wobbly back in college. How long had I been ignoring what was right in front of me because I didn't want to see it?

He should move on and find a girl without the baggage I came with. But why did my heart drop at the thought of that too?

He took a step toward his car, but I wrapped my arms around him in a hug, which lingered. He pulled back to look at me, and our faces moved closer together, my concerns lost in the feel of his embrace until—

"Mommy!" Bobby's voice called from the doorway. "Grandma can't find the Hershey's syrup. Do you know where it is?"

I shook myself out of Eddie's arms, all too aware that my chest was rising and falling heavily with the struggle to breathe. "Coming," I said huskily. I turned back to Eddie. "I—"

"Go," he said. "It's fine. We're fine."

I patted his arm—a terrible consolation—and went to the door, glancing over my shoulder as he watched me walk away.

Bobby was waiting by the door. "It's in the refrigerator, on the door," I said, heading toward the kitchen. "You couldn't find this?" I asked Ruth, plucking the yellow can from the spot where it always resided.

"Go back to the table," she told Bobby, who did as she asked.

"I could find it just fine," she said with her eyebrows raised. "But I was watching out the window and didn't think you wanted the whole neighborhood seeing what I was seeing."

"Two friends hugging after one rescued the other when she had a flat tire and needed to pick up her kids?"

Ruth eyed me knowingly. "If that's what you want to call it," she said. She took the Hershey's syrup from my hand and dumped a small lake of it into each bowl of ice cream. No one was going to accuse dessert of being dry at least.

47

I allowed Ruth to help with bedtime, and we divided and conquered getting the kids bathed and down. It briefly reminded me of when they were little. I would bathe Susie while Harry fed Bobby a bottle, then we would trade off, me bathing Bobby, while he read Susie a story. Maybe Janet was right—maybe no one could do it all alone. Yes, Ruth had, but she only had one child. Besides, it was pointless to compare our situations. No one ever won a medal in the grief Olympics.

Once they were both asleep, I asked Ruth if she would like to join me in the kitchen for a cup of tea. She followed me downstairs, and I put the kettle on.

"I'd rather have sherry," she said.

"When you left the hospital against Dr. Lefkowitz's orders? Absolutely not."

"Spoilsport," she muttered.

"Another thing," I said. "It may not have been your heart, but that doesn't mean it won't be next time. Your weight is good, but you're going to take longer walks daily—you can bring Pepper with you. And we're starting on the heart diet that Harry used. All of us."

"Much good that did him," she said.

The kettle started to whistle, and I poured water into the two waiting cups.

"You're not trying to get rid of me, then?" she asked.

I turned to look at her, wondering if she was being flippant. But her face was serious. "No," I said. "I told you that. You're welcome here as long as you want to be here."

"Thank you," she said. Then she looked down. "I have a confession." I studied her, curious. "I may have . . . misled you a little bit."

"About what?"

"The house."

"This house?"

"No," she said, shaking her head. "Mine."

My eyebrows went up. "You mean to tell me that you could have gone home this whole time?" Maybe I could still rescind that open invitation if this whole thing had been an act.

"No," she said again. "But I fibbed a little in implying that I lost it. I didn't. I sold it."

"You sold your house?" I repeated. "Why?"

She looked down at her hands on the kitchen table. "In case you needed anything. I wanted to be able to help immediately." She brought her eyes back up to mine. "Remember how I told you everyone is leaving the neighborhood to move up here and it's hurting property values? I didn't want you to have to sell it and get pennies someday when I'm gone."

I contemplated what she had said. "When?"

"Right before I moved in," she said. "The rest of my things—the things I thought you or the kids might want someday—are in storage." She swallowed. "I'm sorry for not telling the truth. I was afraid you wouldn't let me stay if you knew I had the money to leave." She seemed smaller confessing this. Frailer. This brave, brave woman had been through so much, yet I was the one who made her worry. A wave of guilt washed over me, knowing that I had made her feel like she couldn't be honest with me. Yes, the early days of her residence were fraught, but I was ashamed at the memory of standing in the living room telling her she had to leave. That wasn't who I wanted to be.

I brought the teacups to the table and sat, reaching across the table to put my hand on hers. "You're not going anywhere anytime soon."

"I can," she said. "I figured I would stay here a couple of months and then rent a small apartment nearby with money from the house."

"You didn't have to sell. I know how much that house meant to you."

She shook her head. "It had become a mausoleum. It was time. And I promised Harry . . ." She trailed off.

I squeezed her hand. "What did you promise him?"

Ruth looked up at me, her eyes brimming with tears. "He knew. Oh, Barbara, he knew the clock was ticking. It's why he bought that insurance policy. He came to me and made me promise to give you a couple of years to mourn, and then he wanted me to help you move on."

"Move on?"

She nodded. "He didn't want you to be alone, like I was. He wanted you to find happiness again."

I remembered a conversation, when Susie was a baby lying in a bassinet next to our bed. I had been exhausted, but content, until he brought up that very subject.

"You're not going anywhere," I told him, snuggling a leg against his.

"I hope you're right," he said, wrapping an arm around me. "But if you're not, I don't want you to be alone."

"Sure," I said, teasing. "I'll bring a date to your funeral."

"That's my girl," he said, kissing my forehead. "But I still mean it."

"Stop being morbid," I said. "You told me you were too stubborn to die."

Then Susie started to cry, and he got out of bed to change her diaper, leaving me more time to rest. Once she settled into his arms, I drifted off to sleep, the conversation all but forgotten. Until now.

Ruth was still talking. "He said, 'Ma, she's not going to want you there. She's so independent. She won't say it, she's too nice for that. But you have to stay anyway and help her move on.'"

I shook my head, my eyes now filled. "I'm not ready," I whispered. "I know it's what he wanted, but . . ." I couldn't continue.

"You'll never be ready," Ruth said. "I'm not ready."

Talking about her was safer territory. "Ruth, it's been decades. And Mr. Greene is crazy about you."

"And what happens in a year or two or ten when he dies too?" she asked. "No. I can't do that again."

"You could go first," I offered helpfully.

"There's the old joke about that," she said, wiping at an eye. "Why do Jewish men die before their wives?"

"Not so funny in our situation."

"No," Ruth agreed. "But we had two of the good ones."

I thought about the story of how she and Abe met. How he dumped his fiancée after meeting Ruth. Harry always said he absolutely doted on her. Then again, our friends likely said the same thing about Harry with me. I didn't see how anyone could ever love me the way Harry did.

"That we did," I agreed and took a sip of my tea. Then I stood up and crossed to the liquor cabinet. "Hell with it," I said. "This conversation needs a splash of brandy. Just don't tell Dr. Lefkowitz when you check in tomorrow."

Ruth smiled sadly but conspiratorially as she held her cup up to me. "Deal." I poured a tiny dollop into her cup. "Don't be stingy now," she said, continuing to hold it up. I sighed and added a little more, then put some in my cup before placing the bottle on the table and returning to my seat.

"Look," I said. "If you don't have feelings for Mr. Greene, tell me that, and I'll leave it alone. But I don't think that's the case."

She took a sip of her laced tea and sighed. "It's complicated."

"It doesn't have to be."

She set her cup down and spread her arms. "Look at me. I'll be sixty years old next month. The last time a man saw me naked, I was your age. What could he possibly want with me?"

"I have no idea," I said.

She chuckled, then leaned forward and smacked my arm.

"You're supposed to argue with me."

"Have you tried arguing with you? It's impossible." Ruth smiled. "But I've seen how he looks at you. Honestly, I'm surprised he didn't try to run off with you years ago."

Ruth shook her head. "He would never do something like that."

"A third good one," I said. "What are the odds?"

"And what about you?" Ruth asked, sitting up straighter.

"Me?"

"Apples don't fall far from trees. I've seen the way you and Eddie look at each other."

I studied my cup and didn't respond.

"Oh, so something *did* happen," Ruth said softly.

"Nothing happened," I said defensively.

"Barbara, in my experience, a man doesn't go out of his way to help a woman as much as Eddie does if he isn't madly in love with her."

I closed my eyes and exhaled forcefully. "I know. He . . . he kind of said . . . something . . . to that effect."

"What did he say?"

I took another sip of tea to fortify myself, then grabbed the bottle and took a swig directly from it. "I asked what happened when he met the right girl. And he told me the right girl thinks of him as a brother."

"Are we sure he didn't mean Janet?"

"Ruth!"

She chuckled. "I'm teasing. Even if he hadn't said a word, the truth is, he's too far gone to look at anyone else. The kids love him. What's the problem?"

"Me," I said with raw honesty. "I'm the problem."

She reached across the table and put her hand on mine. "Then we really are destined to live together until I go, and you become Susie's problem. Maybe we deserve each other." She withdrew her hand, put it in her pocket, and returned it with a gold ring set with a large emerald, surrounded by diamonds. "This was my mother's," she said. "When we left Russia, we grabbed what we could. My parents knew things were getting bad, and my mother had sewn most of her jewels into our clothes. We didn't even know we were carrying them—she distributed them evenly in case anything happened to one person. This ring was her grandmother's. A gift from the czarina, if you could believe my grandmother. Which you shouldn't. The woman lied. She stayed behind because one of my aunts was pregnant and couldn't travel." Ruth shook her head. "We never saw or heard from either of them again."

I sat in silence, trying to imagine losing my own grandmother that way. Then again, mine was still terrorizing her neighborhood in Philadelphia. The Russian army may not have stood a chance against her.

"When we got here, my parents sold her jewelry, piece by piece, when we couldn't make ends meet. This was the last piece. The one my mother wouldn't part with, even if it meant boiled cabbage for another week. She gave it to me when she got sick, telling me I would have a daughter. That it had to go from daughter to daughter." Ruth smiled sadly. "She couldn't have known I'd never carry another child to term."

The *to term* part struck me. There had been other babies, then. How much could one woman endure and still wake up in the morning?

But before I could find the words to reply, she reached out again and took my hand, opening my palm and pressing the ring into it. "I want you to have it."

I looked at the ring in my hand. "I'll save it for when Susie is old enough," I said. "Thank you for entrusting it to me."

"No," Ruth said, shaking her head. "You don't understand. You'll give it to Susie someday, but I want *you* to have it now." She swallowed. "When Abe died, I thought I'd never have a daughter. It took losing Harry to realize I do have one."

My eyes overflowed, tears streaking down my face again. "Ruth, I—"

"It's okay," she said. "But you have to promise to give Eddie a chance. Or if not Eddie, someone else. For Harry."

I slipped the ring onto my right hand, my wedding ring still on my left. It was a perfect fit. I closed my eyes to compose myself, then looked back at Ruth. "I will," I said. "But only if you promise to give

Mr. Greene a chance. A real one." I reached back across the table and clasped her hand, the ring sparkling on mine. "For Harry."

"I miss him so much," Ruth said, her own eyes watering. "I pray you never have to feel that pain."

"I do too," I said. "Both parts. But I think—I think he's happy right now."

"I talk to him sometimes," Ruth said. "And Abe. And you're right."

"I do too," I confessed. Then I looked up at the ceiling. "You wanted this, huh?" I turned back to Ruth when there was no reply. "Now what do we do?"

"I suppose I need to go shopping for some new brassieres," she said. "If someone is going to be seeing them."

A giant belly laugh sounded, and for a moment, I thought it was Harry responding, before I realized it was coming from me. "You're paying for those," I said, still laughing. "With that house money."

She made a disgusted noise. "Fine."

"Harry always said he wanted you to find someone too."

This surprised Ruth. "He did?"

I nodded. "He may have sent you for more reasons than he told you."

"He's still looking after us, even now, isn't he?"

I reached across the table again, and Ruth put her hand in mine. Her eyes were shining, and I could feel my own filling. "He is. And I, for one, am glad he is."

"Me too," Ruth said, squeezing my hand. Then she took hers back, drank the rest of her tea, and stood, announcing she'd had enough excitement for one day.

I watched her lumber up the stairs, marveling at how quickly life could change once again.

48

I told Ruth that I would take her to the hospital to check back in with Dr. Lefkowitz, but that I was staying with her, not working.

"There's no need for that," Ruth said. "I'm completely fine."

"Ruth," I said warningly. "If I have to accept that I need help sometimes, so do you." She looked like she was going to give a sarcastic response, and I aimed a finger at the ceiling with a pointed look.

"Fine," she said, rolling her eyes. "But if they try to make me stay, I expect you to fight it."

"I listen to doctors—one of us needs to."

"What doctor?" Susie asked as she came into the kitchen.

Ruth jumped up from her seat at the table and busied herself getting Susie a glass of orange juice, leaving me to answer the question.

"At work, darling," I said. "You know how your grandmother is. Always thinks she knows better than everyone else."

"And you know your mother, the ultimate rule follower," Ruth said, bringing Susie her juice. "She ought to live a little."

Susie looked from me to her and back again. "I can't tell if you're being funny or if you two are fighting," she said.

Ruth and I looked at each other and started to laugh.

"A little of both," Ruth said eventually.

"But with love," I reminded her, cupping Susie's chin in my hand.

"Whoa. Where'd you get the ring?"

I held my hand out for Susie to see. "Your grandmother gave it to me," I said. "It's a family heirloom that goes daughter to daughter. And someday it will be yours."

"Grandma in Philadelphia sent it?"

"No," I said. "It was this grandmother's."

"But you're not her daughter."

Ruth smiled, wrapping a companionable arm around my waist. "She's the closest I've got."

∼

Ruth said she was going to take Pepper on a walk around the block before we went to the hospital. When I opened the front door to herd the kids toward the elementary school, a small brown paper bag was on the doorstep. Curious, I peeked inside, assuming it was a gift for Ruth from Mr. Greene.

But the bag contained two yellow cans of Hershey's chocolate syrup.

I pulled one out and looked at it for a long moment. Eddie must have brought it by sometime in the night when he thought we might be out.

"Did you get more?" Bobby asked. "Grandma said she found an extra can in the cabinet."

It was another few seconds before I could reply. But then I called back into the house. "Ruth—I'm going to run to the grocery store after I drop the kids off. We'll go to the hospital after I'm back."

Ruth came to the door and saw what I was holding in my hand. "What do you need?" she asked.

I smiled. "A fourth good one."

She pulled me in for a quick hug, which seemed to stun the children.

"Why are you and Grandma being so weird today?" Bobby asked once we were in the car.

"I wouldn't say we're being *weird*. We had a long talk last night and . . . well . . . I think we understand each other a little better now."

"Then she's not moving back to her house?" Susie asked.

"No," I said. "She's staying with us for as long as she wants to."

Both children seemed to relax at this answer. Harry knew what he was doing.

∽

But once the kids were in school, and I started to drive toward Greene's, I got nervous, eventually pulling onto the shoulder, not far from where I had stopped with the flat tire the day before.

"You're sure this is what you want?" I asked the roof of my car. There was no reply. "The *least* you could do is send me some kind of a sign before I go do this. I know what you told your mother, but there's a big difference between planning for something and it actually happening." Still nothing. "I'm scared, Harry. I'm scared I'll get hurt. I'm scared the kids will get attached, and then it won't work. I'm scared they'll think I'm replacing you. I'm scared it *will* work, and then I'll lose him too."

I chuckled mirthlessly. "I don't know what I expected you to do. I don't even know if you can hear me, let alone send signs." I sighed. "But I don't think you'd want the kids to grow up without any kind of a father figure. And you did tell me you didn't want me to be alone, even if I didn't want to hear it." My eyes welled up slightly. "I wish you'd made me listen more. But we were young and stupid, and we thought you were invincible." I wiped at my eyes. "*You* didn't though, did you? It was just me who thought that."

Shaking my head, I let my gaze drift toward the store. It was so much easier to keep everything as it was. There was no risk if I didn't go in there.

But no reward either.

I thought about the night Janet and I met Harry and George. Risks hadn't scared me back then, as Harry caught me with a paintbrush in my hand, vandalizing his fraternity house lawn. He called me a spitfire that night.

Granted, I'd had a few drinks before grabbing that can of paint. This was different.

"Couldn't you have wanted something easier?" I asked the empty car. "We got a puppy."

I leaned my forehead on the steering wheel, trying to work up the nerve to go inside the store, when a distinct feeling of being watched made me pick my head up. All I needed was Eddie to come out and find me upset in my car again. I didn't want to be a damsel in distress. I wanted to be me. Doing this my own way.

But all I saw was a bright red bird sitting on the hood of my car, regarding me with great interest. The same color as the paint I used the night I met Harry.

A cardinal. A male one. And maybe they all looked the same, but I could have sworn it was the one that had taken up residence in our backyard.

I heard Susie's voice in my head. *Grandma says they're a message from someone who's gone.*

"Harry?" I whispered.

The bird tilted its head, then it seemed to nod slightly before inclining its head again, directly toward the store.

"Okay," I said. "You win. But if this ends badly, I'm looking up recipes for cardinal stew."

The bird chirped a small "ha" sound and then flew off toward the store, where it perched on the sign, a tiny fleck of red on the line of the *G* in *Greene*.

I put the car in drive and turned into the parking lot. Then I took a deep breath, got out, and marched into the store.

On Mondays, Eddie was typically by the front, as if he were waiting for me. Which, I now realized, he likely had been. But this wasn't my normal day for shopping. And after the evening he'd had, it was entirely possible he had chosen to take a day off or come in late. I hadn't thought of that, and I briefly debated going back out to the parking lot to look for his car to see if he was there before I searched the store for him.

No. If there was ever a time for a grand gesture, this was it.

There was no one behind the manager's counter, and I glanced around to see if anyone was looking. No one was. I was a regular. No one would think I'd cause trouble.

But they hadn't seen what I could do with a can of red paint and a brush. I cocked my head, looking at the microphone for the public address system that Eddie had installed a few years earlier. That would have to do.

Ducking under the counter gate, I grabbed the gooseneck microphone and flipped the switch to "on." I had seen Eddie use it before, but there were buttons that I hadn't paid attention to. With a shrug, I pressed the green button and spoke into the microphone. "Eddie Greene, report to the manager's counter. Eddie Greene, you're needed at the manager's counter immediately."

Every head turned to look toward me.

I took a deep breath. Maybe he really wasn't here. "Eddie Greene, we need to talk about a can of Hershey's syrup," I said quickly as Lloyd, his assistant manager, strode purposefully toward me.

Then I saw Eddie rounding the corner of the cereal aisle just as Lloyd reached the counter. "Here," I said, thrusting the microphone at Lloyd. "I'm done anyway." Then I ducked under the counter again, moving swiftly away from him and toward Eddie.

"Barbara," Eddie said. "What on earth?"

"I'm only here for one thing today," I said, putting my hands on my hips.

"Look, I'm sorry if the syrup was too much. I just thought—"

"I'm not here about the syrup."

"You're not?"

"No," I said, taking my hands from my hips and wrapping my arms around his neck. "I'm here for you."

"Me?" he asked hoarsely.

"Eddie Greene, if you changed your mind after—"

His lips stopped me, though I tried to continue my sentence until I realized what was happening.

A cheer erupted from the customers and staff, save Lloyd, who still looked annoyed when we broke apart. I could feel my cheeks coloring now, after the fact, at how brazen I had been. But it seemed everyone else approved.

"Janet is going to kill me," Eddie said, then kissed my forehead.

"I'll handle Janet," I said. "Besides, maybe she'll be happy."

"Are you happy?" he asked. "That's all that matters."

"I am," I said, truly meaning it for the first time in two years.

We were going to be okay. All of us. Because none of us had to do it all alone.

Epilogue

February 1964

I zipped Ruth's dress for her, then put my hands on her shoulders, smiling at her in the mirror. She reached up and put a hand on top of mine.

"Do you want your mother's ring for today?" I asked. "I'm happy to lend it to you so it's like she's here."

"No," Ruth said. "I want you to wear it. She's always here with us. They all are."

I thought of the cardinal on my car the day that I first kissed Eddie. So much had happened since that June morning. Both for us and the world. It took several months for Joseph (he insisted I no longer call him Mr. Greene considering he would be my step-father-in-law—and potentially, someday, my father-in-law as well) to wear Ruth down. And the subject of when Eddie would officially join our family had started to come up with the kids with some frequency. None of us, myself most surprisingly, seemed to mind.

Originally, Ruth and Joseph were slated to get married in December. Just a small ceremony in the rabbi's study with us, Eddie, Janet's family, and the two nonrelated witnesses to sign the ketubah that Judaism dictated were necessary. But the events of November in Dallas left no one feeling festive or ready for even such a small group, so Ruth and Joseph decided to wait an additional two months.

And if I was being perfectly honest, I didn't really mind the delay. I had grown accustomed to Ruth's presence and the extra set of hands. Though her cooking . . . well . . . I wouldn't miss that.

When Joseph learned that Ruth had sold her house, he decided to do the same with the house Janet and Eddie had grown up in. I was surprised, but he said they deserved a truly fresh start. And the new home that he purchased was just a few blocks over from us and Janet, so both grandparents would continue to be present in their grandchildren's lives, even if Ruth was no longer living in our house.

"We're really going to miss you," I said, finding that I meant it.

"You should come for dinner . . . probably every night. I don't want the children to starve."

"Oh, don't worry. I have the whole book of recipes that you made for me." It was the size of a Torah scroll. Filled with advice like sticking pasta and tuna fish into a Jell-O mold and other suggestions that would make the kids run gagging from the table.

"Follow the directions to the letter," she warned. "No improvising. You can't improve perfection."

"No," I said, holding her hair back as she fastened her necklace. "You can't." She turned to face me, and I told her she looked beautiful, which she did. No, she wasn't the fresh-faced nineteen-year-old she had been at her first wedding. But her face was softer than it had been when she moved in, the lines of grief easing as she learned to love and laugh with someone new again. As we all became a real family. "Are you ready?"

"As I'll ever be."

I made final adjustments to the children's clothes, and then we left the house, Ruth turning back to look at it one last time. "I remember the day you moved in," Ruth said wistfully.

"And the day you did," I added. "But this isn't goodbye."

"No," she said. "It isn't." And she reached up to pat my cheek. I held her hand to it, marveling at how far we had come together.

"I love you, Ruth," I said.

She smiled. "The best daughter I ever had."

"Technically, the only daughter you ever had."

"Shhh," Ruth said. "Don't spoil the moment."

I laughed as the kids ran past us to the car. "Shall we?" I asked. Ruth nodded and walked down the sidewalk. I followed and sat in the driver's seat. "Everyone ready to see Grandma get married?"

"Mama, look," Susie said, pointing out the front windshield. On the hood sat a bright red cardinal. And from the way it looked at me, I knew it was the same one.

Ruth's mouth scrunched up slightly as she regarded the bird. Then she nodded, and the bird nodded back. She blew a quiet kiss, and the bird looked at her again, looked at me, and then flew away.

"Let's go," Ruth said. "It's my wedding day after all."

 ～

We celebrated that night at Janet's house with dinner, dancing, and extended family merriment. But as the party began to wind down, I snuck outside to find Janet leaning against the patio wall, smoking a cigarette. Pulling my coat around me in the cold night air, I plucked the cigarette from her fingers and took a puff before offering it back.

"We're sisters now," I said, bumping my shoulder playfully against hers as she took the cigarette from me.

"We are," she agreed. "And look, you didn't even *have* to cozy up to Eddie for that to happen."

"Janet, I—"

"Shh," she said. "I'm teasing." She turned to look at me in the light that spilled out of her living room. "Are you happy?"

I nodded. "But I won't be if you aren't."

Janet sighed and then smiled, though it was tinged with sadness. "Do you know, I was actually jealous when Ruth moved in?"

"Jealous?" I couldn't imagine why. She had been more than clear that she couldn't stand her own mother-in-law.

"I know it doesn't compare to losing Harry," she said. "But losing your mom, especially when you are one, is . . ." Her voice broke a little as she trailed off. "It was really, really hard," she said eventually. "It's still really hard."

I wrapped an arm around her shoulder, feeling my eyes fill as she leaned into me.

"Well," I said. "You have Ruth now too."

Janet laughed, wiping at her own eyes. "And you have my annoying brother."

"He's not *that* annoying."

She looked at me. "Neither is she, if we're being honest. Though the Eddie thing is a *little* incestuous now."

"You're really okay with us being together?"

"Barbara, I love you like you're really my sister. So yes. Because he makes you happy."

I smiled, my eyes watery again. "He really does."

Janet nodded. "And on the plus side, if he ever messes up, I won't go to jail for punching my own brother."

I laughed. "Come on," I said. "Let's go eat some cake."

～

Eddie drove us home from Janet's. The kids had fallen asleep before we left, and he had carried them to the car, then accompanied me so he could help get them inside as they were far too heavy for me these days.

As he pulled into the driveway, we looked at each other for a moment and smiled. "What a perfect day," I said.

Eddie took my hand and kissed it. "I can only think of one that will be more perfect."

"I'd say you should ask my father for permission, but I think those two"—I gestured toward the back seat—"are the ones who actually need to grant it." Eddie chuckled and turned away. "What?"

"They cornered me before the cake tonight and asked when I was going to marry you."

"They did not."

He mimed locking his lips. "I was sworn to secrecy."

"You didn't do a very good job of that, did you?"

He squeezed my hand. "You told me no more secrets, about how I felt or anything else." I *had* said that. "Would it have made a difference? If you'd known how I felt earlier?"

"I don't know," I said honestly. "But I think everything worked out exactly as it was supposed to."

"I agree," Eddie said, then he turned off the car. "Let's get these two to bed."

Eddie carried Bobby in, while I woke Susie just enough for her to walk up the stairs. I got Susie into her pajamas and tucked in, then came to Bobby's room and changed him, still asleep, while Eddie took Pepper out in the backyard.

When they were both in bed, I came quietly down the stairs just as Eddie brought the dog back inside. "Want a drink?" I asked.

He wrapped an arm around my waist and pulled me in to kiss me. "Don't need one," he whispered into my hair.

Then we both jumped as the phone rang. "Who on earth is calling this late?" I asked, dashing toward the kitchen to keep it from waking the kids.

"Ruth, I'd assume," Eddie said.

I picked up the receiver just as it started to ring again. "Hello?" I asked.

"Barbara, darling," my mother said. "How was the wedding?"

"Small," I said. She had been a little miffed at not being invited, but it was just immediate family. "But lovely."

"And they're all moved into their new house?"

"Ruth has a few boxes left that we'll bring over this weekend," I said. "But mostly."

"Listen, I was thinking. Now that Ruth is gone, why don't I move back in for a while? I can help with the kids again. So you don't have to do this alone."

I shook my head, but I was smiling. "Mom, you're welcome to visit anytime you want. And I'll call you if I need you. But I have help down here. I'm not alone. And I can do this."

"You're sure?"

"I'm sure," I said, as Eddie came up behind me and kissed my neck. "But listen, Mom, I've got to go. I'll call you tomorrow."

She started to say something else, but Eddie's lips on my neck were more urgent, so I said goodbye and hung up.

"While I'm on the phone with my mother?" I asked, spinning in his arms. "Come on!"

"Sorry." He grinned, looking anything but.

I shook my head. "You're incorrigible." I leaned in to kiss him. We moved to the sofa, where I found myself sitting on Eddie's lap, and then—

"Mommy?" a sleepy voice called from the top of the stairs. "Can I have a glass of water?"

I quickly wiped at the lipstick on Eddie's face, then gave up and laughed as I stood to get Bobby some water. "To be continued," I told Eddie.

"For the rest of our lives, I hope," he called after me.

I knew now that the rest of my life likely wouldn't look the way I ever imagined it. But I was ready to see what it *would* look like.

"I'm going to need a more formal proposal than that," I said as I passed through the living room to bring the glass up.

"Noted," Eddie said. "Any particular time you'd like me to do it?"

"Surprise me."

I touched the picture of a cardinal that Susie had painted in school, as I did every time I passed it. And in the dim light of the hallway, I could have sworn it smiled at me. The hole Harry left would never be gone. But as Ruth had predicted, my heart had grown around it. And there was room for Harry, Susie, Bobby, Eddie, and Ruth. And maybe, someday, even more.

"Thank you," I whispered to the picture.

"Who are you talking to?" Bobby asked.

I handed him the water and ruffled his hair. "No one, darling. Go back to bed."

Author's Note

This book began with something Julia Whelan said at a writing convention that we both spoke at. (She was the keynote. I was a lowly panel member.) But she said that we as authors needed to think about how our story is uniquely ours—how we are the only one who can tell it.

I went back to my hotel room that night and thought about stories that are mine. *For the Love of Friends* was my story—my best friend, to whom this book is dedicated, knows why. *She's Up to No Good* was, in many ways, a love letter to my grandmother. *Don't Forget to Write* was mine again—a girl who didn't quite fit in trying to figure out how to live her life on her own terms. *Behind Every Good Man* was a combination of all three things. But what other stories could only I tell?

As I pondered that, half watching a movie on Prime, a forgotten incident with my other grandmother, my father's mother, forced its way into my brain. It was before I was born, but she was volunteering at a hospital and encountered an anti-Semitic woman—no, she didn't befriend her, but the conversation about Chinese food did happen. My grandfather died in 1960, when my father was nine years old. And she raised my father, taking in boarders and working while he was in school to make ends meet. My great-aunt Bessie and great-uncle Irving helped significantly, and my aunt Dolly and uncle Marvin (my research team!) became his second set of parents. Raising children with a partner is daunting enough. But raising a child on your own when you can't even get a credit card yourself? How?

Neither Barbara nor Ruth is my own indomitable grandmother, though both get little pieces of her story woven into theirs. And neither of them is me, though they both share pieces of my story as well. Because you have to start thinking about the what-ifs once children are involved, which is very much the stage of life that I'm in.

I am also someone who would rather carry the weight of the world than ask for help. And I'm slowly learning, as Barbara does, that you can't exist in a vacuum. In Barbara's case, the time period traps her. In our current day and age, I think a lot about the meme where a mother says she's drowning, and society high-fives her and tells her she's a superwoman doing it all herself as she slips under the waves. Because this is HARD. For everyone, whether they post about it on social media or not.

Of course we had some fun cameos, between Beverly and Stuart, and readers who have been with me since the beginning hopefully got a chuckle at Evelyn saying that Joan (Lily's eventual mother from *For the Love of Friends*) may not be cut out to have kids.

But I think overall, this is a story about learning to lean on others and let them lean right back on you, like Bob Fosse and Gwen Verdon somehow staying upright in "Who's Got the Pain." (Google it if you don't get the reference.)

Thank you for coming on this journey with me, and let me assure you, I'm just getting started.

—*SGC*

Acknowledgments

This book began, as mine all now seem to, with a late-night text to my agent extraordinaire, Rachel Beck, saying, "POSSIBLE book idea . . ." As I make more author friends, the complaint I hear the most is that their agents take forever to get back to them. Whereas Rachel and I have three constant conversations going between email (professional), Instagram (reels and normal memes), and text (unhinged memes, mom ramblings, and everything in between). Thank you for guiding me on this journey of a lifetime—I couldn't imagine doing this with anyone else by my side!

Thank you to my now-former editor, Alicia Clancy, for buying this book before I wrote it and for setting me on this path where I now get to call myself a full-time author. I am forever grateful.

Thank you to my new editor, Nancy Taylor Holmes, for your wisdom and guidance. I love how instantly we clicked and became wedding/Jersey Shore/Springsteen-sighting buddies—and now basically family. We're making Domingo happen somehow!

Thank you to my developmental editor, Christina Henry de Tessan, for making this book sparkle. While making cuts often feels like trimming off body parts, your insight was exactly what this story needed, and I'm so happy that I got to work with you!

Thank you to the entire team at Lake Union and at Liza Dawson Associates. You all are perfect and amazing. Zero notes.

Thank you to my publicist, Ann-Marie Nieves, for making sure people know who I am and for being the best of cheerleaders in publishing and life.

Thank you to my husband, Nick, for keeping the house and family running while I'm working and traveling and for cleaning everything when I'm in the zone. And, you know, considering this book, for being here. Love you, honey.

Thank you to Jacob and Max, for being my everything—even if Max is no longer allowed on the microphone at book events. (And thank you to Gracie and Sandy, for cuddle breaks and making me stroke you like a Bond villain while I do virtual events. And even thank you to that stupid immortal fish!)

Thank you to my mother, Carole Goodman, for being my alpha reader, my babysitter, my personal shopper, and my person who screenshots and sends me every single mention of me on Facebook. I couldn't do any of this without you.

Thank you to my father, Jordan Goodman, for knowing all of the things. And for always knowing who to ask about the handful of things you don't know. Sorry about the Amazon bill!

Thank you to my brother, Adam, sister-in-law, Nicole, and nephews Cam and Luke. I think my favorite texts are when your friends get to the end of one of my books and realize I wrote it and freak out to you. Love and miss you!

Thank you to my grandmother, Charlotte Chansky, for letting me mine your life for comedic gold and for being the only person in my whole life who has told me that I always do my best and that is always enough.

Thank you to my aunt and uncle, Dolly and Marvin Band, for being my research team. Trying to write a book a year about a time period I didn't live through while momming and teaching would absolutely not be possible without you! Thank you for always taking my calls and texts to share your wisdom with me.

Thank you to my aunt and uncle, Mike Chansky and Stephanie Abbuhl, for your constant support and generosity. Speaking in Avalon was an absolute highlight of my life, and it would never have been possible without you.

Thank you to my cousins Allison Band and Andy Levine, Ian and Kim Band, Mindy and Alan Nagler, Andrew and Dani Chansky, Peter Chansky, Ben Chansky, Shira Pomeroy, Maddy Levine Holt, Jolie Band, Trevor Band, and Matthew Nagler for being excited for every step of this journey with me.

Thank you to Mark Kamins, for loving me like your own child and for managing my money so I don't have to learn how to do any of it myself.

Thank you to Jennifer Lucina, for being my lifelong lifeline. I don't know how it's been thirty years (especially because we're both twenty-nine!!!), but I am so grateful that I have you every single day of my life. You're my lobster.

Thank you to Sarah McKinley, for being the best in every possible way, whether it's saving me a trip to the doctor, dropping off hand-me-down snow pants, letting me bounce ideas off you, or being my most excited beta reader. I am better every day because of you.

Thank you to Jeremy Horton, for keeping me grounded (figuratively), while making sure I'm never grounded (literally). And for being someone I can always count on to show up and remind me that I matter.

Thank you to Kevin Keegan—when I emailed you all those years ago and said I hoped you wouldn't be disappointed that I was going into education instead of becoming a journalist, you replied and said that on the contrary, you couldn't be prouder of me because I was following in your footsteps. And somehow you *were* even prouder when I stepped back from teaching to write full-time. Thank you for thirty years of mentorship, support, and friendship.

Thank you to Haben Asghedom, for being the best next-door neighbor and friend on the planet. You make this whole motherhood journey better every day, and I am so, so grateful that I have you. And thank you to your entire wonderful family, Mike, Aurora, Elena, and my little bestie, Zara. We are all so lucky that you chose to be our neighbors, friends, and maybe future in-laws? Lol.

Thank you to Jessica Markham, for being an absolute inspiration in every way. I honestly don't know how I survived before you were in my life. Thank you for being my beta reader, sounding board, fashion maven, legal research expert, and dear friend.

Thank you to Sonya Shpilyuk, for being the Ann to my Leslie and the Leslie to my Ann. You beautiful musk ox.

Thank you to Sue Perez and Luisa Ramos, for keeping me looking good!

Thank you to Helen Laser, for being the best narrator on the planet and bringing these characters to life!

Thank you to my friends: Joye Saxon, Christen Dimmick, Jamaly Allen, Caroline Dulaney, Katie Stutzman, Sarah Elbeshbishi, Reka Montfort, Katie Samsock, Jennifer Kramer, Kim Thibault, Mary Dempsey, Kerrin Torres, Laura Davis Vaughan, Jan Guttman, Max and Angie Giammetta, Jenna Levine Liu, Brittany Rassoolkhani, Heather Bergman, Alex Tsironis, Beth Davis, Sandy Young, Nicole Lau, Brigid Howe, Elyse Blocher Brum, Rob and Diana Pajewski, Steve and Carolyn Korman, and Sam and Jodi Lish.

Thank you to my author friends, who have made this journey so much sweeter: Jean Meltzer, Aimie Runyan-Vetter, Annie Cathryn, Heidi Shertok, Meredith Schorr, Felicia Grossman, Stacey Agdern, Sam Greene Woodruff, Alison Hammer, Lisa Barr, Rochelle Weinstein, Lauren Parvizi, Helen Laser, Jane Rosen, Zibby Owens, Pam Jenoff, Ellen Won Steil, Rea Frey, Georgina Cross, Jaime Lynn Hendricks, Dara Levan, Harper Kincaid, Erica Mae, Jacqueline Friedland, Jenn Bouchard, Lindsay Hameroff, and Jessica Guerrieri.

Thank you to my literary "big sis," Andrea Peskind Katz, for being the best champion ever.

Thank you to Renee Weiss Weingarten, for all of your support and for creating one of the best book corners on the internet—and thank you to all of Renee's Reading Club!

Thank you to my beloved Peloton Moms Book Club. I'll see you on the leaderboard!

Thank you to Melody Wukitch, Sarah Rifield, and the whole team at Park Books. A lot of indie bookstores won't touch an Amazon author, and I appreciate you supporting authors over industry more than I can ever say.

Thank you to the Confino family.

Thank you to my bookstagram family (I apologize in advance for anyone I leave out—this is a long list!): Kelly Kervin, Stacy Smith, Jamie Rosenblit, Susan Zabolotzky, Susan Peterson, Moran Vidaletz, Kelly Mikolich, Chase Waskey, Leslie Zemeckis, Christine Adams, Danielle Medina, Dara Granoff, Leighellen Landskov, Leslie Shogren, Michelle Jocsun, Sophia Becker, Susan Ballard, Kate Vocke, Cheryl Koch, Alexis Campbell, Jennifer Hecht, Fay Silverman, Aimee Fogel, Ticey Geyer, Katie Polito, Larry Hoffer, Lauren Margolin, Emily Halperin, Ginny Velazquez, Jessica Roy, Liz Gerke, and Kristy Barrett.

Thank you to all of the students I have taught—stepping away was hard, but I hope you can all follow your passion as well.

And finally, thank you to all of my readers, for making this dream of mine come true.

Book Club Questions

1. Barbara describes sending her mother home as wanting to try to do this by herself. Why do you think this independence is so important to Barbara?
2. Is Ruth passive-aggressive or just blunt but trying to be helpful?
3. Have you ever talked to someone who was gone? Did it ever feel like they responded?
4. How would this situation play out differently today? Do you think Barbara would let Ruth stay if it wasn't a time period when women couldn't get credit?
5. Both women claim the other's cooking is atrocious. Who do you think can actually cook?
6. Barbara stops Ruth from revealing details to Susie of the pogrom she and her family fled. How do you think these early events shaped Ruth's view of family?
7. Barbara's job is still something of a novelty for a woman with children in that time period. She doesn't need the money, so why is this position so important to her?
8. Mrs. Kline provides a glimpse of the antisemitism of the early 1960s, and Ruth disarms her fairly easily considering all of the trouble she's given the hospital staff. Why do you think the two women connect beyond their shared trauma?

9. Dr. Harper knows Dr. Howe is harassing women on his staff. What responsibility does he have for this situation?
10. At one point, Barbara wishes Janet could see through her veneer and know she isn't okay. Yet when she sees Janet isn't okay, she doesn't say anything. Do you think they find a path to more open communication by the end?
11. The concept of "bashert" (when something is destined or meant to be) comes up in the novel. Both Barbara and Eddie and Ruth and Joseph had strong connections to each other in the past. Do you think it was bashert that they returned to each other?
12. Was Joseph interested in Ruth while his wife was still alive? Or does their shared loss now bring them together?
13. Is the cardinal a coincidence? Or do you think it's actually a sign from Harry? Or is it Abe?
14. Mother/daughter relationships and the loss left in their wake feature prominently in this novel, despite the main relationship being an unrelated pair. How is Barbara doing with her own kids in your opinion?
15. Is Barbara right to nudge Ruth to go out with Joseph?
16. Is Barbara actually ready to date Eddie? Or is she appeasing everyone around her (Harry included)?
17. Has Barbara dealt with her own grief enough to actually move on? Or, like Ruth says, do our hearts grow around our grief?
18. Do you think they see the cardinal again after Ruth marries Joseph? Or does it fly away?
19. Is Janet actually happy about the ending? Or does she feel excluded?
20. What do you think Barbara learns about herself and life by the end of this novel?

About the Author

Photo © 2022 Tim Coburn Photography

Sara Goodman Confino is the bestselling author of five novels: *Don't Forget to Write, Behind Every Good Man, She's Up to No Good, For the Love of Friends,* and *Good Grief.* After spending more years than she's willing to publicly admit teaching high school English and journalism, she is currently writing full-time and trying to make a living off the crazy stories in her head. She lives in Montgomery County, Maryland, with her husband, two sons, two miniature schnauzers, and a goldfish that seems to be vying for the world record of longest-living fish. When she's not writing or frantically parenting, she can be found on her Peloton, at the beach, or at a Bruce Springsteen concert, sometimes even dancing onstage.